Bare, Bear Bones

Bare, Bear Bones

written by

M. SUSAN THUILLARD

"Cover illustration by Afton Corbett"

authorHOUSE®

AuthorHouse™
1663 Liberty Drive
Bloomington, IN 47403
www.authorhouse.com
Phone: 1-800-839-8640

First published by AuthorHouse   05/21/2011

ISBN: 978-1-4634-0954-8 (sc)
ISBN: 978-1-4634-0955-5 (ebk)

Library of Congress Control Number: 2011907766

Printed in the United States of America

Bare, Bear Bones
Main Characters and Chronicles:
    Anderson Baines Cole Davis (Andy)

Born in Seattle, WA on April 4, 1964. He was always big and awkward as a child, and very shy. Other children often teased him about his shyness and about his name. He seemed to bear these indignities quietly and with dignity, often walking silently away. At home he spent hours reading in his room or played basketball at the local park when he knew other children would be home having dinner. His parents got him exercise equipment when he showed an interest in working out. He used his equipment religiously and became well muscled and toned in his teens. He still kept to himself. Others still teased him, but not as often. He was big and found that a steady stare usually intimidated people. He never dated during his school years. He had trouble with acne in his early teens, but by the time he graduated from high school, he had overcome the problem. He was ruggedly handsome with black wavy hair and crystal blue eyes. He stood 6'6" tall, his body lean and toned. His hands were large and made him seem clumsy with smaller instruments like pencils. After the death of his father, he and his mother moved to Missouri to live in her family home with her sister, Andy made trips to visit his brother in 1982 (stayed 6 months), in 1984 (stayed a year), and then moved to his brother's house in 1986 until his brother's death in 1988. He then sold the family home and moved back to Missouri where he lived in a small bungalow on a country road a mile from his mother's house until his mother and aunt died leaving him the family farm. He moved his own family into the farmhouse where they lived until 2004.

Camden David Davis

Andy's father, factory worker, quiet, unobtrusive man, died April 4, 1974 on Anderson's tenth birthday.

Anita Carol Cole (Baines) Davis

Mother, took in sewing for side income, strikingly beautiful woman with black hair and intense blue eyes. She took in borders after her husband died, then moved to Missouri to be near her unmarried sister, Suzanne Sarah Cole Baines. They opened a Rooming House in the old Baines family farmhouse. She died of a heart attack in 1984.

Allen Benson Christopher Davis (Allen)

Brother, 12 years older than Andy, doted on his little brother, buying him gifts and candy all the time. He worked as a parts deliveryman for a tool company and lived in the family residence in Seattle after his mother and brother left. Allen drank heavily, never married, and finally committed suicide on April 4, 1988, Andy's 24th birthday.

Alice Bonita Carol Davis (Carole) and Abigail Barbara Camille Davis (Camille)

Twin sisters, born in 1970, died in an automobile accident the day Anderson was born, April 4, 1964.

Anna Betsy Carmel Davis (Betty)

Sister, 10 years older than Andy, she mothered Anderson, as she always called him. She was often harsh with her younger sibling. She married and moved to southern Illinois in 1978.

For more about Andy's life, see notations at back of book.

Part One

THE BEGINNING AND THE END

April 6, 2005
Henderson, LA

In the misty grey of predawn, two nondescript men in their canoe slithered almost silently down the dark waterway, eyes alert for alligators and the nutria, or swamp rats which told of the reptile's presence. The men were brothers, twin-like in appearance. Their weathered faces were beardless and seamed with wrinkles and lines from long years of toil and exposure to the elements. They were dressed in old jeans, long-sleeved denim shirts, and canvas fishing vests, their hands protected by leather gloves, with the fingers cut off. Their hair was brown with graying streaks worn long and tied loosely into a single braid. Jacques was the youngest by a year at 42. His arms bore the scars of many battles with the gators and turtles they hunted in the swamps. The thumb on his right hand was missing. Paul was taller by a couple of inches, but he'd lost a leg in a gator battle when he was ten and he seldom stood to his full height. He sported a handmade prosthesis, the third one he'd made over the years.

Long tendrils of Spanish moss hung from skeletons of trees whose roots lay just beneath the surface of the still, black water. "Umph," grunted Paul in the prow of the canoe. His left arm shot out and forward. Jacques, in the stern smiled grimly, adjusted the blade of his paddle, and headed the canoe in the direction indicated. There was gator noise up ahead. It would be a profitable morning after all. They cruised their canoe as close to the sounds as they could, their eyes squinting in the dim light to see the cause of the ruckus.

Bump! The canoe was rocked by the hard, scaly back of an alligator skimming alongside their craft.

Jacques spat a long stream of black juice into the water, barely missing the reptilian. "They got somet'in up der?" He asked in a tone barely above a whisper.

His brother grunted again, using his own paddle to slow their progress, pausing, then suddenly pushing forward with a deep thrust. They hit the marsh edge with a rush of scraping and scratching as their canoe shot onto the ground, completely out of the water. There were six or more gators gnashing and writhing on the ground around them, disturbed by the sudden appearance of the men. "Hi-yi-yi!" They yelled in unison as the gators reluctantly moved back into the water. The blackness swallowed them with a hiss as their bodies splashed away. Only one eight-foot monster turned back to roar a challenge before he, too slithered silently into the cold, dark liquid lapping along the shoreline.

The two men had jumped out of the canoe, waving their paddles, still chirping their battle cry. One of the brothers produced a shotgun which he trained on the water behind them and to their right. The gators were scared off for now, but there was something here they wanted, and they'd be back.

"Cest qua ce, Mon Ami?" (What is it, My Friend?) Asked Jaques.

"Applle les gendarmes," (Call the police.) His brother Paul answered. He shined his flashlight over the bodies lying along the marsh. They were human bodies, bodies of girls. Jacques dug his cell phone out of his pants pocket and made the call to 9-1-1.

While the men waited, they built a series of small fires between the bodies and the water to discourage the gators from coming back. They didn't talk, having developed a simple camaraderie over the span of their lives where doing was more important than saying. When the fires were sufficiently strong for their purpose, they sat nearby waiting for help. Paul got out a crude flute and began playing a melancholy tune as Jacques watched for varmints that might sneak back to the scene of death.

Later in the day:

Federal Marshall Mack Johnson was called to the scene of the crime. He was a tall, athletic man in his late 50's with short, graying hair and intense, intelligent eyes. He'd been a homicide detective for over 20 years. He wiped his face with his right hand as he listened to one of his team describe what the area and terrain were like.

"Marsh and swamp along the river here," he indicated with a sweep of his arm. "A couple of tracks off into the trees there to the left, where folks launch their boats and whatnot. Those two Cajun fellows over there found them early this morning. They were having themselves a little early morning canoe ride when the noise of the gators brought them here."

"They look good for it?" Mack queried.

"Naw, they're swamp rats, but this doesn't seem like their style. They called it in to the local police as soon as they had the gators off the bodies."

As he walked up to the crime scene, one of Mack's aides started filling him in on the details of what he was about to see. "Four bodies, two of them are children, the other two women. Gators got to 'em, so it's pretty grizzly. One of the kids . . ."

"That's enough!" Mack barked as they approached the crime scene, already swarming with technicians, police of all types, and news people. "What've you got, Jenny?" He asked as he strode up to the team's medical examiner. He scanned the scene with relief when he saw the covered bodies. He didn't want to lose his lunch.

Jenny Gibbons smiled up at 'The Chief' as his team referred to Mack. "Hey, Mack. I thought you'd be along." She indicated the body nearest her. "Thirty year old, white female; asphyxiation is the cause of death. Gator took her foot and part of her arm. No obvious sexual trauma." She pointed to the next body, laid out beside the first. "Another female, this one Caucasian also, I'd guess five or six years old, asphyxiated, most of the lower half of her body has been eaten, so I don't know about any other trauma." She moved to the third body bag. "Two to three years old, another guess, female Caucasian, also asphyxiated from what I can tell. No other signs of trauma right now. I would say a mother and her children." Jenny moved off into the trees about 60 yards to the fourth victim. This body wasn't bagged and lay on the marsh as though asleep. Her arms were folded across her chest, making her look peaceful. "And here we have another female. This one is, as you can see, a black female, maybe 20 or 21 years old." She pointed to the marks on the dead girl's neck. "She was strangled, and this was left under her hands." She handed the detective a Louisiana Driver's License for a Xenia Davis. Her name was circled in red ink.

"That's it? No ID's on the others?" He asked no one in particular. His aide was quick to confirm his question about ID with a shake of his head.

"Can we move them?" Jenny looked up at Mack from her crouch next to the fourth body.

"Yeah, get them outta here!" He barked at the hovering team. He turned from the crime scene and strode to his shiny red SUV. "Kids!" He muttered in disgust. "Why is it always kids?" He wiped his face on a large white handkerchief and nodded as the Assistant Medical Examiner shouted after him.

"I'll have a lot more for you in the morning!"

He turned and walked backwards a few paces. "Did the murders occur here?" He waved his left hand at the surrounding trees.

"I'm not sure!" She shouted at his retreating figure. "This may have been just his dump. They were left here for the gators on purpose, I'd guess."

He turned back around and pounded a fist onto the hood of his vehicle. "Why?" He asked of no one in particular. "It's always why." He barked a few orders as he climbed into the driver's seat with two of his closest colleagues.

Meg Riley was busy on her computer generating investigative work for their arrival at the office. His senior agent, Jared Sanders, stared out the window as they bumped along back roads, then sped down a secondary road toward the city. He was a handsome man with a boyish face and blonde, wavy hair. His white polo shirt stretched over large shoulders and chest, narrowing into khaki colored slacks.

"Jared!" Mack said in his loud, abrupt voice. "Have you solved the case yet?" He smiled slowly, showing even, white teeth.

Jared was slow to respond, but finally looked at the Chief and then at Meg who had quit typing for a moment to listen to his answer. "Remember that case a few years ago about the bear?"

"Well . . . what? Tell me what you're thinking."

"Didn't they find a few bodies or bones and some ID's?" He shook his head. "I'll have to dig that old file out. There's something familiar about this scene. I can't quite remember . . ." His voice trailed off as he looked again out the window, the swampland fading into concrete, pavement, and tall glassy buildings.

August, 2002
Bitterroot Mountain Range

A large marauding black bear wandered along a forest path in the mountains of Montana. She was an old bear, her eyesight fading and her long teeth worn down from years of gnawing on bones and tearing apart stumps and logs. She stood for a moment by a dead pine tree, reaching up as high as she could to feel the old scratch marks of other bears in the vicinity. Plopping back down on all fours, she stood for a moment, rubbing first one side on the tree, then turning and rubbing some more against the smooth old trunk. She snorted and harrumphed into the still morning air until a whiff of something on the slight breeze caught her interest. She stood on her hind feet and sniffed long and deep. Humans were at the campsite in the valley splayed before her. She couldn't see them, but she could smell the smoke of their recent fire. She licked at her thin hairy lips, drool induced by the familiar smells, hanging sloppily from her jowls.

Ever so slowly, the old bruin made her way down the mountainside to the creek, where she cautiously crept closer to the quiet camp. She walked around the three tents, sniffing at each one. There was only the man smell. She scratched absently at the damp coals in the fire ring before inspecting the two vehicles parked nearby. A noise from one of the tents caused her to drop down on all fours and move silently behind the vehicles, slipping back down the slight incline to the creek, which she crossed quickly. She walked up through the trees and along a boulder-strewn path to a rocky out-cropping high above the camp. There, she lay down on a protruding ledge, her head resting on her enormous paws. She watched as the morning sunlight brought out the campers.

Five men eventually emerged from the tents to have a hearty camp breakfast before they wandered into the forested hills to hunt. That was it, the fire was reduced to smoke and ashes and no other movement caught her interest. No, there were only men in the camp this time and they were careful with their food, not leaving even scraps for her to forage. As the sounds settled to stillness, the bear arose and meandered higher into the mountains in search of whatever she could find to eat. She wandered aimlessly into high meadows where she pounced almost playfully onto unsuspecting mice and voles. Her wandering led her back to a high rocky cave a few miles from the valley floor. She rested in the cave for a night and a day before slowly making her way back down through the rubble of shale and rock to her favorite hunting grounds. In one secluded spot she snuffled and dug around the boulders and windfalls for any morsels she might have missed in times past. As she batted around the bones and dead tree limbs, a skull clattered over a short ledge onto a grassy patch a few feet below. It was a human skull . . .

September, 2002

"Are you sure this is safe?" Called Linda Owens. "We're a long way from anything!" She looked behind her at the meandering mountain trail they had climbed from their car, now hidden from view.

Dan Owens laughed. "You're such a scaredy-cat!" He called back. "Come on! These old logging roads are easy hiking! I could take you up there if you want some real exercise!" He pointed to the craggy mountain on their left.

"Okay, okay," I'm coming!" She laughed into the bright morning sunshine and crisp mountain air. It was their honeymoon of hiking and camping and she would follow Dan anywhere. She smiled at his boyish enthusiasm as she hitched up her small pack higher onto her shoulders, then forged ahead along the old roadway, still far behind her husband.

"There's a little grassy place up here a ways," he answered. "We'll stop there for a few."

She waved him on and walked along the road about a hundred yards behind him, now. "This is going to be a honeymoon to remember," she muttered to herself. "The week of a thousand hikes." She rounded a bend in the road and stopped at the beautiful scene before her. With a rocky hillside for a backdrop, this grassy park-like area was breathtaking. Stately pines arose on her right and ahead, cutting off her view of the road. And there in the middle of it all sat her handsome husband of only a few days, smiling like he'd created this spot just for them. "This is beautiful," she said, coming to sit on the log next to him. "You're right, it was worth the effort."

He did a mock bow including his best Elvis imitation. "Thank you, thank you very much."

She pushed him back and he did a slow motion roll onto the grass behind the log. "Ow!" He yelped, reaching up to rub his head.

"Watch out for the rocks," she teased.

"Right," he said slowly. "Only this isn't exactly a rock." He held something in his hand for her to see.

"What is that?" She asked, frowning.

"I think it's a skull," he answered lamely, not believing what his eyes were telling him. He peered closer, but it didn't help. It still looked like a person's skull.

"Not, no you don't mean a human skull, do you? Surely it's from a bear . . ." She could see that he did mean it was human, but the reality just wasn't making sense. They both looked around them like something sinister was going to reach out of the trees for them. "What should we do with it?" She asked in a whisper.

"I'm not sure," he stated flatly. "But, I think we need to get the police or something." They stared at one another for a few seconds, the skull looking at them both through blank pits of eye holes.

He laid the skull back into the grass and backed away from it, pulling his wife with him. It took them only a fraction of the time to reach their vehicle as it had to hike up to the grassy knoll. They scrambled into their jeep and drove madly down the mountain roads.

"My God, Dan, someone died up there, all alone. What on earth could have happened? Do you think a bear attacked someone?"

Her husband was shaking his head as he maneuvered the jeep around the steep dirt roads. "I don't know, Linda. The creepy thing is that there was just the skull. I didn't see any other bones, just that one lonely skull."

Hours later, a dozen or so vehicles made their way to the remote area. They combed the grassy park, but could find no other bones, human or otherwise, just as Dan Owens had told them. One man, Lieutenant Kenneth Barnes, stood looking up at the rocky cliff behind the park-like scene.

"What'cha thinkin', Lieutenant?" One of the officers asked.

"Is there some kind of trail to get up there?" He pointed at the cliff before him.

The officer looked up at the cliff some forty feet above them. "Yo, guys! Let's see if we can get up here!" He pointed toward the top of the bluff.

"Back here, there's a path back here!" Someone else shouted after a few minutes.

In seconds, five of the team swarmed up the path and onto the ledge. "You aren't gonna believe this!" Someone shouted down after a few minutes had lapsed.

"Is she up there?" Lieutenant Barnes asked.

"Maybe," the officer wiped his sweating face. "There's at least ten skeletons strewn around up here." He paused. "Hang on a minute, someone's found something."

Lieutenant Barnes never moved. He stood rooted to the spot his anxious face turned upward, waiting for the latest news. Finally, after a two-year hunt, they may have stumbled onto Hannah's body. He closed his eyes remembering his teenaged daughter, her innocent bright eyes and long blond hair always in her face. She'd just turned eighteen and was headstrong, often defying her parents as she felt her way toward adulthood. They'd had numerous confrontations about her lifestyle and the late nights she was keeping. *If only she'd listened just once,* he thought now. *I might not be here finding her remains. She'll never have a wedding, a family . . .* He knew these thought wouldn't help now. "What's going on up there?" He shouted in his frustration.

"I'm comin' down, Lieutenant! Just a minute!" The young officer ducked his head and was lost to sight. In a short time he was handing the Lieutenant his findings. "Twelve bodies, well just bones, up there, but we've found these." He handed the Lieutenant a few driver's licenses and ID cards.

Kenneth Barnes frowned at the cards splayed in his hands. "What's this?" He threw out the question to no one in particular. All of the licenses were marked with a red circle around the names. Half way through the stack he found his daughter's driver's license. A tired sigh escaped him as he folded the cards together neatly and wiped at his suddenly perspiring face. "How many body bags do we need?" He asked in a choked voice.

"Twelve, Sir." came the quiet reply.

"Twelve women?" The Lieutenant croaked.

"Well, twelve skulls, Sir. The bones are scattered everywhere. There's a cave just above that looks like a bear den. We've only found nine ID's so far. That's what I gave you, there."

"I'm going back to town. Bring me whatever you find." He turned to leave, but turned back. "No clothes or anything, just these?" He held up the cards.

"There's some clothing scraps, hair, and a few teeth, Sir. We'll get everything. I think a couple of the guys went up to the cave in case there's more up there."

"What about purses or wallets?"

"No, Sir, nothing like that. Just some ripped up jeans mostly; parts of one or two shirts, I think."

Back at the police station, Lieutenant Barnes started looking through his missing person's files. Six of the names were there, six women who had gone missing from his own area over the past two or more years, his daughter among them. He had his sergeant check the national database for the other names. By the next morning, they had all dozen ID's and names, three from California, two from Washington, his daughter Hannah's along with five others from Montana, and one more from Oregon. Their ID's were all intact and obviously belonged to the remains found on a remote ledge in the forests of Montana, prey to bears and other animals.

"Sergeant, where's the name of that truck driver we questioned when Hannah went missing? The one who drove her car to the restaurant, you remember?" He asked.

"It's there in the file, I believe, Sir."

"Get it for me, will you? Let's see if we can find this guy and question him again." *I remember him,* he thought. *Baines Anderson from Seattle or Missouri or somewhere in between. Yeah, I remember the smug snake.*

March, 2003
Helena, Montana

The ruggedly handsome man brought his semi-truck to a stop in the police station parking lot. "A-D Trucking, Seattle, WA" announced the bold, black lettering set upon a white magnetic sign on the door of the shiny red cab.

Detective Lieutenant Kenny Barnes watched as the green and gold reefer trailer behind the red cab came to a stop in the back lot where he stood near the open fire door of the stationhouse.

The truck driver sat quietly in his cab for a full ten minutes before he finally slid out of the truck onto the pavement of the deserted parking lot. He shut the door and dusted his hands along the front of his worn Levis. He hitched up his pants then slicked back his black hair, a ritual of long habit.

Kenny Barnes clenched his jaw as he watched. He wanted to rush forward and slam Baines Anderson against his polished red truck. He'd been thinking of this man for almost two years, ever since his precious Hannah, only 18years old, had gone missing. A single tear coursed down his weathered cheek at the thought of his beloved only child. If all went well today, it would finally be over. He snapped the pencil he'd absently picked up when he walked to the open door. As the seconds ticked loudly by on the clock in the room behind him, he rubbed his free hand across his face. He went over in his mind how he would stop the guy if he got back into his truck and tried to make a run for it. But, he needn't have worried. The man walked up to him and stopped, his right hand offered in greeting, a slight smile playing across his face.

"Lieutenant Barnes," Baines acknowledged with another smirking smile.

"Mr. Anderson," Lieutenant Barnes nodded as he moved aside to let the younger man pass. He didn't touch the proffered hand. A desk sergeant looked up as the two approached.

"My name is Baines Anderson," he said. "I'm here to visit with Mr. Lieutenant Barnes, here behind me."

"Yes, Sir, we've been expecting you," answered the sergeant, glancing up at the detective.

Detective Barnes carefully placed a hand on the man's shoulder. "This way, Baines," he said. "Come down this hallway with me." He turned to walk through a doorway, down a corridor, and into a small interrogation room on his right. Baines Anderson looked after him, shrugged nonchalantly, and followed him into the room beyond.

"Have a seat, Baines." Lt. Barnes indicated a chair behind the table. A bare table and two hard chairs were the only furniture in the room. A two-way mirror reflected the two men from the far wall.

"Do you have coffee?" The trucker asked as he took a seat across the table from the officer. "I missed my coffee there at the truck stop when your <u>kind</u> officers told me I should come on over here to chat with you." He smiled. "nice of them to escort me over here, like."

"We'll get you some," Lieutenant Barnes stuck his head out the door and gave an order for coffee and rolls to the desk sergeant. Turning back to the table, he carefully closed the door and addressed his subject. "Get comfortable, Baines, this might take awhile."

"Is that a fact?" Baines seemed calm and collected. He leaned back in his chair and put his hands on top of his head. "Your men been waitin' at that truck stop long? Cause I ain't been out this way in a long while. Your department must have money to burn."

Lieutenant Barnes ignored the idle chatter. "Do you remember the little talk we had about a year or so ago?" He asked as he sat heavily in his chair.

"Sure, at the little café there along the interstate, that the time you mean?"

"Yes, that's the one."

"Yep, I remember." He sat up, putting one elbow on the table, his fingers rubbing his clean-shaven chin. "Ended up that little talk right here in this room, didn't we? Did you ever catch that guy? The one you were asking me about."

The Lieutenant took a breath and let it out slow. "We might be close," he acknowledged with a slight nod. He looked down at the thin file he had in front of him, tapping it thoughtfully.

15

"We'd like to tie up some loose ends, Baines, and I think you can help us with that."

"Oh, do you?"

"Why don't you tell me your story again?"

Baines Anderson laughed lightly, sitting back once again and tapping the tops of his thighs with his big hands. "From a year or more ago? What're you, crazy?"

"You don't remember what you told us at the time?"

"From a year ago? I don't think so. Can you remember what you said a year ago?" He indicated the unopened file. "Without looking at your crib sheets, I mean?"

"We can just go over the questions again, if that's what you want to do."

"Nah, not me." He scooted his chair back, both hands flat on the table in front of him. "If we're done here, I have work to do."

"We haven't even started, Baines."

"Are you arresting me or holding me on some kind of charge?" His vibrant blue eyes were icy cold as they pierced into the heart of the Lieutenant.

"We want to close this case, Baines."

"Good, you go do that. It's got nothing to do with me." He shrugged and paused. "I believe that that's what I told you way back when."

"You admitted to dating my daughter, remember?"

Baines sat back in the chair and looked closely at the officer. "Yeah, I remember."

"Tell me again why you were driving her car."

"You ever take a girl out and let her drive?" Baines smiled.

"We have your fingerprints in her car," Lieutenant Barnes said quietly. He was sweating. His anger was rising and he knew he couldn't go on with this banter. *Here's the man who killed my daughter, right in front of me, and he acts like he's an innocent bystander.* Suddenly, he got up. "Hang tight there a minute," he said as he left the room, shutting the door behind him.

In the viewing room, Lieutenant Barnes confronted his Captain. "I can't do it. I thought I could, but I just want to strangle him and his smirking face." He fell into a chair near the desk.

"It's okay, Kenny. I'll take over." Captain Jones said, glancing at the man through the glass.

Baines smiled broadly as the Captain came into the room. He rested his chin on his clasped hands, elbows on the table, and waited for this new interrogation to start.

"Mr. Anderson, I'm Captain Jones," he offered a hand to the man opposite him. "I don't think we've met before."

"All right," Baines answered, shaking the hand offered to him. *These stupid backwoods cops don't even know who I am,* he thought to himself, a slight smile playing around the corner of his mouth.

"You can understand that Lieutenant Barnes is a little close to the subject of this investigation," he paused for effect. The younger man didn't respond, so he continued. "Well, as he was telling you, we need to clean this up and put it to rest. We believe you can help with that."

"A year or more later," Baines mumbled.

"Well, it's been complicated, but I guess I should tell you that a team is out there searching your truck right now. Here's the search warrant that allows us to do that." He shoved a folded piece of paper across the table.

From behind the glass, Lieutenant Barnes watched. "Please, please let them find something in that truck!" He mumbled. "Any scrap of a thing that he might have kept of hers, anything!"

Baines smiled again. "Okay," he said, laying the papers on the table in front of him without opening them.

"We don't want any mistakes now, Baines. You understand what I'm saying?"

"Nope."

"Is there anything new you'd like to add to your story from last year?"

"Nope."

"Did you have anything at all to do with Hannah Barnes?"

"Is that a trick question?" The handsome man frowned slightly.

"It was pretty straight forward."

"Answered all that the last time. How long is this gonna take? A man's gotta make a living."

"Well, you dated Hannah, right?"

Baines closed his eyes and breathed slowly. *This too will pass,* he thought. *Sit tight and ignore them. There's nothing for them to find. You'll be home in a couple of days. Be still now. Be still.* "Where's that coffee?" He asked suddenly.

Captain Jones sat back pondering the situation. *We might lose this guy,* he thought. *Please let them find something, anything, in that truck! But, after a year?*

Almost immediately a knock came at the door, and the desk sergeant appeared with coffee and donuts. "Thanks, Tom," said the Captain.

Baines occupied himself with the food. It was a welcome diversion while he waited. He could almost drown out the stupid rhetoric being spouted out at him as he concentrated on his chewing.

"We found her body, you know, Baines. Out there in the forest where you left her."

No response.

"Her neck was broke. Did you do that? Maybe she fell when you were hiking with her or something. Anything sound familiar yet?"

No response.

"You remember that you confessed to dating her and driving her car, right? Your prints were all over the car, Baines."

No response.

"Why don't you just tell me about that date, okay?"

The man they called Baines Anderson looked deadpan at the Captain. "You guys must be desperate." He said before eating the last of the donuts.

"Forensics has put together a good case for us. We just need a little cooperation from you here, Man."

Baines quit chewing and looked again at the Captain. "Who you fooling? If you got this wonderful case, why ain't her killer behind bars? And, what do you need me for?" He busied himself again with the food. "You gonna drink that other cup of java? Cause I'll down it, if not."

"Go ahead," he pushed the cup closer to Baines. Captain Jones looked up at the observation window, then closed the file he'd opened only a few seconds earlier. Without another word, he got up and walked out the door.

"Kenny," he said, controlling his mounting anger. "I thought you said we had a good case here." He tapped the file he'd laid on the edge of the desk. "I opened this in there and there's nothing but a bunch of blank paper in it, not even a copy of his original statement, nothing!"

"I know." Lieutenant Barnes wiped his face with his hand and bowed his head almost to his knees. "We do have a case, but we can't put a collar on him. Not yet, we can't. I hoped he'd cave when you told him we were searching his truck. I didn't put anything in that file that he might get a hold of."

"Geez, Kenny!" The Captain started to walk to his office. "Have they come in yet?"

"Yeah," Lieutenant Barnes said dejectedly. "It was clean."

"Of course it was clean! How long do you think he would keep evidence hanging around? Go cut that man loose!" He barked the order over his shoulder as he stomped his way into his office and slammed the door.

Lieutenant Barnes told the desk sergeant to let the suspect go as he walked through the hallway and out to the parking lot where he sat dejectedly in the driver's seat of his green sedan. "I know he did it, Hannah," he breathed. "But, how do I tie him to it? There are no clues, Hannah. He broke your neck and there are no clues." He wiped at the tears spilling down his cheeks.

Two years later and they had to let Baines Anderson go again. Kenny Barnes knew Anderson was the killer, but there was absolutely no proof. The only link he had to any of these remains is that they were all in the same place, on a cliff ledge in the middle of nowhere, and Hannah was with them. Hannah had dated Baines Anderson once or maybe twice and she'd let him drive the car. His fingerprints were naturally in the car. That was the only link he had for the man. He put the files back on his desk in their special place, where he pored over them whenever he could. He knew someday he'd get his break.

April, 2005
Granite City, IL

"Well what in the world is this?" Betty Myers muttered, looking at the scrap of paper in her hand.

"Well, what is it?" Asked her husband, Ben, as he rustled the morning papers he was reading.

"It's a note from Anderson, but it doesn't make any sense at all." Frowning deeply, she sat across the table from him. "I'm gonna call him."

She tried his cell phone, but there was no answer. "Anderson," she said to his message service. "This is your sister. You call me and tell me what this silly note means. This doesn't mean anything to me. What are you talking about? Are you and Denise still in Louisiana? Call me back soon." She hung up and turned the envelope over. "Well, this is from Missouri. What's he doing back in Missouri?"

"Call the house. Maybe they moved back or came up to check on the old place," offered Ben.

"He's had such a hard life," she mused, worry etched into her face.

"Uh-huh," he murmured.

"Ben, please pay attention! I think something's wrong!"

"Yeah, yeah, why don't ya just call the house?" He peered at her over his glasses, then rattled the papers once more as he tried to read the sports pages.

"I thought he had a job down there in New Orleans." She was still looking at the note, scrawled in pencil on just a scrap of paper. *Something isn't right,* she thought. She looked up his old home phone number and called the family home in Missouri. "There's no answer," she said absently. "Ben, something's wrong. I can feel it." She directed to her husband who sat at the kitchen table in their house trailer, still deeply involved in his morning paper and drinking his coffee.

"Yeah, well no one ever said Andy is in his right mind, you know. He moves around almost as much as he drives around the country. Can't keep that boy pinned down for a minute." Ben said.

"No, I know he travels to escape real life and that he's got his problems, but . . ." she paused, lost in thought. "I think someone should check the house. I'm afraid, Ben, I truly am. This note is just so queer."

"Well, call the police out there and have them do a wellness check, if you want. But, maybe they're just out getting groceries or something. After all, if they've moved back, there would be plenty to do." He paused, laying the paper out on the table over his coffee cup. "Look, here's a plan of action. Wait a couple of hours and call again. Just keep calling until he or Denise answers. If there's still no answer by tomorrow noon, then we'll call the police and have them check. Does that make you feel better?"

"No," she sighed. "But, you're probably right."

Betty called every two hours until midnight. She finally couldn't leave any more messages on his cell phone and no one ever answered at the house. *The message thing is probably full*, she decided. She and Ben went to bed, but Betty didn't sleep soundly at all. There was something about that note . . . It was a poem like the nasty little rhymes the bullies used to chant at Anderson when he was a child. That wasn't like Anderson to make up rhymes himself. "Why mother and dad wanted to do the alphabet thing with everyone's names is beyond me," she mumbled into her pillow. "It hurt Anderson so."

Finally morning came. "I'm calling the police now, Ben," she told him as she handed him his morning coffee.

"Go ahead," he answered. "All your mumbling and tossing and turning last night's got me thinking maybe something's wrong, too. Let's get it over with."

"Town Marshall's Office," answered the disembodied voice at the other end of the phone.

"This is Betty Myers, Marshall Weston. Could you check on my brother for me? I think something might be wrong out at the home place." Betty said to the familiar voice.

"Who's this? Oh, is that you, Miz Betty? You mean out at Andy's place, that is, yore mama and auntie's old farm? Heck, Ma'am, they up and left nigh onto a year ago, you know. The place is all boarded up. I don't think there's . . . uh, what's that?

Just a minute, Ma'am, one of my deputies is a-saying something to me." There was a pause while Betty listened to muffled voices in the background. "Well, Miz Betty, excuse me. Officer Oscar Carter, here, just told me he saw some lights on out there at your old mama's place a couple of night's ago on his way home. I'll send him out to see if old Andy's moved back." He laughed heartily. "That ole boy's harder than a coon at midnight to keep track of, ain't he?"

"Yes he is, Sheriff. Could you call me right back when your man checks out the place?" She asked.

"Why shore," the Town Marshall answered, waving a hand at his only officer to get him moving. "I'll call you as soon as he comes back, maybe an hour or so, okay?"

"Thank you, I'm probably worried over nothing, but you know how worrisome Anderson can be."

They said their good-byes and Betty sat rigidly with the portable phone in her lap. She read the note again. *And now I've made my A-B-C's, Aren't you very proud of me? Only 20 years to find them all. Now it's over. I'm the last to fall.* It was simply signed with the letter *A.* Betty looked at it over and over. *That's always how he signs his letters,* she thought. *It really is from him. Oh, why doesn't that man call?*

Over an hour later, Officer Carter made his report to the Marshall. "Somebody's been there. Andy's car's in the barn. One of the living room windows has the boards took down and there's a light on in the kitchen, but the doors are all locked and the house and everything's quiet. Didn't look like vandals been there or nothing."

"You say his car's in the barn? His old Chevy?" The Marshall asked.

"Yep, expired plates and all. There's some tracks in the dust, so it's been put in there recent like. I knocked on the doors, but nobody answered. It's as quiet as death around there. Mustn't be nobody around the place."

"There wasn't Loo-see-ana plates on the car?"

"Nope, just his old Missouri ones from last year. Car seats are still in the back and everything."

"Was his truck parked out back?"

"No, Sir. Didn't see hide nor hair of his big rig."

"Well, that explains it, then." The older man smiled at his deduction of the situation. "They've come home to roost, but gone out on a run somewhere. They've done that lots of times. His old sister's worried for nothing." He reached for the phone as he thanked the deputy for his diligent work. "We'll have to talk to that boy 'bout those expired plates when he comes home." He laughed aloud at his own words.

Betty answered the phone on the first ring. "Hello, Marshall Weston, is that you?" She asked anxiously.

"Hello, Miz Betty. Now, I want you to listen to me, and calm down some. Andy's been out to the place, but it looks like he and the missus and the children must've gone out on a truck trip. Their car's in the barn, but the truck isn't there. They opened up the house, so I'm sure it's him and not some vandals. You can rest easy that all's well. Okay, now?"

"Oh, thank you, thank you so much! That does make me feel somewhat better." She said, expelling a long sigh. "He's not answering his phones, but if Denise and the girls are with him, maybe he just turned his cell phone off. Thanks again. Sorry I bothered you with this."

"Not a problem, Miz Betty. Not a problem a-tall. That's what we're here for, to serve our fine citizens."

"Yes, well thank you again." She hung up, not waiting to see if he had anything else to add.

"What'd he say?" asked Ben.

"Says Anderson and the girls must be out on a road trip somewhere. His car's in the barn and the house is opened up, but his truck isn't there." She answered.

"Well, that sounds all right, then," he nodded.

"Except for the letter," she said, holding up the paper from her lap.

"He'll probably call in a few days. You know how he is sometimes." Her husband consoled her. He pulled the letter from her fingers and read it for himself. "Hm-m-m, this does sound strange, even for Andy," he said frowning but offering no more insight. He cocked his head to one side and looked up at his frowning wife. "What's this rhyme thing about?"

"That's what I've been trying to tell you," She snatched the letter from his hands in exasperation. "When we were kids, the neighborhood children used to follow Anderson around and make fun of him. He was shy and would cry easily and that made them do it all the more. There was one girl, what was her name? Oh yes, Donna O'Neal. She was especially mean and made up rhymes like . . . *A,B,C,D, here comes creepy!* Stuff like that." She sniffed and dabbed at her eyes with a handkerchief. "Anderson would cry himself to sleep, and wet the bed."

"I guess I never knew this about him. I just always thought he was a tough-guy teenager who kept to himself all the time."

"Really Ben, you never have paid attention." Betty shook her head, making her curls bounce above her ears. "No, Anderson was so shy it was painful. I took care of him as much as I could, but he turned on me one day when he was about sixteen or so. I didn't have much to do with him for five or six years, well until after Al died, you know."

"Yeah," he nodded. "He did start coming around sometime after all that. That's when I thought all his problems started, his brother dying on his birthday and all that."

"Papa, too," she nodded sadly. "Papa died on Anderson's 10th birthday." She sat in a nearby chair and sighed. "And the twins died in the accident on the day he was born." Tears flowed freely down her cheeks. "Oh, poor Anderson! It's a wonder he survived at all!"

April, 2005
Houston, TX
Lead Investigation Team, South-Central District

"So, what've we got?" Mack Johnson came into the conference room like a whirlwind, as he always did.

Jared Sanders was writing on the display board off to the left of the door. Meg was, as usual, working on her laptop. The last of the sun's rays were streaming in the windows across from the door making the room bright even without the help of overhead lights. Mack looked at the display as he sat at the head of the table, waiting for his colleagues to talk. All eyes turned to Jared Sanders.

Time Line (missing women)

State	Sep 2001	Apr 1999	Jun1998	May 1997
Montana	12			
Oregon	–	4		
Washington	–	–	5	
Wisconsin	–	–	–	4

Our Time Line (bodies found)

State	Apr 2005	Mar 2003
Louisiana	4	
Montana	–	12

All of these murders had the same MO—strangulation. ID's were found at all sites with the names circled in red marker. Bodies were left for wild animals. All cases remain unsolved.

Jared finished his writing before he began to explain. "There was a similar case to ours in 2003 from Montana." He used a pointer to indicate the information on his drawings. "Hikers found a skull and that led to the remains of twelve bodies, well mostly bones and teeth. But," he paused for emphasis. "They recovered twelve ID's all marked just like our Xenia Davis's ID was." He paused again to look at his boss. There was no response, so he continued. "One of the bodies was a cop's daughter who'd been missing for about two years. When she went missing, they questioned a truck driver she'd dated a couple of times, but couldn't tie him to her disappearance. They questioned him again when they found the pile of bodies or bones, but still couldn't hold him on anything."

"What do we have on him?"

"From Montana we have prints in the name of Baines Anderson, and his signed statement saying he didn't do anything but date one of the victims. Can't really read the signature, it could say anything from Boss Hogg to Who Knows What. But, he is an owner-operator of his own truck, one of those independent drivers, it says here . . ." he shuffled through his papers. "A-D Trucking out of Seattle, WA." He paused as he read a little farther in his notes. "No company was listed in Washington State under that name, but there was a Baines Anderson who had a license and permit from Bend, Oregon from 2000 to 2002. He looks to be our man." He paused and looked up at his boss. "I like him for it, Mack. I sent the prints to our database. There's nothing yet."

"Montana must've liked him, too." Mack commented.

"Yeah, I talked to Lieutenant Barnes out there. He's got a deep, gut feeling, you know. It was his daughter this guy killed."

"His gut's been rumbling for, let's see, four years, right?" Mack asked with his traditional sarcasm. "Now yours is rumbling, but no solid food in sight." He rubbed his hands together expressively. "Let's have some meat, Boy!" His wide grin was infectious and everyone around the table was smiling at Jared.

"I'm working on it, Mack." He said as he pointed to his chart, tapping on it with a pen.

"Just don't lose sight of OUR murders, Kid." He paused. "If that's all there is, I'm goin' home. Call me when somebody here has some work done."

"Well, here's something we DO know!" Jared was quick to add.

Mack stopped in mid-stride and looked back. "Well?" He prompted.

Jared was again shuffling papers. "Xenia Davis was a local waitress, born and raised in Louisiana. She'd never been in trouble, but had been seeing some white trucker for a couple of months."

Mack smiled as he walked back. "Now see, that wasn't so hard, was it? That's the kind of ties I'm lookin' for. What else?"

Jared cleared his throat, trying to hide the smile of satisfaction that was bubbling to the surface. "We traced dental records for the white family. Denise <u>Davis</u> and her girls were new to the area . . ."

"Whoa, whoa, whoa!" Mack held up his right hand. "Another Davis? All these dead people are named Davis?" He scratched his head. "What's up with this?"

"I know, I know," Jared answered. "But, Davis is the name. They came from outside Joplin, Missouri. They're not related to Xenia. We're trying to contact Denise's husband, Andy. He's a truck driver."

"My, my, my!" Mack clapped his hands "Don't you love it when things just come together like that?" The sudden, sharp slap of his hands nearly made Jared drop his pointer. He quickly laid it on the table, embarrassed that he'd been still holding it.

"Here's something for your board," Meg said quietly from behind her laptop. She absently pushed her glasses up and looked at the two men like she just noticed they were there.

Jared grabbed his marker and waited for her to speak as Mack eyed her curiously. Meg had worked for his team since the beginning. She was older than his other team members, somewhere in her late 50's. She rarely spoke, but when she did, it usually was worth listening to. Mack held her in great respect and the other team members did, too. She was the 'mother' figure for them all.

"How you got that timeline running?" She squinted at his display board.

"Descending," he answered.

"Okay then," she looked back at her screen. "October, 1997 in Pennsylvania there were 5 corpses found, same M.O. as ours. From what could be told, they were all strangled and left in the mountains for animals to scavenge. ID's found were circled in red. They had all been there for three to four years, just left for bears and whatnot."

"That's a 10-year gap and clean across the country, Meg . . ." Mack started.

She waved an impatient hand at him. "Quiet now, quiet," she said. "Okay, now in 1993, let's see, that'd be September, there were five more old corpses found, maybe dead for three or four years again, up in Tennessee. These were found because a bear attacked a bunch of campers for no reason. Again, it's the same M.O. as our case here. They liked a truck driver back then named Cole Davis, but never tied him to more than the fact that his regular truck route was along the Appalachian Trail and it was known he had dated one of the girls in Pennsylvania."

"Let me guess," Mack put in. "She was a local waitress."

"Nope," Meg smiled at him, looking over the top of her glasses. "She was a housekeeper at a motel connected to the local truck stop."

"Have they got any evidence we can use?"

"I'll call on that. The file indicates a smudged set of prints and a tread mark that came from a big rig out in Tennessee. There's nothing listed from Pennsylvania, but I'll see if they can dip up something."

"Trucking company?"

"He was an independent. Didn't even have a sign back then. But, it was licensed in West Virginia to Cole Davis from Seattle, WA."

Jared was busy bringing his charts up to date with this new information.

Time Line (missing women)

State	Sep 2001	Apr 1999	Jun1998	May 1997	Oct 1994
Montana	12				
Oregon	—	4			
Washington	—	—	5		
Wisconsin	—	—	—	4	
	—	—	—		5
Pennsylvania	Sep 1993				
Tennessee	5			—	

Our Time Line (bodies found)

State	Apr 2005	Mar 2003	10 yr gap	Oct 1994	Sep 1993
Louisiana	4				
Montana	—	12			
Pennsylvania	—	—		5	
Tennessee	—	—		—	5

↑   ↑
Suspect-Truck Driver   Suspect-Truck Driver
Balnes Anderson   Cole Davis

All of these murders had the same MO—strangulation. ID's were found at all sites with the names circled in red marker. Bodies were left for wild animals and all of the cases remain unsolved.

Mack looked at the new information on the board, his head back and nostrils flaring with the effort of his thoughts. "Write this down, Jared-My-Boy," Mack leaned back in his chair, stretched his arms above his head, and rubbed his fingers through his hair as his feet landed comfortably on the corner of the table. "Heading will be Truck Drivers. List the names, Cole Davis, Andy Davis, and Baines Anderson." He spouted as he looked at the names on the board. "Now, doesn't that just jump right off the board at ya'?"

"Yep, there's sure a lot of Andy's and Davis's showing up," Jared commented.

"Hm-m-m," Mack contemplated. "Is he related to any of our girls? At least some of them, maybe?"

"My thought, too," answered Meg.

"Yeah, they're all from Missouri except the local gal, I don't think that's a coincidence. "I wonder if he got some kind of perverse pleasure out of the black girl's name being Davis," he paused and looked at his co-workers. "You know, just before he killed her or something." His voice trailed off into silence.

"Who's gone to Missouri to find our own Mister Andy Davis?" Mack asked after a considerable pause.

"Mark and Sarah," Meg answered.

Mack nodded. "Well, let them do their hunt. After they question him we'll tell them he's looking like a man with a mighty lot of coincidences in his life. Call me." With that, he planted his feet back on the floor, stood with a flourish, and swept out of the room.

"Whew!" Jared collapsed into a rolling chair, spinning slightly across the floor in front of his display board, and looked at Meg.

Meg smiled. "Quit tryin' so hard. He's noticed you or you wouldn't be here right now. You'd be out there doggin' some illusive truck driver."

Jared laughed. "You're right. I know you're right. But, I want this one almost bad enough to go out there myself." He looked at his board again. "Ten years," he mumbled. "What'd you do, Andy Davis, for ten years?" He absently tapped the empty space with the end of the pointer.

Meg looked up. "My question is, what'd he do before 1993? I don't think he just popped up one day and killed five women. There has to be more to this story, and I'm gonna keep diggin'."

May, 2005
Granite City, IL

Betty Myers couldn't get her thoughts to settle anywhere but on the strange letter she'd gotten from her brother over a week ago. She worked in her flower garden and thought about their years as children. It seemed so long ago since she was a child. She sat back on her knees, trowel in one gloved hand. Her thoughts carried her away into their past. *I was ten years old when Anderson was born,* she thought. *And Allen was fourteen. It was such a sad time.*

On the evening of April 4, 1964, a very pregnant Anita Davis had taken her twin girls to a dance lesson. Betty wasn't feeling well, so had stayed at home, and Allen was attending football practice at the school. Camden Davis, her husband, was bowling with his friends. A terrible storm blew up out of nowhere, wind whipping and rain pelting as hard as sleet. Anita was driving slowly, barely keeping up with the mad rush of traffic when screeching tires caused her to panic and swerve to the left. Her station wagon slammed into another vehicle, while yet another slammed into her car. It became a multi-car pileup on the Interstate where she and her girls were pinned in the wreckage waiting for emergency workers to get to them. Anita drifted in and out of consciousness, alternately aware of the screams of her daughters and her own pain, then falling into a black abyss. The last time she regained consciousness, there was only silence from the back of her car. She tried to turn around and look for her daughters, but her own pain was too intense and she drifted back into unconsciousness from the effort.

The Davis family gathered in the waiting room at City Hospital. They'd been there for several hours already, Camden pacing, drinking one cup of coffee after another. Allen slept on the sofa and Betty tried to read a magazine so she wouldn't cry anymore. *My two sisters are dead,* she thought. *I should have been with them. Maybe I could have helped and there wouldn't have been any accident. Oh, look at Papa! He's so sad and hurt looking. And Allen's only sleeping so he won't be seen crying. Mama's just got to live! She's got to!*

Finally, a doctor in a white coat came into the waiting room. "Mr. Davis?" He asked in a deep, quiet voice.

Camden Davis nodded and Betty stood up to be with him.

"Your wife and baby are both alive. The baby is very small, but we think he'll survive. If he makes it through the next 48 to 72 hours, he'll have a very good chance. Your wife has multiple broken bones, but she's resting comfortably right now, under a lot of medication. You and your children may see her for a few moments." He put a friendly hand on Camden's shoulder. "Then why don't you go home and get some sleep? I'm so sorry about your two youngest daughters. They were dead before the medics got them out of the car. Go home and rest, Man. You're gonna need it. Your living children are gonna need it, too."

Mama did eventually recover after months of therapy, although she was really never the same as before. The deaths of her daughters had taken a toll on her emotionally, Betty had to admit. Betty had taken care of little Anderson with the help of a nurse who came once a week, back then. Papa worked harder than ever, seldom spending time with his family. Allen buried himself in football until he graduated high school. After that, he went off into the Army.

Anderson was such a puny little thing, with the biggest hands and feet. He looked all out of kilter until he was fourteen or so and started getting some height. The neighbor children just teased and tormented him almost every day . . .

Betty stifled a sob as she sat on her knees in her beloved flowers while her mind shifted to another era. "All those years of torture as a child, the rhymes, the teasing; it all made Anderson such an angry teenager," she mumbled to her begonias. She touched the delicate buds showing up among the bright greenery. "He was so much better after he returned from the Army, but he was still sullen. I wonder why he and Al ever got on so good back then. Of course, Anderson kept coming back to Mama from time to time. Maybe he and Al didn't get on so good." She looked up, staring at nothing. "I remember when the youngest O'Neal girl was murdered. When Anderson came home shortly after that, he laughed. Her sister had hurt him that bad. He just laughed at their tragedy. It fairly gave me the chills." She rubbed at her arms as the memory of his laughter ran through her mind causing goose-flesh to pop up. *"Little pimple-face deserved what she got," He'd stated. "Did you know her?" She asked, with a frown. Anderson just smiled and walked away. She thought he'd said no, but she wasn't sure. He might have just snorted at her questioning him.*

Betty looked at the soil in her hands. "Why am I digging up all these old hurtful memories?" She asked as the dirt slipped through the fingers of her gloves. "There were happy times, too." She looked up at the sun high over the sycamore tree in her yard. "I remember so well when Denise Johnson's family moved here." She looked down the street at the brick house, now vacant. She smiled at the memory of the young woman who went door to door trying to get laundry to do. *"It'll just help out my mama,"* she'd smiled at Betty. *"Well, they're hiring waitresses over there at the café,"* Betty smiled back at her. *"It's my brother's favorite place to eat."*

Betty settled against a large rock and put her feet out in front of her. Her mind wasn't on gardening, that was for sure. "Denise was so much in love with you, Anderson," she mused. "She still is. You're all she ever talks about, you and those two little girls." A frown crossed her forehead as she thought about her nieces. "I wish they hadn't named them Carrie and Brianne," she mumbled. Putting the little family together, that meant their four names started with A, B, C, and D. Betty shook her head sadly. "He just never gets away from it. The alphabet follows him every day. I wish it didn't bother him so badly. Now, he sends me this crazy note. What does it all mean?"

Betty got up from her gardening and put the tools away in the shed in the back yard. As she walked to the screen door, she began formulating a plan. "I'll just go out to the farm and clean it up for them if they've come home," she smiled in joy for the first time in many hours. "It'll also clear my mind of disturbing thoughts and let me have some peace." She hummed a little tune as she began preparing supper for her husband. It was a nonsensical tune, one made up by Anderson when he was a child. He always whistled it when he was clearing his mind and trying to deal with some problem or other. Betty didn't notice that she too, often hummed the little ditty as she sorted through life's problems.

April, 1999

Denise

Denise Jackson was a petite girl with flowing strawberry blonde hair and wide hazel eyes. In the summertime, you could see the light sprinkling of freckles across her nose and cheeks. She looked younger than her twenty years, but that was sometimes an advantage. Like the first time she met Anderson Davis. He seemed mesmerized by her youthful looks saying she reminded him of a child he once knew. She wasn't sure if she should be flattered or angry, but he was so handsome and attentive that she decided he was actually flirting with her. He drifted in and out of her life because of his truck driving work, but he always seemed to look her up when he was home in Missouri. Of course she knew that her Mama and his sister Betty had been hoping they'd get together. After all, Betty helped her get this job where she knew they'd be sure to meet. And Mama pestered her day and night about 'that handsome brother of Betty's.' She'd say "Betty and Ben are so nice, why Anderson must be about the most wonderful man you're ever likely to meet!" Denise would smile In her shy way and answer, "Yes, Mama."

"I am the luckiest girl alive," Denise Jackson sighed now at her reflection in the mirror. She'd been dating Anderson Davis off and on for over a year, and now, it was to be her wedding day. "I can't believe he loves me!" She smiled the radiant smile that only brides and new mothers have.

Yet, a slow frown crept onto her face. It hadn't been very romantic, no talk of love. He just walked into the restaurant and blurted. "Let's get married or something." She'd stared at him like he was a stranger. "Today, Denise. I want you to marry me right now."

"All right Anderson," she'd answered. Of course it took longer than one day, almost a month to be exact. Anderson had been so impatient about all the planning and organizing it took to just get married. Of course they couldn't elope, it would have broken Mama's heart if her only child just up and ran off to marry.

"Besides, Mama loves him almost as much as me," she sighed. She lifted her chin and erased the frown from her face as she moved into the chapel to marry Anderson Davis, his brother-in-law walking her down the short aisle of the little country church in place of her father who'd left when she was a small child.

Their honeymoon was short. They spent the weekend at a local resort where they could swim. Anderson taught her to golf on the second day. She never dreamed it could be so much fun, and her love deepened as he treated her with patience and love.

Denise was pregnant within the first weeks of their marriage. It was all she ever thought of as a young girl, being a mom and having a little house in the country to care for. She was happy with the small, white house she and Anderson shared. It had a picket fence around the front yard and a space for a garden in the back. Anderson was gone a lot, so Denise threw herself into gardening. She grew roses and had a productive vegetable patch. When Anderson was home, he was attentive to her, and a good dad, too. He named the baby Brianna, called her Breezy, and carried her around with him whenever he was home. Denise never knew a man who loved his child so much. Two and a half years later, she gave birth to another baby girl. Anderson was gone again when baby Carrie was born, but Denise didn't mind. He was such a good father when he was home, she knew he'd be pleased with their new infant, too. And he was. He got down on the floor and played with both girls whenever he could, even had tea parties with them and played with their dolls like he was one of their friends, not a father at all.

Life wasn't without its challenges, though. Mama died a few weeks before Carrie was born. It was a real blow to Denise; she and Mama had been close, like best friends rather than mother and daughter. Denise didn't make friends easily, so she got lonely sometimes with Anderson gone so much. She visited Betty once in awhile, but it wasn't the same as it had been with her mother.

Since Anderson had named their first-born Brianne, and Denise liked the alphabet pattern their names seemed to be taking, she was excited to name their second daughter. "A, B, C, D," she announced one evening at supper. "We just all belong together, like the alphabet, don't we, Dear? Your name, and our names together." She quickly looked down when she saw the look on his face, then hurried on. "I mean, I know you had some trouble with that when you were growing up, but now it just seems to make us a unit. You know, like we are together because of it . . ." her voice trailed off.

Anderson stared at her like she'd lost her mind, his face contorted as he fought to contain his rage, and his eyes, dark and ugly. "How could you, Denise?" He said in a hissing voice she'd never heard before. She glanced at him, then down at her hands again. "I married you because you're not like all the others." He shook his head slowly and got up to leave the room. He stopped in the doorway and turned to face her. "I can't . . . you're my wife Denise, I can't think of you being like that." He rubbed a hand over his face and stared at her for a long minute. Finally, a kind of weak smile formed on his face and he blew out a big breath before leaving the room. Denise didn't know if he was angry or just thought she was foolish, but he didn't bring up the subject again and she left it alone, too.

Anderson seemed to be sensitive to Denise's loneliness because he started calling home more often, even inviting her and the girls to come out on some of his trips with him. Denise and the girls especially loved the time they went out to California to visit Anderson on one of his trips. They stayed in a motel while he drove up and down the coast. He got her a rental car and encouraged her to take the girls to Disneyland and Knott's Berry Farm. He only spent three days with them, but took them to see the sights in Los Angeles when he was there. They walked on the Avenue of the Stars and shopped on Rodeo Drive.

On another trip to Montana he left her in Livingston where they could take side trips to Yellowstone Park. They went camping in the famous park, and Anderson taught her about trees and wild plants. It was a side of him she'd never known before where he played games with them and climbed trees with the girls. She knew he was smart, but she hadn't known that he had such a love for plants and trees. It made her feel good inside to know that he shared her love of plants, although for her it was gardening and flowers and for him it was trees and wilderness flora and fauna.

There was one moment though, the first time she felt fear . . . They were hiking far from camp when they chanced upon a bear. Denise and the girls were terrified, huddling together on the path, close to a towering old pine tree. Anderson seemed entranced by the encounter. He stood apart from his family, across the path. He didn't make a move to protect them, but stood staring, first at the bear, then at Denise and the girls.

"Anderson," Denise said in a half-whisper. "Do something!"

Still; he stood still as a statue, a small smile forming on his lips. The bear stood up on its hind legs and sniffed the air, huffed loudly as he came back down on all fours, and suddenly roared fiercely at them as though he would eat them all right then, and just as suddenly turned to saunter off the trail into the trees.

Anderson grinned at Denise who stared back at him in horror. "Heh-heh," he laughed lightly. "That was a close one. C'mon, Girls, let's go back to camp."

They followed him silently as he turned around and headed back the way they'd come. Denise walked woodenly between the girls, holding their hands tightly. But, Anderson walked briskly ahead and whistled his little tune as though there was nothing wrong. He never looked back to see if they were following or safe, just walked along, arms swinging to the tune he cheerily whistled. Denise would never quite forget that he didn't come to the rescue.

Other times, Anderson would just call her out of the blue and arrange for her to fly to meet him, sometimes taking just her on camping and hiking trips in the mountains or all of them on river rafting trips and trail rides at dude ranches. She felt the trips almost always strengthened their marriage. He was normally such a loving and devoted husband and father. True, she still spent a lot of time alone in motels and strange cities, and she had the niggling doubt about her safety with him, but he would usually spend weekends or a few days here and there with them, completely devoted to having a good time. He was never stingy with money, either. Denise wasn't the type to spend foolishly, but he would sometimes impulsively buy them all clothes or take them out to expensive restaurants.

The only drawback seemed to be when he would take the rental car for a few days. He would be moody and angry and she knew he would take the car for some kind of mysterious drive alone. She only asked once about his taking her and the girls with him. That was the second time she saw the dark, strange look come over him. It was like he went into some kind of trance or something, not knowing she was even in the room with him. Like the time he stood useless when the bear scared them. "No!" He barked at her, causing her to jump and the girls to cry out in alarm, before he fled out to the car, spinning the wheels and driving recklessly out of the motel parking lot. She never brought it up again. Whatever was eating at him from time to time, he couldn't share it. She reflected on his childhood and the stories his sister had told her. It would bring tears of pain to her eyes and an ache to her heart to know he kept that part of his life buried.

"It's probably what makes him boil over with anger and his 'moods'", she said to the mirror. Besides, even if he was moody and withdrawn sometimes, he was also fun at the most unexpected times. "It's been a good life," she whispered. "if an accident or something happened right now . . ." she paused. "Well, we've had a good life together. He's a good man, as Mama would say."

The year before, sometime in the fall, maybe, he began acting differently, though; just after Labor Day, she reflected. *Yes, something is different and strange, even for Anderson,* she thought to herself. He seemed to be hiding something and she suspected that he might have a girlfriend somewhere out west. She didn't ask, preferring not to know and not wanting to make him angry. After all, he always came home to her and the girls. He was still a devoted husband and father when he was home, just moody. He wasn't making as much money either, and that might be the reason for his moods, she reflected. The more she thought about it, the more she was able to convince herself that money and bills were the issue. He took care of all that, giving her a generous allowance, so she didn't really know if they were in some financial trouble or if he was just getting tired of being on the road so much. Secretly, she hoped he would find a local driving job and be at home to help with the garden and some repairs the house was in need of. She looked around at the cracked plaster and a window broken during a hailstorm. The old farmhouse needed painting, too, and one of the back steps was broken. She glanced out the window at the clapboard barn and scrutinized it, too. *Yes, the old barn needed a lot of repairs, maybe even a coat of paint.* She smiled wanly.

Late in 2003, he completely surprised her. He stayed home for several days before he told her what was on his mind. "I'm thinking of moving," he said calmly at dinner one night.

"Where to?" She asked around the lump in her throat.

"Maybe down to Louisiana or Mississippi." He looked idly through the newspaper in his hands.

"You really mean just up and move, sell the house and everything?"

He looked over the paper at her. "I'll never sell this place, Denise. Besides, if things don't work out, we'll need to come back home."

She breathed a slow sigh of relief. He'd said home, so this was just a temporary move. And he wanted her and the girls with him instead of going off driving alone again. "How soon?" She asked timidly.

"Next week, I think. I'll board up the place and we'll see if we can make it down south for a little while."

"Are you having trouble finding jobs?" She hurried on to explain. "I mean, you usually just go off and work out west or something, we've never moved anywhere before . . ." Her voice trailed off.

Anderson frowned slightly before he smiled disarmingly at her. "Not to worry. I need a change, that's all. I've called about a couple of loads out of Texas to go to New Orleans. I'll get us a house to rent down there for you and the girls, mostly. Then I think things will get back to normal." He studied the paper and she studied him.

"Okay, Anderson. That sounds like a plan. I'll get one of the neighbors to clean out the garden while we're gone. Sheri and her kids are always needing extra food."

"Yeah, yeah, that sounds good."

So it was that they moved south. He was true to his word and in only a couple of weeks of living out of the truck, they had a small house in the country near Lake Charles, Louisiana. Denise liked it there. People were friendly and she soon had a part-time job as a waitress. Anderson was angry over the job, so she quit when he came back from one of his trips. It didn't seem to take much to make him angry these days. It was the first time she thought that their marriage might be in real trouble. The problem was Denise didn't know what the problem was. All she knew was that he had been going through some kind of life change that started in Missouri, or on his last road trip, and now things weren't too good here either.

"You can't outrun misery," Mama would say. "Cause you always take yourself with you wherever you go."

Denise gained a little hope during the Christmas season. Anderson was home and they decorated the house together, something they'd never done before. He seemed extra attentive to both her and the girls, taking them out shopping and to restaurants like they had all the money in the world. His new mood seemed to last right up to Mardi Gras, then he came crashing down into what she believed to be depression. He started talking about going home to Missouri, but said he had a project to finish first.

"I thought we were doing really good here," she said.

"I told you we'd go back to Missouri someday," he snarled.

"But we haven't even been here a year, Anderson. I'm sure if we give it a couple of years or more, things will be better." She wished she'd kept her mouth shut.

He got right into her face with that black look she'd come to fear and hate. "I can't explain this to you," he said. He grabbed her by the arms and held her still in front of him. "You . . . you just . . . I can't tell you!" He let go of her and she fell back, knocking over a lamp which hit the floor with a crash. "I'll be back!" He yelled over his shoulder as he rushed to the door. He stopped with his back to her and his hand on the doorknob. "I've got something to finish and then . . ." he paused before opening the door, slamming it behind him. She couldn't figure out what any of that meant, but then Anderson took care of everything and she never had the worries that some of her friends seemed to have, like money worries or a drunken husband. No, Anderson was almost always good to her and she chose not to think about negative things. She absently rubbed her arms where he'd gripped her so tight. It was the first time he had ever physically hurt her. As she bent down to pick up the pieces of the lamp, the girls came whimpering to her and helped. She sat with them on the floor for a moment and held them close. "It's all right," she crooned. "It's all right."

"Why was Papa so mean?" Carrie asked.

"Yeah, mean," repeated 2-year-old Brianne.

"Hush now," Denise answered, pulling them closer. "Just don't fret. Papa has work worries and he's not himself right now. It'll be all right soon." She smiled. "He's thinking maybe we should go home to the farm soon."

After they picked up the broken lamp, she fixed them a snack and they talked a little about going home, maybe painting their room again.

"Can I help?" Brianne asked with a hopeful look.

"Me help, me help," echoed Carrie.

Denise smiled and nodded. "Let's read a story," she said.

Carrie chose a book for them and Denise tucked them into bed for a nap as she started to read to help them feel drowsy.

Over the next few weeks, Anderson came and went, obviously driving locally, but not discussing his jobs with Denise. That was normal behavior and she began to relax, thinking that whatever had caused his moodiness must surely be over. As a family, they went to the coast on weekends and on a shopping spree to Baton Rouge. He didn't mention moving again, so she thought maybe he'd decided to take her advise after all. She felt better as she looked at his smiling face when they drove home late one night. The girls were asleep in the backseat of the car. On an impulse, she reached out for his hand. He surprised her by grasping her hand and kissing it lightly, winking at her, and smiling his beautiful, crooked smile. She couldn't help it, a sigh of contentment burst forth as she basked in his loving attention. *Everything's all right,* she thought. *We're okay and life will just smooth out.*

A few weeks later, Denise Davis looked into the mirror in their Louisiana apartment. "Six years," she whispered. She turned to look lovingly at her two young daughters, still sprawled on the bed, wrapped in the sheets. She turned back to the mirror. "Six years and two children, and still he returns home to me, loves me." She smiled sadly. There was something different now, she had to admit. His moods shifted so rapidly. He seemed happier, yet there was something . . . if she could just put her finger on it . . . "Well, never mind," she said softly. "He'll find a permanent job here soon or a long haul, and we'll be okay. He'll be driving steady for somebody soon, back to travelling all over the place like he likes to do. He's so good at finding jobs and loads for his truck." She turned from the mirror and smiled at her sleepy girls.

"Up and at 'em, Girls," she jostled them awake. "Papa's promised to take us for a hike somewhere today. Let's get up and around to make him happy, okay?" Anderson had been pouring over maps, looking for trails in the swamps to take them on. Evidently, he'd found what he was looking for, because he'd made her promise to be ready this morning when he returned to the little apartment. She smiled again. "I'm ready, Anderson." She said softly. "Whatever your surprise is, we'll be ready to go!"

End of April, 2005
Rural Missouri

Agents Mark Stevens and Sarah Eagen flew to Springfield, MO where they rented a white SUV to drive to their destination, a small town a few miles north of Joplin, near the Missouri/ Kansas state line.

"There's the local Marshall's office," Sarah indicated with the wave of a finger.

"Yeah, let's see what he knows about Andy Davis and his family. Maybe there's a missing person's report or something."

They angle parked their rig in front of the small stone building and got out. Up and down the street, people had stopped to stare at them.

"Looks like we're popular," Mark mumbled.

"More like we're bugs under the microscope, I'd say," Sarah answered as they walked into the old building. The sign beside the door was in need of paint, but you could still read the words 'Town Marshall.

They stood for a moment inside the doors and stared at the counter separating them from the rest of the room. Behind the counter were two desks, a set of lockers, an open, walk-in closet, and two empty jail cells. "Wow!" Breathed Sarah.

"I wonder if Barney Fife is in?" Mark smiled at her as he walked up to the counter and rang a bell.

A door from the back of the closet opened and a heavyset man entered. He was in his mid-to-late fifties, graying at the temples. A smile was soon replaced by a frown as he observed the strangers across the counter from him. He hitched up his gun belt and walked forward. "Can I help you folks?" He looked first at Sarah, then at Mark.

"Yes, Sir," Mark began, observing the words 'Town Marshall' on his sleeve. "We're hoping you can." He and Sarah both flashed their badges. "We're Special Agents from Texas," Mark resumed. "We're investigating a quadruple homicide in Louisiana . . ."

The Marshall broke in with a guffaw and a hand slap to the counter. "Wait! Wait, wait, wait! You all want me to believe that some murder in Loo-see-ana has a bunch of Texas wanna-be

Rangers here in my little neck o' the woods?" He turned toward the back of the building. "Hey, Oscar? Come out here and see the show, would-ja?"

Another officer immerged from the closet. He was a tall, lanky young man with a napkin stuck in his shirt collar and a piece of fried chicken dangling from his left hand. He wore a blue uniform, half tucked into some wrinkled, patched jeans. He seemingly hadn't seen a comb in a few days, but was clean shaven, or maybe didn't need to shave yet. He was all arms and legs with no body fat. His hatchet-like face was greasy around his mouth where a wide, lopsided grin greeted them.

The Marshall waved at his guests. "This here's, well shoot! I don't think I even got yore names." He looked expectantly at the pair of city officers.

"Sarah Eagen and Mark Stevens," Sarah offered, pointing at her partner. "We're here to see if you know where we might find Andy Davis."

The Marshall and his cohort looked warily at one another for a few seconds. "Ole Andy?" The Marshall asked. "Heck, he lives just outta town a few miles. What 'cha want with him?"

"Just routine questions," Mark Stevens put in, looking from one man to the other. "Can you give us directions to his house?"

"Well, sure, but it won't do you no good to go out there." Marshall Weston shook his head and rubbed at the stubble on his ample chins. "His ole sister called the other day a-lookin' for him, too. But, he weren't to home. Was he, Oscar?"

"No, Sir," said Oscar, wiping at his mouth with an already greasy sleeve. "I went out there, but the house was as quiet as a cemetery."

Mark and Sarah exchanged glances. "You want to draw me a map?" Mark asked quietly.

"Sure, sure!" Marshall Weston nodded as he grabbed a pen from his pocket and pulled a pad of paper from a drawer behind the counter. He paused, tapping the end of the pen lightly on his puckered lips. "You know, Andy moved down to New Or-leens, or somewhere awhile back. I know he's a queer duck, but yore not thinkin' of him as a suspect now, are you?"

"Does Mr. Davis have a family?" Sarah asked, ignoring his question.

"Yep, he sure does," Oscar offered. "He's got him a perty little wife and two little girls that look just like their Mama."

"And there's his old sister, Betty Myers," added the Marshall. "She lives over to Granite City. Comes over to visit from time to time. This here place . . ." he indicated the paper he'd started drawing on. ". . . it belonged to their Granddaddy, then their Auntie and their Mama lived there 'til they met their ends. Andy had him a little place down the road, oh, 'bout right here, I 'spect," he put a small square on the drawing. "But after his Mama died he up and sold the little place and moved to the old homestead."

"Did he grow up here?" Sarah asked, pen poised over her notebook.

"Naw," the Marshall looked up at the ceiling, hitched his gun belt, and sat on the edge of his desk. "Now, let's see, his mama grew up here. She took up with some guy from out west somewheres . . . Oscar, where'd Al live, Seattle was it?"

"Yep," Oscar nodded.

"Then, after their daddy died, Mama Anita and two of the kids come out here to live with Andy's Auntie, that'd be his mama's sister, over there at the old home place." He tapped the note pad still in his ham-like fist, indicating the bigger square that represented the farm. "I think he was back out there on the coast when his brother Al killed hisself, isn't that true, Oscar?"

"Yes, Sir. Then he came back out here after he sold that place and bought the little farm."

"Yeah, yeah, I think that's right. Somewhere's in there ole Betty married up with Ben Myers and moved away. Andy took that a might hard, I think. He and Betty were always real tight. She's kind of a quirky old gal, but she's got a heart of gold and she loves that brother of hers. Always takes up for him, kinda protective-like, you know?" He paused for a few seconds. "What was it that set her off the other day? Oh, yeah a letter or something from Andy, that was it."

The younger man brightened. "Yes, Sir, you had me run out there to check on the place. His ole car's in the barn and the house's been opened up." He looked at the investigators.

"Like I said, he and his family'd moved down to New Or-leens, but I guess things didn't go too good, 'cause they're back right now."

"You've seen him, then?" Mark asked, anxious to get out to 'the ole home place' himself.

"No," Oscar shook his head. "But, he'd boarded up the house last year when they left, and the boards are off the front windows now. And, of course the car's in the barn."

"But nobody was there?" Mark persisted.

"No, Sir . . ."

"It's all right, Oscar," the Marshall broke in. "Ole Andy's a truck driver, you see. His big rig's gone, so it seems likely they all went on a little road trip for some cash, you know?"

"Who's he drive for?" Sarah asked quietly. Her mouth was dry as she wrote in big letters, TRUCK DRIVER.

"Aw, he ain't never drove for no big outfit," Marshall Weston laughed. "He's one of them independent drivers. Has him a little sign on his truck, reads A-D Trucking or some such thing. Think it might even still say See-attle on it, don't it, Oscar?" He looked askance at the obviously nervous young officer. "Seems to do right well for hisself, being independent and all that."

"I think yore right, Mr. Weston, Sir," Oscar nodded emphatically. "I think that sign does still say See-attle."

"You all think he might know somethin' about this murder in Loo-see-ana?" The Marshall asked too casually, once again hitching his gun belt.

"We'd sure like to talk to him and his wife," Mark said.

Sarah looked at her partner thoughtfully. "Yes," she said with a nod, "and to see the two little girls."

"Well, don't rightly know when you might catch him out there, but here's the map," Marshall Weston pointed at the paper in Mark's hand. "You want us to come along?"

"No, no, that's okay," Mark waved them off. "But, you wouldn't happen to have the phone number for his sister, now, would you?"

"Oh, yeah, I do. Get that for 'em, would you, Oscar?" He laughed a little bit. "Be prepared to talk and talk with that one. She's got plenty to say." He laughed at his own words.

Sarah thanked them as they turned to walk out the door. They walked silently to their car and didn't break the silence until they were driving down the street, headed out of town. "What'll we find, do you think?" Sarah asked.

"Well," Mark studied the road before him, maneuvering a right turn onto a gravel road. "Let's just wait and see. Why don't you call the sister and see what she's got to say?"

"No answer," Sarah said after trying to call the number the officer had given to her. "Maybe she and her husband work or something."

"We'll have to talk to her some time or other, I do believe." Mark smiled as he turned the car down a long driveway. They could see the old farmhouse at the end of the lane, with a small barn off to the left. It made a picturesque site. There was a car ahead of them, two people getting out and heading toward the house. "Might be we'll get our chance right now," Mark observed, indicating the middle-aged couple standing on the porch.

* * *

"Now, who's that?" Betty asked her husband. They turned to greet the two people getting out of their dusty, white SUV.

"Don't rightly know," answered Ben. "But if I was a gambling man, I'd say they're cops."

"Andy's in trouble," Betty breathed. "I just knew that note meant trouble. What do you suppose he's done?"

Ben shrugged. "Could be most anything, I guess. Howdy, Folks," he smiled at Mark and Sarah. "Can we help you with something?"

Mark ran lightly up the porch steps and reached out a friendly hand. "Are you Andy Davis?" He asked.

"Oh, no! No, but this here's his sister," he indicated his wife standing a little behind him.

"Hi," Sarah spoke up. "I'm Sarah Eagen and this is my partner, Mark Stevens. We're special investigators from Texas. Is this Andy's house? We'd like to ask him some questions about a case we're working on."

Betty relaxed and smiled. "Yes, this is where Andy lives," she looked lovingly at the old clapboard house. "I'm forgetting my manners. I'm Betty Myers and this is my husband, Ben."

"Is Andy home?" Mark asked casually.

Betty smiled sheepishly as she turned to unlock the door to the house. "I don't know," she said. "I was about to go in and see if anything needed done. They've been gone for awhile and . . ."

"Now, Betty, these here are the police." Betty turned to look at her husband.

"Yes, I know."

"Well, let's tell them what we know and what you're thinking," he smiled apologetically at the investigators.

"Is there something wrong?" Sarah asked.

"Well, let's just go inside and sit down . . ."

"Now, Betty, let's sit right out here on the lawn chairs where it's nice and cool." Ben led his wife to the chairs. "That house's been shut up and bound to be stuffy as anything in there."

Betty dug into her purse for a moment. "Here's a note I received from Anderson a few days ago. It's been worrying me because I can't seem to get a hold of him and well, here, you read it and see what you think." She thrust the paper into Sarah's hand.

Sarah read the note and handed it to her partner. Mark frowned as he read, then reread, the scrawled letter. He looked up at Betty, then looked down and read the note one more time. He and Sarah exchanged a long look.

"Mrs. Myers, what do you think this means?" He held the letter back out toward her.

"Well, I just wish I knew," she began. "When we were children, Anderson was picked on by others because of his name, you know. It was always the alphabet thing. I don't know what possessed Mother and Father to do that . . ."

"The alphabet thing?" Sarah asked, suppressing a chill that ran down her back.

"Yes, well, Mother's maiden name was Baines, you see. Anita Baines. And Father's name was Camden Davis. A-B and C-D, you know." She paused for acknowledgement from the others. "So then, they named their children that way, too. Allen Benson Christopher, Anna Betsy Carmel, that's me, then there was Alice Bonita Carol and Abigail Barbara Camille, and then of course, our beloved Anderson. His full name is Anderson Baines Cole Davis. For some reason, he took all the A-B-C stuff seriously and he was tender hearted, so the teasing of the other children was just too much. They made up little rhymes, you know." She screwed up her face and recited in a sing-song voice. "*A, B, C, D, Here comes creepy.* That was one of them. And, *Andy-Dandy, moldy candy; Baines-Rains, body pains; Cole-Pole, dirty old mole, Davis-Mavis, someone save us!* He never did make friends all those years. He used to hide after school until everyone else had left, or else he'd run clear out around the neighborhood and then come from the opposite way."

"Well, it didn't help with everybody dying on his birthday and such, either," piped up Ben.

"Excuse me?"

"What did you say?" Mark and Sarah asked at the same time.

"Oh my . . . you see, the day Anderson was born our mother had been in an automobile accident and our sisters both died. We thought Anderson would die, too. But, he fought and struggled to survive. He was such a tiny thing. But, as a boy he had these big hands and feet. Made him seem out of kilter, sort of, you know?"

"I see," Mark nodded.

"Oh, that's not all," she waved at him and went on with her story. "Our father died on Anderson's tenth birthday. He had a heart attack just after the cake and ice cream. Just keeled over on the couch and never moved again." She clucked her tongue and shook her head. "I don't think Anderson ever forgave him." She looked up as tears streamed down her face. "Then Allen went and hung himself when Anderson turned twenty-four. He was living out in Seattle with Allen then, Anderson was. Came home from a weekend away that day, with a pizza, and found our brother hanging out in the garage. Something happened to him that time, I guess. He got the idea that he was somehow bad luck, everybody died on his birthday, the rhymes that were nasty and cruel, that kind of thing, you know?" She was quiet for a few moments and no one had the heart to break into the silence. "Of course it wasn't true," she stated suddenly. "But it always worried him about the number 4, you know. April's the 4th month and so many things happen to him in April. Then the alphabet thing . . ." Her voice trailed away.

"So now, you're worried about him because of this letter?" Mark asked.

She looked forlornly at the paper in her hand. "Yes, this paper has worried me a lot. Anderson doesn't make up rhymes, can barely stand it when someone else does it. So, for him to rhyme tells me that something is wrong. And what's he talking about with this 'the last to fall'? I just don't know what can be wrong. He hasn't answered his phones in days, and I haven't heard a word from Denise; that's his wife. She usually calls me and lets me know how things are going." She looked at the paper once again. "I wish she'd named the girls differently . . ."

Sarah frowned. "What?" She asked. "What are the girls names?"

A small snort escaped Betty. "Carrie and Brianna. Denise thought it was cute, Anderson, Brianna, Carrie, and Denise Davis. It's the whole alphabet game all over again. It's a wonder it didn't drive Anderson completely insane a long time ago." She shook her head and wiped at her eyes with the hem of her long, old-fashioned apron.

Mark looked at Ben and motioned for him to follow him out to the cars. Sarah stayed and made small talk with Betty.

"Ben," Mark began. "I think you and I need to look in the house. I have a feeling there might be something in there that Betty needn't see right now."

Ben frowned. "You think the ole boy did himself in, don't you?"

Mark threw up a defensive hand. "Maybe I'm wrong, but my gut's telling me that there's something very wrong in there."

Ben stared at Mark for a long moment. "Just what are you here for, Mr. Stevens?" He asked. "You come here to arrest my brother-in-law, is that it?"

"Really, Sir, I came here to ask him some questions about a crime down south. But, after listening to your wife, I feel just like she said; that she might be right, you know? Something could be wrong, very wrong, if you take my meaning. I don't like this letter he wrote, either."

Ben nodded. "I just brought her out here to ease her mind. She's been driving me half crazy with talk about what Andy might do to himself." He paused and stared at Mark. "Now, I half believe it myself. Let's go in and take a look, shall we?" He headed toward the porch again with Mark half running to keep up.

Betty arose as the men approached. Ben was quick to grasp the key from her hand and gently push her back toward her chair. "Just let me and this here young fella go in there, Dear. We'll let you know if everything's all right."

Betty sat back with a look of fear, one hand flying to her mouth. "Oh, Ben," she breathed. "Oh, Ben . . ."

Sarah put a hand on Betty's shoulder and nodded at her partner. He nodded back at her and the two men disappeared into the building.

They entered a dusty, but neat dining room, a large living room opening to their right. Ben led the way through a closed door straight ahead. It led into a bright kitchen. The smell got to them before they got to the pantry door, which stood slightly ajar.

"I'll get it," Mark stepped ahead of Ben and pushed him back against the table. He opened the pantry door cautiously. A single light bulb illuminated the small room full of shelves and a freezer. A rod had been fastened across the room, balanced on the top shelves of canned goods. A bucket was turned over and had rolled against the door. Anderson Davis hung from the metal rod, held there by a nylon rope. He's been dead for a few days. Flies were crawling on him. Mark stepped back and closed the door. "Call the sheriff," he said before he got to the kitchen cupboard and vomited his breakfast into the steel sink.

Ben stood for a few seconds, then, wiping a hand over his sweating face, he marched out of the kitchen and reached for the wall phone in the dining room. Mark could hear him as he talked. "Billy Weston, this here's Ben Myers. You'd better get out here to the old Davis place and bring the county sheriff with you too," he said. "Yes, it's an emergency." Pause. "Well, you better bring the Coroner with you, I guess." Pause. "Yes, I said bring the Coroner." Pause. "Cause there's a dead man out here, that's why." Pause. "Yes, you did hear me right, Weston." Pause. "Good. That's good, then. Goodbye." He pulled a handkerchief out of his pants pocket and wiped his face and neck dry. "Oh, Lordy," he breathed as he walked slowly to the porch door.

Betty stood and met him at the door. "What's he done, Ben? What's Anderson done?"

Ben looked at his wife through the screen door for a moment. Then pushing it open, he gathered her up in his arms as tears coursed down his cheeks. "Now, Betty-Girl, I don't want you a-goin' in there."

"Just tell me, Ben." Her body shook against his. "He's all I have left of my family. Tell me what he's done."

Ben nodded. "Well, he hanged hisself in there, yonder." A sob caught in his throat. "He's been dead a while, I'd guess."

As the couple cried together, Sarah eased past them and went into the house. She found her partner, leaning against the counter, wiping his ashen face with a towel. "What's up, Mark?" She asked with a frown of concern. She pointed behind her toward the door. "He says Andy Davis killed himself. Did he?"

Mark pointed toward the pantry door. "Yep, he's hanging in there. Been there a few days. Flies all over the place . . . oh!" Another wave of nausea threatened him, but he coughed into the towel to ward it off. "Can't you smell it?"

Sarah nodded. "Yep, I can," she said over her shoulder as she opened the pantry door. She held her face in her elbow and propped the door open. Shooing flies away, she looked at the decaying corpse. She backed out and looked at her partner through eyes blurred by tears. "We sure it's him?"

Mark nodded. "Close that door, will you? Yep, Ben says it's him."

Sarah complied. "Whoa, that's bad! I hope Ben doesn't let Betty come in here. She doesn't need to see that."

Mark pointed at the table. "He left a journal," he said.

Sarah picked up the book and nodded. She and Mark walked outside together.

Betty and Ben were sitting side by side on the porch swing, holding hands, heads bowed. They looked up expectantly, as one person. "Where're the girls?" Betty asked. Grief made her voice high-pitched, thin, and reedy.

Mark turned abruptly and marched back into the house. Sarah let him go and sat in one of the porch chairs. Mark walked through the living room and up a flight of stairs. He cautiously opened every door and looked in every closet and cupboard, but all the rooms were empty of people. *Or bodies,* he said to himself. *Let's face it, you're looking for bodies here, unless that's who he left out there in the swamp for alligators to eat. His own wife and kids! Man, how's a guy do something like that?* He turned around and headed outside to join his partner. He could hear sirens and see a cloud of dust in the distance. They'd be in for a circus for the next few hours. He and Sarah needed to get the Myers' off by themselves for some deep discussion. "Sarah . . ." he started.

"I know, I know," she waved him away, her nose stuck in the journal from the table. She looked up at him briefly. "We've got to call in, Mark." She pointed at the book. "This is full of stuff."

"Yeah, well we've got to tell them about the rest of their family," he indicated the worried looking couple now talking with a very animated sheriff.

"I'm calling Mack," Sarah announced in response. "Let him handle all of this stuff. He's gonna be mad as it is that we've let the locals come in here and mess everything up."

"Sarah," Mark started, sounding agitated. "Go get your camera and do some work. I'll hold off the Marshall and Deputy Fife, and whoever else shows up, as long as possible while you get the scene on film. Here's a bag for the stupid book." He handed her an evidence bag from his jacket pocket.

Sarah jumped up and headed for the car, dropping the book into the evidence bag as she passed her partner. "You're right. Listen, ask Betty if Andy has more of these journals. This one's only for this year and I don't think he just started making these notes. There's a chart on the back flyleaf that Mack will want to see, too. It's creepy . . ." Her voice trailed off as she went down the steps and marched to their SUV.

Mark took out his cell phone and called Texas. "Hey, Meg," he said. "We've got something big up here. Tell Mack to get his sorry butt up here if he wants a clean crime scene." Pause. "Yeah, the guy's here. He killed himself." Pause. "No, we're fighting off the locals and getting pictures as we speak." He waved Sarah past him into the house. "I'm pretty sure he's our man. Looks good for those murders down there." Pause. "Yeah, his wife and kids." Pause. "He left a note for his sister that's kind of an admission." Pause. "Okay, it's about an hour's drive from the airport, listen to my directions . . ."

*   *   *

Marshall Billy Weston hitched up his gun belt, fished a toothpick out of his shirt pocket, and stuck it in his mouth. He looked up at the Davis house and winced. There sat Betty Myers and her husband on the porch swing and it looked like the old gal had been crying. That self-important investigator and his Gal Friday were talking together on the porch. When she started down the steps, he watched the fellow get out his phone.

"Geez!" He muttered. "We don't need all these high-falutin' city folks out here. If ole Andy's gone and killed hisself, we need to just get him buried and his sister through her grief." He looked at his deputy who was looking mighty worried, with a frown as big as all of Missouri etched on his forehead. "Kid, you stay with the old folks up on the porch and take some notes from them if you can. I'll deal with the city slickers and find out what this is all about." He frowned as the lady investigator ran past them, back up the steps and into the house carrying a big silver case and what looked like a camera bag. "So much fussin'," he hissed under his breath. "And find out where Andy's ole lady and kid are, too!" He whispered to his deputy.

The two lawmen walked up the steps and went right to Betty and Ben Myers. "Howdy, folks," Marshall Weston nodded. "My good man here will take your statement. I'm sorry about all this."

Betty Myers looked at her old friend first with disdain, then with a softening of her features. "I know you do the best you can, Billy Joe."

"Well, Oscar here didn't go into the house t'other day," he answered. "I'm surely sorry 'bout it. Should've come out here myself, I 'spect." He puffed out his chest as he spoke. His deputy looked sufficiently ashamed and moved the toe of one boot in little circles on the porch floor.

"Now Billy, these folks are here because Anderson did something far worse than take his own life, far worse." She looked up at him out of the depths of sorrow and grief. "They weren't even the least surprised at what he'd done here. I'm so very frightened for Denise and the girls, there's not a whisper of them anywhere . . ." Fresh tears coursed down her weathered face and splashed onto her hands in her lap. "No, no . . ." she sighed into her palms, her head hung down now almost onto her lap.

"There, there now, Dear." Ben put his arm tightly around her and drew her into his shoulder where she sobbed quietly. "Sorry, Billy, but you know as well as anyone that this family's been through hell and back, at least Betty has, over her family. She's the last survivor of a family of . . . well, she's fragile right now."

Betty sat up and wiped at her face. "Oh Ben, how silly you are!" She declared. "I'm not fragile or anything like it. Frankly, I think I'm the only sane one in the family, of us kids anyway. How did Mama ever survive?" She turned her attention to the Marshall, then looked beyond him as Sarah Eagen came toward them. "Is there something new?" She asked the younger woman.

"No, I'm afraid not. But, I do need to ask you a couple of questions if you're up to it." Betty nodded and Sarah went on.

"Do you know where Andy keeps his journals? We've only found the one on the table."

"I didn't know he even kept journals," Betty mused. "Guess I didn't know him as well as I thought." She paused for a moment. "You know, he did have a little metal box he carried around sometimes. Maybe they're in that."

"Any idea where the box might be?"

"Not really. It's just one of those small metal lock boxes. I'm just guessing, of course. Perhaps it's in his truck." Betty frowned and looked toward the barn. "Where is his truck?"

"We haven't seen it since he left for Loo-see-ana," offered the Marshall. "Could be, he left it down there, I guess."

Betty began shaking her head. "He wouldn't leave his truck," she stated. "But, then . . ." her voice trailed off as she looked up at the weathered, old house.

Everyone was silent while the coroner and two local firemen walked by with Andy's body on a gurney. They watched the macabre processional walk to the waiting emergency vehicle where they inserted the body and closed the door.

"Where's Denise?" Betty wailed, looking around the small group.

"Ma'am," Mark began. "We came here looking for a killer. We believe that your brother might have had information about the murders of four people in Louisiana. The bodies of two women and two girls were found a few days ago. They'd all been strangled."

She shook all over, her mouth opened and shut and opened again, but no words came out. A sob caught in her throat and she brought up one fist to stifle the choking sound. Her husband encircled her in his arms, making soothing noises in a low voice. After some time had elapsed, she sat upright again and looked at Sarah. "You think that Anderson . . ." She shook her head once again and swallowed hard. "You . . . was it Denise?" Her voice had become a hoarse whisper.

Sarah nodded. "We believe it may have been. We'll know more when we get autopsy reports."

Betty's head dropped so low it seemed that it would strike the floor. She put her hands to her face and shrugged off Ben's attempts to comfort her. Breathing hard, she rose up and looked again at Sarah, ignoring the men gathered around her. "And those two baby girls?"

"I'm so very sorry," Sarah acknowledged, tears coursing her own cheeks and dripping onto her white blouse.

"Do you know someone named Xenia Davis?" Mark asked. "A young, black girl, maybe twenty or so?"

"No," Betty said. She looked at Ben, but he just shrugged and shook his head, a look of pain and bewilderment etched into his florid face.

"She was the other woman at the murder scene," Mark said gently.

"The only one with any ID," offered Sarah lamely.

Betty nodded, bringing her arms up to cradle her breasts. "It's April," she murmured.

"Ma'am?" Mark queried.

A long sigh escaped her as she looked off across the fields. "I should have come here right away when I got the letter. But then, perhaps it was already too late." She looked at Sarah once again. "Could I look at the journal you found?" She asked.

"Of course," Sarah nodded. She reached into her camera bag and took out the evidence pouch containing the book. She struggled for a moment with the seal, then extracting the book she most reverently handed it over to Betty.

With trembling hands, Betty caressed the front of the book and turned it over, looking at the worn covers. She flipped it open to the first page and looked silently at page after page. Looking up, she said, "This is just an ordinary journal, weather, road conditions, that sort of thing."

"Could you just turn to the back and look at a chart drawn there?" Mark asked. "Do you know what that is?"

Betty looked at the chart, frowning. "The alphabet and check marks. Why are some of these in red or green?" She looked up at Mark for the first time.

"I hoped you could tell me," he answered. "But I realize that he might have been keeping these things very secret." He pointed at the chart as he said, "I know that the fourth person

58

at the crime scene in Louisiana's name was Xenia. It began with an X."

She looked again at the chart. Slowly, with her left hand, she touched the chart. "Denise, Carrie, Brianna, Anderson." She said. She looked up, horror mounting in her eyes, fresh tears flowing freely over her reddened cheeks. "Oh, surely not . . .," she began. A shudder made her nearly drop the book, but she righted her grip and looked at it again, studying the markings. "What're these numbers at the bottom? I mean, of course they're years, but what do they represent?"

"I'm not sure, Ma'am." He swallowed hard and cleared his throat. "But, I think that names, check marks, and letters all might led to dates of uh, well, crimes. The year 1997 seems to have been important to him, but that's purely a guess."

"Do you mean to say you think my brother put a check mark on every letter of the alphabet as he killed someone with a name beginning with that letter?" She looked again at the chart, frowning as she calculated.

"Fifty-six, Ma'am. There are fifty-six checks or letters."

"Fifty-six?" She whispered as she looked out over the overgrown yard. "He can't have . . ." her lips moved but no sound came out. "He would . . . he wouldn't have . . . Oh, Anderson, what have you been doing? Why, oh why, Anderson? Oh my, this can't be true, can it?" She looked in panic at her husband who stared back at her, at a loss for words himself. "All of these years, he's been . . . ?" She shook her head in morbid wonder. Her gaze strayed once again to the yard and the forested hills beyond. "The cats," she said, laying a hand on Ben's arm. "Remember the cats, Ben? He kept shooting them that day." She looked at Sarah once again, desperation filling her hoarse, whispery voice. "Did he shoot anybody?"

"I don't know," Sarah answered with a shake of her own head. "I don't think so, but you can see why we need to find any more journals he might have kept. Maybe, just maybe, he left clues so we can investigate and put this all to rest."

Betty closed the book. "Yes," she nodded bleakly. "I'm sure they must be in the lockbox, but I have no idea where that might be." She handed the book to Sarah without looking at her.

"We'll get this back to you someday, when our investigations are completed." Sarah smiled weakly.

"No! No, don't bother," Betty shuddered once again. "I don't want it. I just don't want it." She reached into the pocket of her skirt and drew out the letter from her brother, shoving it into Sarah's hands. "Here's this, too. I imagine you'll want this."

Sarah nodded, her face infused with kindness. "Yes, thank you. It will help in our investigation."

The forensics team finally arrived and for the next few hours scoured the farm. The empty lockbox was found on a shelf in the barn. The journals were laid out neatly in the trunk of Andy Davis' car. They went back to 1978 when Andy had joined the Army. There were sketchy entries in the books between 1982 and 1988, from the time of his discharge to the time when Allen, Andy's brother hanged himself. It seemed to be the first time a name appeared in the margin; 'Wendy', was neatly printed in bold letters.

*   *   *

Back in his office in Texas, Mack poured over the journals himself. He started with the chart in the back of the current year's journal, then went to the beginning and started making two lists, one of names and one of dates by alphabet, an alphabet which started with the letter E.

In June of 1988, Andy caught up his journals and kept them meticulously from that time forward. He told of a girl he knew from his school years in Washington, Donna O'Neal. Her sixteen-year-old sister, Wendy, disappeared in March of 1988, shortly after her sixteenth birthday. He told of the search for her, of his feelings . . . *"The witch deserved it, her and her little rhymes when we were kids. I got the most satisfying feeling of peace in her fear and tears . . ."* That was the first time a name appeared in the margin of one of his journals. In April 1988, neatly printed in capital letters along the edge of one page, was the name W-E-N-D-Y. A newspaper clipping was taped to a page in the 1989 journal, a story of the discovery of scattered remains in the Snoqualamie National Forest, the remains of Wendy O'Neal. There was just one marginal entry in 1989, in the fall, Tanya. Andy had started a new truck route in the Appalachia's, driving from Georgia to New England.

Mack added a new column to his lists, the names of states. He made a copy of the chart Andy had made and blew it up so he could reference it easily as he checked off names and states. The list of years at the bottom of the chart page at the end of the journals meant something he knew, but what? He went over the notes again, ticking off his ideas. "A green box is next to 1997. A red star is next to the years 1997 through 2004." He sat back in his chair and stared up at the ceiling. "A green box, 1997." He sat up and looked once more at the chart. "Ah-h-h, and a green box around Z!" He frowned as he mumbled at the papers on his desk. "It means something; Z, 1997." He searched through the scattered stack of journals until he came to the one for 1997. There were four names along the page margins, but Zeta's name was in green. "Okay, so the name Zeta in green, 1997, green box around the letter Z . . ." He paused. "The letter Z is the end of the alphabet." He frowned and rubbed his temples. "The alphabet, but only E to Z. A in red, B, C, and D in green, and boxed in red. X boxed in red with a red star."

Mack pushed away from the table and walked to the window where he could see traffic far below. "Anderson Baines Cole Davis. That darned alphabet ruled his entire life." He stretched and walked back to his desk. He bounced a pencil against the papers in a slow cadence. "Once he found Z in 1997, he realized he could kill the entire alphabet, but not A, B, C, or D because that was himself, his family."

"Are you making any progress, Chief?" Jared asked from the doorway.

"I don't know. I think he might have been on a spree to kill the alphabet, but I just don't know. This chart is the key to the whole thing, though. I am sure of that. I think we were right about 1997 and Z being the thing that changed the killing from a random thing to one with a purpose. He felt he had to find every letter . . ." Mack's loud voice faded into the still room.

"Meg's been busy filling in our wall chart and I've been working on names found in his journals balanced against ID's found in various states. He's been a busy boy for the past seventeen years, that's for sure."

"That he has, Jared. Mark and Sarah back yet?"

"Nope, they've gone on to Pennsylvania and then I think they're going up to Canada or someplace cold. What's this?" He asked, shuffling through Mack's notes.

"Making a couple charts of my own," Mack smiled.

Jared grimaced as he read the charts Mack had made. "Our boy should've stayed in the army, made a career of it. He might've gotten to go to war and killed people without doing this."

"It isn't about killing people, Jared. It's about killing the alphabet. The alphabet killed his childhood and he's just getting even." Mack sat up suddenly. "Ah-h-h, once he'd killed X, he was done! Then it was all right to kill A, B, C, and D." He looked through the charts once more. "He could've done that by just killing himself, but there was the problem of his wife. She'd carried on the alphabet tradition, so she had to go, too and of course the girls because they were a part of the alphabet that plagued his life." He nodded and smiled. "I see. Now, I see, D, C, B and of course, A is last, the last to fall."

"Yeah, I see a lunatic who got away with sixty murders, that's what I see. Sixty murders right in plain sight with no one the wiser that it was him."

"Sixty, a number divisible by four, yep that was important to him, too. He wrote once that the number four was a curse to his life. See here now, look at Meg's chart." He dragged out a copy of her work. "Between 1989 and 1993, 4 years, he killed 14 women. There's a four in 14, four years . . . Between 1995 and 1999, another 4 years, he killed 24 women, again a number with a four in it and also divisible by four. Then, between 2000 and 2003, another 4 years if you count all of each year, he killed 16 more women." Mack paused.

"Yeah, I get it," answered Jared. "Sixteen is divisible by four.

Mack resumed, nodding his pleasure at what he presumed was Jared's compliment. "He had two years, 1994 and 2004 when he didn't kill anybody. Both have four's in them so that probably meant something, at least to him." He read through his notes for a moment. "His birthday was on the 4th day of the 4th month, 1964. His father died in 1974, evidently on Andy's tenth birthday. His brother died in 1988, right around the time of Andy's birthday. Eighty-eight's divisible by 4, by the way. His mother died in 1984. Two of his sisters, his father, and his brother all died on or around April 4th, the boy's birthday. Man, he must have hated to see that day come around. When everyone else was having parties and celebrating, he had to wonder who would die next just because it was his birthday. Wow!" Mack looked at the notes and became thoughtful. "Now, he's killed his family and himself in April, and I'm sure he did it alphabetically." Mack slapped the desk and stood to pace. "I'll bet he killed her first!" He exclaimed.

"Who?"

"Who? His wife, that's who, of course he did! D, C, B, and then A for the last of the entire alphabet, just like I was thinking a minute ago." He paused and added softly. "'I'm the last to fall.' It's what he was saying to his sister. It's his suicide note and his confession. I've killed them all and now I'm done with me, too."

They were silent for several minutes before Jared spoke.

"You know, all this stuff that happened to him happened to his sister, too. I mean the teasing and bullying at school, all that stuff. The family deaths did too. I mean, well, I know the deaths weren't on her birthday and all that, but still they were all her family and she's had to shoulder all the grief and guilt. She hasn't gone about killing anybody, or even the alphabet, if that's what you think he's been doing."

"That's true," Mack nodded. "But, there's no telling what the same situation does to each person. We all have different psyches even if we're born into the same family. I know my brother and I are as different as night and day!"

"Well, that much is true I guess, but I just feel sorry for that woman. Her whole family's dead and her brother that she cared for and loved went out and killed 60 people, some of them her neighbors and then her own nieces and sister-in-law. That's almost too much for me to fathom and he's not related to me. She's got memories of him as a baby and a boy. I don't know. This case is really getting to me, I guess."

"Need a vacation?" Mack smiled broadly at his coworker.

"Nah, I'll just get back to work so we can get this thing closed out."

"Have we got Andy tied to all the bodies, now?"

Jared turned back at the door and laid a hand along the wooden frame. "Pretty much; same MO, driver's licenses with the red circle, names matching up with names in his journals, places he's been. His sister sent us a stack of post cards he'd mailed her over the years. They tie him to the areas of the crimes pretty well, at least within a state or two, something he could drive in a reasonable amount of time." He tapped his fingers on the wood. "You know, you can say all you want that this wasn't about killing people, or women, or girls, but that's what he did. He hunted them down, befriended them, then took them out into a wilderness area and choked the life out of each one of them. Then he circled their names in red on their licenses and left that as evidence. Alphabet aside, he was a cold-blooded murderer."

Mack nodded as Jared walked back to the desk. "You're right, Jared!" He yelled after him. "You're right," he mumbled to the papers on his desk. "We're both right, and it doesn't change a thing. Sixty people are still dead."

Part Two

WOMEN AND GIRLS

Wendy, 1975, Seattle, WA

Little Wendy O'Neal hid behind the hedge along the sidewalk as her older sister, Donna, taunted the young boy. He was older than Wendy, but not as old as her sister. She watched his eyes turn from sadness to fright and finally to anger as his body shook with suppressed emotions. Finally, he turned and ran.

"Andy-Dandy, rotten candy! You can run, Anderson Davis, but you can't hide!" yelled Donna at the retreating figure.

"Why do you do that?" Wendy asked as they resumed their walk home from school.

"Oh, who cares? He's just a little creep from a family of creeps," Fourteen-year-old Donna looked back as they walked along, her head held *high, curls bouncing. She was a beautiful girl with golden blond curls and honey brown* eyes. She was already developing a figure although her school uniform hid it from all but the most curious of the boys at school. "Does Mother know you came to meet me again?" She frowned at her three-year-old sister.

Wendy, freckle-faced with red unruly hair, jutted out her jaw as she stared up at her older sister. "Yes," she said with a little stamp of her foot. "She told me I could." Her brown eyes sparkled as she stuck out her tongue for emphasis.

Donna hurried on mumbling something as she went. Wendy skipped along behind her, lost in the thoughts of their neighbor boy, Anderson Davis. She wondered if he was crying. *Maybe he's too big to cry,* she thought. *Only little kids cry and he's kind of a big kid.*

As they turned onto their own sidewalk, Wendy looked back down the street. She ran up the steps to the front lawn and craned her neck back toward the Davis house, downhill from their own. She watched Anderson sit glumly on his porch steps for a moment. He slapped his hand onto the porch railing as he jumped up, lunged for the bushes at the side of the porch, and ran around to the back of their property.

Wendy looked to be sure her sister had already gone into their house before she too, went around to the back where she could see clearly into the Davis backyard. She watched in silent horror as the boy held a screaming, clawing neighborhood cat up in the air by the tail. The glee on the boy's face was frightening, but not nearly as frightening as the sound of his laughter. Suddenly, he flipped the cat over and squeezed it by the neck. It fought, but finally lay slumped over his large hands. *He must have gotten scratched really bad,* she thought. Below her, Anderson shook the dead animal before tossing it over the fence into the alley dumpster. He sat with his head resting on his forearms, propped on his knees for a few moments alongside their dilapidated garage before looking up. At that moment, their eyes met and held. Wendy waved a small hand and tried to smile even though she felt sick at what she'd just witnessed. Anderson rose in anger and ran to the back of his own house, disappearing inside. Wendy shrugged expressively before turning to her own back door.

Wendy, 1981

As eight-year-old Wendy O'Neal walked along the street, going home from school, she noticed a young man sitting on the Davis porch. It wasn't the old guy who lived there, but a teenager. He smiled at her as she walked by. She smiled briefly, but kept walking quickly up the hill to her own house. As she walked up the steps to the porch, she glanced back and saw him standing on the lawn at his house. He waved a little wave at her. She suppressed a smile and waved back. She knew now who it was. It was the boy who killed the cat. *He remembered me,* she thought in delicious secrecy as she pushed open the porch door.

"I'm home, Mama!" She called into the kitchen as she put her books on her bed.

"There's cookies!" Mama called back.

Wendy went into the kitchen and sat at the table. Her mother placed a plate of cookies and a cup of milk before her. "Was school all right?" Mama asked.

"Yes." She answered around a mouthful of cookies. "We went to the library today and I brought home some books to read."

"That's good, Dear." Her mother was busy at the sink. She was a middle-aged woman with graying brown hair and a fully freckled face. Her tired brown eyes made her seem older than she was. She slumped a little over the sink, peeling potatoes for their dinner.

"Mama," Wendy began.

"Yes, Dear?"

"Did Mrs. Davis move back?"

"Mrs. who?"

"You know, down the hill, Mrs. Davis."

"Oh, I don't think so, Dear. Why?" She turned to look at her daughter.

"I just saw one of her sons out on the porch."

Her mother turned from the sink and looked at her daughter, drying her hands on a towel. "Who do you mean? Her son lives there." She frowned.

"No, the other one. You remember the little boy everyone used to tease?" She drank down the remainder of her milk. "I think it was him, only he's a lot bigger now, like a teenager or something."

Mrs. O'Neal frowned deeply. "How do you even know that boy?"

"Cause Donna and the other big kids used to call him names and stuff."

"Donna was a part of that?"

Wendy looked up, pursing her lips at the thought that she might have said too much. She nodded quickly.

"I never knew. The poor boy." Mrs. O'Neal sadly shook her head as she turned back to the sink.

"Anyway, I saw him down there. I think it was him. He waved at me."

Her mother turned back to look at her. "He's a stranger, Wendy. Don't you have anything to do with him. I mean it!"

"Okay," Wendy said meekly. *Why?* She thought inwardly. *He was just a sad boy and he knows now that I didn't call him names, not ever.* She excused herself from the table and went to her room to change from her school uniform.

As the days went by, Wendy looked forward to seeing Anderson at the gate to his sidewalk. He would always speak to her and she would always speak to him. On one such day her mother met her at the door of their house. "Did I just see you talking to that Davis boy?" She asked.

Wendy nodded. "Yes, Mama."

"What did he say?"

She shrugged. "He just said, 'Hello, Donna's little sister.' He always calls me that. I told him my name's Wendy, but he still calls me Donna's little sister."

"Why does an older boy talk to a little girl, that's what I want to know," retorted her mother.

"Cause he knows I never called him names like the older kids did and he's being nice, that's why." Wendy fled to her room, close to tears, although she didn't know why. Mother wasn't mad, but why didn't she like Anderson Davis?

Mrs. O'Neal followed her daughter to her room. "I'm sorry, Wendy-Girl. I didn't mean to upset you. It's just strange, that's all. Your father and I don't want anyone to hurt you and we don't know him very well, do we?"

"Why doesn't anyone like the Davis's?" Wendy asked

"It isn't that they aren't liked. It's just that, well, they're . . . there's just been so much sadness and tragedy in that house. It's made them seem a little strange and they don't mix well with others." She came to sit with Wendy on the bed. "I do remember his mother though. She was a very nice, if sad, lady."

"Why are they all so sad?"

"Well, some of her children died in an accident, then her husband died, too. It was just an awkward time for them all. I think with Anderson being the youngest, he must have grown up in a very sad and strange household. He wasn't always a very nice little boy." She got up and walked to the doorway and turned back to smile at her youngest child. "Not to worry, Dear. But, remember that he and his brother shouldn't be keeping company with a young girl. Okay?"

Wendy nodded. But inside, she knew that Anderson would someday be her special friend. *No use to worry Mama,* she thought as she dressed. *She just doesn't understand. After all, she and Papa are kind of old.*

Finally, school was out and summer was upon them. Wendy spent as much time at the neighborhood park as she could. Sometimes Anderson Davis would be there, too. He pushed her in the swings. He could send her flying higher than anyone, even her father when he had the time to spend with her. A few times Anderson joined the neighborhood children in a game of hide and seek, but Wendy heard her father tell him to go home one night. "You leave these kids be, Young Man. Go find friends your own age!"

Wendy watched as Anderson scowled at her father. Suddenly his head came up and he smiled wickedly before turning around and heading down the hill to his house. As he passed Wendy he winked at her. She smiled secretly to herself as she watched him go. Her father told the other children it was time to go home and she had to go inside and go to bed. But, she dreamed that night; she dreamed that Anderson came into her room and whisked her away on his big white horse. It was a delicious, secret dream.

Soon after school started again, Anderson was gone. He just disappeared as instantly as he'd appeared in the spring. Wendy never knew what happened. She passed the house the same way every day, but he didn't come out. One day she saw his older brother out in the back yard and went down the alley to their fence. "Excuse me, Sir," she began. "Where's Anderson?"

The man looked up at her and blinked. He wasn't like Anderson. He was scary with his unshaved face and messed up hair. He didn't smile or anything. "He's gone back to Missouri," he said. "Now, get away from here!" He waved a hammer in her direction.

Wendy gave a little squeal and ran back home. It was a sad time for her as she tried to understand why he left so suddenly. Anderson was gone and she didn't know why. *What did I do? Wasn't I friendly enough?* That night she cried herself to sleep, her nine-year-old heart broken.

Wendy, 1984

When Anderson Davis returned to Seattle, he was a man. He'd finished school in Missouri and gone into the Army where he found some discipline in his life. After his discharge, he visited his mother for a short time then came to spend time with his brother, a sad drunk of a man who spent his days driving a delivery truck and nights in front of the TV with a bottle of beer, several bottles, in fact.

Anderson began working on the house which was in sad need of repair. He went out and got a delivery job like his brother's, but he worked nights. That way he had his days to fix up the house. He painted and mended, and mowed and planted until the place looked decent again. Allen ignored most of the efforts. He complained when his free weekends were interrupted by the sounds of sawing and hammering or the mower running, but he managed to largely ignore the work, and his younger brother.

One Saturday afternoon, Anderson took a walk in the local park. He watched a group of girls sitting on a blanket playing with Barbie dolls. He smiled at them as he found a bench to sit on so he could watch. Finally, they were all gone but one. He moved to a bench that was closer and smiled at her when she looked up. She frowned back at him fiercely.

"I'll bet you're Donna O'Neal's little sister." He said.

She looked at him for a moment before she tossed her short, red curls, leveling him with a black look. "What if I am?"

"I thought so," he acknowledged.

"What do you want?" She asked putting all the angst of spurned womanhood she could muster into the words. It was all she could do not to stick out her tongue at him.

"Just to say hello," he shrugged.

She turned her head and looked at him with malevolent, eleven-year-old eyes. "And then without a goodbye you'll just go away again, right?"

He laughed, not just a polite little laugh, but he put his head back and laughed right out loud.

Wendy jumped up and gathered her dolls and the blanket. Without another word, she ran all the way home. For a long time

71

she heard his laughter echoing in her mind. *Just like when he killed that cat,* she thought. *He hurts things and he hurts people, and it makes him happy. I was such a child when I thought he was handsome and wonderful! Now I'll ignore him forever!*

She saw him from time to time that long year. She thought it would never end, that he'd never go away again. She took a different way home everyday so she wouldn't have to go by his house because he was always working on it, painting or something. She laughed out loud when she saw him in his Army fatigues, back from some weekend with his unit. She stopped to look back down the street to be sure he'd heard her laughter. He stared at her for a moment before he walked into his house

A few days later he met her in the alley as she scurried home from school. "Is this your cat?" He held a limp animal draped over one hand.

"What happened to him?" She asked in a squeaky voice and with a look of horror.

"He outlived his usefulness," he replied calmly as he threw the dead animal into the dumpster. He smiled at her, gave a little wave, and walked through the gate into his own yard. She could hear his laughter as he walked up the steps and into his house.

Wendy couldn't move. It wasn't her cat, but she was rooted to the spot thinking back to the day she'd watched him kill another cat with his bare hands. "Did you kill this one, too?" She whispered. "Why do you kill defenseless little kitties?" She paused as though there would be an answer to her unspoken question, then she turned woodenly and walked to her own gate. She threw up right there in the alley. Afterwards, she walked into the house and washed her face at the kitchen sink. "I'm home," she said as she wiped her face with a towel.

"Are you sick?" Her mother rushed to her side and felt her forehead. "I do believe you have a fever, and you look all flushed and shaky. What's wrong?"

"Nothing," answered Wendy. "I just want to lie down. I, I puked out in the alley."

"I'll make some chamomile tea," offered Mrs. O'Neal. "You must be getting that awful flu that's going around."

When her father came home from work, Wendy insisted she was well and could eat some of the soup her mother had fixed for supper. She listened but didn't participate in the table conversation.

"Are you feeling better, My Girl?" Her father finally asked.

Wendy looked up and smiled wanly. "Yes, Papa."

"Good!" He looked up at her mother. "Are you sure it was the flu?" He asked.

"Well, it's been going around," she offered in reply.

Wendy sighed. "It wasn't the flu, Mama. I just saw a dead cat in the alley and it made me puke." She said as she pushed at her nearly empty bowl.

"A dead cat?" Her father began laughing with his hearty, booming voice. He was a large man with a protruding stomach and thinning, red-gray hair. His large nose turned red when he talked and almost purple when he laughed. It made Wendy smile to see it.

"Well of all things," Mrs. O'Neal said. "Why didn't you tell me at once?" She was smiling, too.

"I still felt like puking," Wendy answered.

"I'll go take care of it," her father said as he scooted back his chair, scraping it against the tile floor.

"No!" Wendy said too quickly, shaking her head. "I mean, one of the neighbors already threw it into the dumpster. It, it's already gone."

"One of the neighbors?" Asked her mother. She was thinking of all the close neighbors, most of whom were elderly.

"Who?" Her father asked with a serious frown.

"It's the Davis boy, isn't it?" Her mother asked before Wendy could think of an answer.

Wendy closed her eyes to keep the tears from falling and nodded. "Yes," she whispered. "I saw him throw it away and that's what made me sick."

Her parents looked at each other knowingly for a few seconds. "What were you doing in the alley?" Her father asked.

"She's been coming home from school that way for a long time, Dear," interceded her mother.

"I always walk through the alley, Father," Wendy said at the same time.

Mr. O'Neal frowned. "Well, no more. You come home on the sidewalk."

"You haven't been talking to the Davis boy, have you?" Mother asked.

Wendy shook her head. "No. He said hello once during the summer, but I haven't talked to him since then."

Her father seemed to relax. "Good, good, just keep it that way. That man has no business talking to kids. His brother's a no-good drunk and . . ."

"Thomas!" His wife admonished. "Anderson's cleaned up that place all by himself. His brother Allen's lucky to have him living there."

"But, still . . ." He began again only to be cut off by his wife.

"Yes, but he doesn't have any business talking to little girls." She nodded in agreement.

"I'm eleven!" Wendy reminded them in protest.

"The subject's closed," her father said as he arose and went to the living room and the TV where he'd spend the rest of the evening.

Long after supper Wendy laid on her bed in the shadows and thought. *Mother's right. Anderson's cleaned up the place real nice. He isn't a drunk like his brother. I've just been silly. Because I saw him kill a cat when he was a boy is no reason to believe he killed that one today. It probably got run over by a car and he was just throwing it away. Of course!* She sat up and looked out the window over the night-lighted city. *He just laughed because I got sick! I must have looked pretty silly to him. He must think I'm just a little girl, too.*

Wendy went to the bathroom and prepared to go to bed. She stopped by the living room and said good night to her parents who kissed her fondly. Her mother followed her back to her bedroom and tucked her into bed. "Don't grow up too fast, my girl," said her mother. "You're still a girl, still my sweet little girl."

Wendy settled safely in her bed, thinking of white knights and white horses until her thoughts became dreams and her dreams became reality.

Wendy, 1986-1987

She never saw Anderson Davis again. That is, not until she was almost fourteen years old. She was at a beach party with some of her friends when he showed up. He stood by an old car in the parking lot while she and her friends danced in the sand.

"Who's that guy?" Someone asked.

Wendy looked up and saw him. She smiled to herself.

"I don't know," answered another one of the girls. "He's giving me the creeps."

"It's like the guy who watched us in the park all the time a couple of years ago, remember?" Asked the first girl.

"Maybe he's just watching over us," Wendy offered.

"Why would he do that?"

Wendy shrugged. "I'll go and ask him."

"Wendy O'Neal!" Her friend said in horror. "You'll do no such thing! Your dad would kill us if we let you talk to a stranger."

Wendy was already on her way. She laughed over her shoulder. "He's not a stranger, Stupid," she said. "I know him."

Andy Davis watched as the girl walked toward him. She was becoming a woman. He'd waited a long time for Donna O'Neal's sister to become a woman. *Just a while longer,* he thought. He smiled and raised one eyebrow as she came nearer. "Hello," he offered quietly.

"Hello, Anderson Davis," she said coyly.

His smile widened. "Seen any cats around here?"

Her mouth dropped open in surprise. "What? Oh! You are an evil man!" Her eyes told him that she didn't really think he was so evil. Or, that she liked the evil.

His tongue touched his lips as he considered the girl-woman before him. She wasn't as pretty as her sister, but that was all right. He crossed his arms and rested them on his knee as he put one foot on the bumper of his car. "You girls know it's almost dark?"

"Yeah, why do you care?" She retorted.

He put his foot down and started for the driver's door of his car. "You better go home before the boogey man gets you." His laughter floated over her like a soothing balm. She watched him start his car and back away.

"Who was that?" A voice startled her from near her right shoulder.

She looked at her friend and smiled. "Just an old neighbor."

"Old is right," offered her friend. "What'd he want?"

"Oh, um, my parents are getting worried. It's getting late and we need to go home before the 'boogey man' gets us."

"That is so stupid!" Her friend said in disgust.

"I know, but it probably is time to go before my dad comes down here himself." She looked at the retreating car and smiled again, biting her lower lip to keep the smile from spreading all over her face.

"That is the guy from the park," said another friend. "What is he, a spy for your dad or something?"

Wendy nodded. "Something, like that, it's a fact," she said.

Wendy was a busy teenager. She wasn't especially popular in the large high school she attended, but she wasn't shunned, either. She was involved in band and choir and the drama club from her earliest junior high and high school moments. She went out with friends to the beach and to movies and to the local soda shop, but she never thought about any one boy seriously. She reserved her heart for someone special and dreamed her secret dreams.

Wendy often saw Anderson Davis in the distance, watching as usual. He always sat not too far away at the movies or at sports games. She missed his surveillance when he was gone in his truck for weeks at a time.

"Where's your body guard?" Someone would ask.

She'd just smile. "Oh, he's around," she'd say.

As she approached fifteen years old, her parents sat her down for a talk. "Wendy," began her father. "Does Anderson Davis bother you?"

She frowned. "Who?"

"You know who Anderson Davis is, Wendy. Don't play games with your father," her mother added.

"Yeah, but what are you talking about?" She asked, still frowning. *Oh-oh,* she thought. *Where'd this come from? Who's been talking?*

As if reading her thoughts, her father continued. "Some of us parents have been talking and we're afraid that this man's been following you and your friends around. Is it true? Have you seen him?"

Wendy appeared to think for a moment. "Not really," she began. "Well, I've seen him around at games and stuff, but then I see most everybody from the neighborhood at those things, too." She looked innocently at her parents. "Why, is there a problem?"

"You don't think he's been following you around?"

"Yu-u-ck!" She screwed up her face for emphasis. "He's like old enough to be our parents, almost!"

Her mother smiled and her father seemed to relax. "How often do you see him hanging around?" Her father persisted, but more calmly than before.

"I don't know," she whined. "I'm a teenager. Why would I notice that? Why are you being mean about this? Have I done something wrong?"

"No, no, Dear," her mother came to the rescue. "Your father and I just became concerned when we heard things from other parents. It's nothing you've done, Honey." She turned and looked at her husband. "Thomas, I think this is enough, don't you?"

Thomas studied his daughter for a moment. "I suppose," he conceded. "But, if you see him anywhere around you girls, I want you to come right to me and tell me, do you hear?"

"Yes, Sir," she nodded, tears dropping to her hands in her lap.

"There, there, Dear," crooned her mother, rushing to hold her daughter. "Don't cry. Thomas, you've made her cry."

He flashed a look of irritation at his wife. "Tears or not, that boy doesn't have any business hanging around teenaged girls!" His voice boomed out.

"I know, I know," she nodded, holding her daughter to her bosom. "It's all right, Wendy. Father isn't mad at you."

"He, he isn't exactly a boy, Father," Wendy managed to squeak out.

Thomas O'Neal was about to rise from his chair, but stopped and looked closely at his daughter.

She bit her lip before explaining. "Well, really, Father, he's an older man, you know. He just doesn't have any family of his own yet. Maybe he feels like he should look after the neighborhood teenagers or something." She shrugged, trying to look innocent.

"Huh!" Her father exploded. "Let him go look after the teenaged boys, then. He's spending too much time trailing after young girls." He rose and started for the kitchen. "And you're right about one thing! He's an older man! He needs to go back to Missouri or Mississippi, or wherever his Mama took him!" With that, he left the room.

"Really, Mama," Wendy said as she stood and went to her room.

"I know, Dear. I know," her mother smiled sadly.

Once alone in her room, Wendy paced between the bed and window. "That was too close for comfort," she breathed. Andy, as he'd insisted she now call him, had bought her sodas a few times and they'd sneaked away to the beach twice, walking in the freezing, pelting rain. He treated her as if she was an adult, not a child, like her parents did. "If only they could understand," she whined to the mirror above her dresser. "But, they're so old! They haven't a clue what it's like to be young anymore." She walked to the window and knelt on the floor, looking out over the city. "Andy and Wendy," she sighed. "It goes together beautifully."

Just this afternoon, when they'd met behind the cedars along the alley, Andy had asked her when her birthday was.

"March 26," she'd said. "Why?"

"I'll have a surprise for you," he answered.

"What kind of surprise?" She clapped her gloved hands in delight. "I can't wait another two whole weeks! Please tell me!"

"Stop," he'd been kind of stern. "It's a surprise and that's how it'll stay. I'll be back from California just in time."

"You're leaving again?" She'd pouted prettily.

Anderson looked at her and smiled to himself. He brushed her pouting lips lightly with his own. "Just be patient, okay?"

In breathless wonder, she nodded. *Did he just kiss me?* She thought as she watched him walk down the meandering path through the cedars toward his back gate.

Later that night, as she looked out over the city from her bedroom, she relived the moment once again. She felt a strange tingling come over her body. *This is what it's like to be in love,* she thought, hugging herself tight. *I'll bet my parents never knew anything like this!* She looked up at the night sky, the city lights drowning out the starlight. *It's a dream come true. It's what I've been waiting for since I was three years old!*

It was a night filled with delicious, secret dreams.

Wendy, March 26, 1988

The long anticipated day finally arrived. It was a Saturday so Wendy slept until 9 o'clock. Her parents planned a family picnic in the park, weather permitting. Donna arrived from her home in Portland for the big day. Her mother always made a special fuss out of every holiday and birthday. But, Wendy was thinking only of Andy. He'd promised her a surprise on her birthday. She wondered how he'd manage it since there would be so many people around.

Donna was a secretary in some big office in Portland. Their parents spent every moment whenever she was home talking about how important her older sister was. Wendy finally asked if she could go to the park at about noon. *Maybe Andy will surprise me there if I'm available and alone,* she thought. She wiped the back of her hand slowly across her mouth at the memory of their first kiss.

"Not yet," mother said. "We'll all go around two o'clock. That will be soon enough. Come and visit with your sister."

Wendy sat glumly on the couch.

"Oh, she's very much a teenager, isn't she?" Donna commented.

Wendy made a face at her. "I'm in the room. You can talk to me like I exist."

Their mother laughed. "Yes, well too much so, I'm afraid. Not like you, Donna. You weren't so outspoken, at least not to your parents."

Donna looked hard at her younger sibling. "Yes, well I'm afraid it's that way with all teenagers these days. They don't know when to be quiet." Her smile was acidic and made Wendy cringe.

"Well, at least I'm not mean to the little neighbor kids like you were," she retorted.

Donna laughed without any humor. "I've heard how kind you've been to little Andy-Dandy," she said. "Mother's told me he practically worships you."

Wendy looked horrified at her mother. "You said that?"

Her mother began to protest. "Oh, well, no I don't think I said anything like that. Donna, really, you shouldn't tease."

"No, she didn't!" Donna laughed openly at her sister's discomfort. "But it got you going, didn't it?"

"Let's get ready to go to the park," their mother interjected. "I know it's still early, but it's nearly time. Your father will be back from the store soon."

Wendy sighed in relief as she jumped up to help her mother. Donna laughed quietly, following along to the kitchen.

"You aren't really flirting with that guy, are you, Little Sis?"

"What guy?" Wendy frowned to hide her anxiety. She was sure her sister could hear her heart beating, it was pounding so loudly in her own ears.

"Andy Davis, of course." Donna gave Wendy a little shove with her hip. "Mother's worried, you know."

"Geez, Donna, he's practically as old as you." Wendy flipped her head and walked out the door.

Donna looked thoughtfully after her younger sibling. "H-m-m-m-m," she uttered toward the door.

The picnic was a fine event. Mother had invited many other families of girls Wendy knew. They played kickball and ate lots of food. The girls played tag and used the park equipment like they were little girls again. Finally, there were just Wendy and her friend, Cynthia left. They sat together, slowly drifting on swings. "It's kind of like saying goodbye to childhood, isn't it?" Wendy asked.

"Yeah, like this is our last time to act like little girls. It does seem like that." Answered Cynthia.

"Do your parents know you've been sneaking around with Eddy?" Wendy asked.

"I don't think so." She shook her head and pumped herself higher in the swing. "Anyway, we're breaking up. He acts like such a jerk sometimes."

"What do you mean?" Wendy dragged her feet in the sand to stop the swing. "I thought you two were gonna run away as soon as you turn fifteen."

"Well, he acts like such a boy, you know, like my brothers. I get enough of that from them. I think I might like to get to know someone older."

"That's what I've been thinking, too," Wendy swiveled in her swing. "My mom married an older guy and that's worked out okay."

"Some of the Senior boys are cool," Cynthia slowed down and dragged her feet in the sand to stop near Wendy. "If we could ever get them to notice us, that is."

"Yeah," Wendy admitted idly.

"Oh-oh, it looks like our folks are getting ready to go."

Wendy looked at the picnic area where the adults were packing up the trash. Her father was returning from the car and waved at her to join them. "C'mon, Wendy!" He called.

"Maybe they could go on home and I could walk you half-way to your house and still get home before dark," Wendy suggested.

"Sure, okay, if they'll agree."

The girls linked arms and waltzed over to their parents. "Can we walk?" Wendy asked.

"Walk where?" Her father asked. "It's almost dark already."

"We're not done talking. Can we walk half way to Cynthia's house? I'll run all the way back home right after, I promise." Wendy put on her best pleading face.

"I don't know, Wendy . . ." began her father.

"Ah, let the girls have their fun," chimed in the other adults.

Donna laid a hand on her father's arm. "Really, Dad, let them have some more time together. She's gonna grow up too, you know."

"Huh," he answered. "All right, then, but come straight home. No more than an hour, do you hear?"

"Yes, Father," Wendy answered, all smiles. "I hear you and I'll be home right away, I promise." She saluted to give her answer emphasis.

The girls watched the adults go before they turned to walk across the park in the opposite direction. "Is someone following us?" Cynthia asked, looking into the trees along the edge of the park as they chattered their way along.

"Where?" Wendy craned her neck to see. "I don't see anyone, do you?"

"No, I guess not. I just thought I saw someone moving over there by those trees." She pointed to their left.

Wendy seemed disappointed. "Probably just someone out walking a dog cause it's getting too cold for anyone else out here. I should've grabbed my sweater." She shivered and rubbed her hands over her bare arms.

"See?" Her friend pointed at the trees. "There's someone over there!"

Wendy peered past her friend. "I can't see anyone. Besides, this is a park. People are always walking around out here. What's got you so scared?"

"I don't know. I just want to get home. Come on, let's run for a little bit."

They started running toward the trees and the park edge. In a few moments they would be saying goodbye and turning toward their own homes. Wendy kept looking toward their left, but couldn't see anything in the shadows. Suddenly, she came to an abrupt halt, ramming into her friend who had stopped and was staring down at the ground.

"Oh, yuck! It's a dead cat! That's disgusting!"

Wendy looked down at the ground between them. Sure enough, there was a dead cat lying at her feet. *I'll bring you a surprise, he'd said.* Her mind went to Andy's last words. "No!" She screamed. Without saying another word she turned and ran out of the park and up the street, leaving her friend behind. She turned sharply into the alley her feet slipping on the stones, her sobs making her hiccup. She could barely see for the tears flowing from her swollen eyes. It was too cruel. She couldn't believe he'd do such a thing, but it was a dead cat and she knew he killed cats . . .

"Whoa, whoa, where you going?" Andy grasped the running girl by the arms just as she was passing his garage. "Hey, Birthday Girl, what's wrong?"

Wendy beat at him with her fists, pulling to free herself from his grasp. "Let me go! I got your surprise. You're crazy and I'm going home. Let me go!" She pulled and shoved for all she was worth, but he kept her easily in his grasp.

"Stop, now. Just stop and tell me what you're talking about. My surprise for you is sitting right over there by your gate. Talk to me, come on, slow down and talk to me." He held her tight against his chest until she stopped flailing her arms and calmed down.

"What, what did you say?" She peered up at him. "My surprise is where?" She looked beyond him at a cardboard box that was sitting next to their backyard gate.

He smiled down at her and nodded. "I left it there because I know your folks don't want me to talk to you. Now, what were you talking about?"

Wendy closed her eyes in embarrassment. "In the park," she mumbled. "There was a dead cat, and I thought . . ." she put her head down in shame and shook it gently. "I'm so sorry."

Andy held her out at arm's length and looked hard at her tear-streaked face. "You thought I left you a dead cat for your birthday? And you thought I left it in the park?" He suddenly smiled, and just as suddenly burst into his maniacal laughter. "Go home, Little Girl. Take your present and go home." He shoved her away from him and slipped quickly to his own yard and inside his house.

Wendy approached the closed box slowly as his laughter still rang in her ears. She kicked at the box with her toe. From inside she heard the plaintive cry of a kitten. Bending down, she tore at the lid and opened it. A fluffy white kitten jumped up on the edge of the lid. "Meow," it cried. Wendy sat on the ground and picked up the little cat. "I'm so sorry," she muttered through her tears. "I'm so sorry I hurt you like that." She looked toward the Davis house, but it was shrouded in darkness. She took the kitten inside. "Look, someone left a kitten in the alley. It's like a little birthday present."

"Absolutely not!" Her father was adamant. "We've never had a cat and we're not starting now. There's too many of the darned things in the neighborhood as it is. No, I won't have one, and especially not in the house!"

Wendy spent the better part of two hours arguing off and on with her father over the fate of the white kitten. "I'll keep it on the porch until I find a home for it," she finally said in resignation.

"Fine!" Her father shouted. "But, if it isn't gone by mid week, I'll get rid of it myself."

Wendy went to the alley for the box to place inside the porch. She set it up on its side and lined it with an old towel, and she got the kitten a small bowl of warm milk. He lapped it up greedily as she sat with him on the cold floor. "We mustn't ever let him know, Candy," she crooned to the small bundle of fur nestled in her lap. He purred in contentment.

Her mother appeared at the door. It's cold, Wendy. Come in and get ready for bed."

"Yes, Mother. I'll be right there," she sighed. She placed the kitten on the towel in the box and petted it until it settled down to sleep. Then she tiptoed into the house.

*　　*　　*

Andy Davis slipped inside the kitchen door and closed it gently. He could hear the television blaring in the living room where he knew Allen would be lounging with a couple of beers. He sighed at the messy kitchen with its pile of unwashed dishes in the sink and the greasy top on the stove. "Allen, you're a pig," he mumbled.

"Better a pig than a cradle robber," came the slurred voice of his older brother.

Andy frowned. "What?"

"What'cha doin' hanging around that little girl?"

"Who?"

Allen swung his bottle toward the wall. "That little girl up the hill; you lost your marbles?"

"If you were ever sober, maybe I'd try to explain it to you."

"Huh! I know what I know and I see what I see about you, Baby Brother. What I don't get is why you spy on little girls. You're a good-lookin' sort of guy, I know you date women, so what's the big deal?"

"It's better if you don't know." Andy's face was a mask of innocence. No emotions played across his handsome features and no feelings reached his cold eyes.

Allen shivered suddenly as he peered closer at his brother. "You're as cold as a snake, Boy." He shook his big head slowly and went back to his chair. "As cold as a snake and as deep as a river."

Andy followed his older brother into the living room and sat on the arm of the sofa across from Allen's recliner. He grabbed the remote and used it to turn off the TV. "Doesn't it ever bother you that everyone around here makes fun of us? They always have, but now that we're all adults, they talk behind their doors and peek out their windows, and they still make up stories and hate us."

"Aw, that's just crazy talk, Andy. Nobody cares about us."

"That's true."

"I didn't mean that. Ma and Betty, they always cared, you know that."

"Maybe it was different for you. Maybe nobody called you names and made up rhymes with your name."

"When you gonna grow up?"

"And be a real man?" Andy exploded. He rose from the couch and paced the floor. "What's it take to do that? I joined the army and my name became a cadence! How long do I have to wait for people to stop calling out the alphabet every time I sign a paper? When do I get to walk down the street like a normal person without some kid-girl making up rhymes about me?" He stopped and sat down again, a wicked smile replacing the anger. "Never mind. It'll be over soon. Miss Donna O'Neal will get hers."

"Donna? Is this all about the older sister? Is she the one who used to beat you up and call you names?"

"Shut up, Allen. You don't know nothing."

"So, you think terrorizing the little sister with dead cats and stuff is somehow payback?" Allen burst out laughing and took another swig of his warm beer. "Geez, you're such a dork, Andy. Like I said before, grow up."

"Well, we'll see," Andy said calmly. "We'll see what happens." He slapped his palms against his knees. "Guess I'll go to bed as soon as the dishes are done," he hinted.

"Hm-m-m," Allen answered, already back to watching his beloved TV. He cradled the remote in his lap.

On Tuesday, Andy waited in his car at the end of the block. When he saw Wendy he waved at her, pointed toward the park, and drove away.

Wendy watched him go with a light heart and great excitement. She ran home to change from her uniform. "There's cookies," her mother called out when she heard the door close.

"I'm going for a run in the park first, okay?" Wendy yelled as she rushed to her room and hastily changed into some slacks and a turtle neck sweater.

Her mother appeared in the doorway. "Home work first, Dear."

"I don't have any tonight, just a library book. I promise to read before bed."

"Why all the excitement to go to the park?"

"Mom, it's the first really warm day and it'll be getting dark soon. I want to try out some moves to maybe be a cheerleader or something. Okay?"

"Your sister's coming to stay for a week."

"Why?" She frowned, wrinkling her nose.

"Wendy! Your sister loves you."

"I know, sorry. Can I go?"

"Only for an hour, no more."

"Okay," she kissed her mother on the cheek. "I promise."

Without another word, she was out the door.

The hour passed, then another. By the time her husband came home from work, Mrs. O'Neal was angry at her teenager. They ate supper, discussing various discipline methods when their girl would come waltzing in the door with whatever excuse she'd have. As the hours rolled on, they became worried, then frightened. By eleven o'clock that night, they were frantic. They'd called the police and hunted everywhere they could think of on their own. Mrs. O'Neal had called all Wendy's classmates, but no one had seen her after school. No one they met remembered seeing her in the park at all that afternoon or evening. By Wednesday morning, the whole neighborhood turned out to look for the missing girl, but there was no trace.

On Saturday morning, most people had gone on with their lives, the police were pursuing more recent events, and there was no solace for the O'Neal family. A small group of neighbors met in the park where evening was drawing into night and still there was no clue to Wendy's whereabouts. Donna approached Andy Davis. "Thanks for your help, Andy. You've been here everyday."

Andy eyed her with a bemused look. "No problem. Wendy was always <u>nice</u> to me."

Donna didn't meet his gaze. "Yes, she's always nice to everyone. She's a child."

"You weren't nice to me when you were a child," he said softly.

Her eyes flashed with menace. "Are you holding a grudge against me?"

"Nope," he shook his head slowly. "Are you?"

Tears washed down her face. "No, Andy, I'm not. My baby sister is missing and I'm suffering almost as much as my parents." She turned slightly and motioned at them.

Andy smiled but said nothing. He looked steadily at the ground.

"Your brother never came out to help," Donna observed, turning back to look at him.

"My brother is lost in a bottle of booze when he isn't at work. He doesn't know what goes on in his own house, much less in the neighborhood."

"Oh . . . sorry," she mumbled. "He always was kind of reclusive."

"Yeah, well he doesn't like people much," he paused. "Me neither, for that matter."

"Just little girls?" She taunted.

"Especially not little girls," he answered calmly. "They're mean and nasty. Kind of like cats, you know?"

Donna frowned deeply. "Is that what you thought of me when we were children?"

Andy stood to his full height. "Still do," he said, turned on his heel, and walked away.

Donna returned to her parents. "That guy is a creep," she whispered to her mother.

Mrs. O'Neal looked after Andy's retreating figure. "He's been here looking, every day."

"Did the police search his house? His brother's a drunk and all. They've always been kind of strange, I think."

"Yes, Dear, your father insisted on their place being searched, first thing. He never trusted the boy, what with him always seeming to be around the girls when they were out." She sighed. "He and his brother may be strange, but Wendy wasn't there. I don't think she ever went to their house. No one does. She was never seen there, at the house, I mean. She did talk to Andy a couple of times out in the alley on her way home from school and he was seen quite a lot wherever the kids were gathered." A shudder passed over her bent and slight form. "They didn't find her or anything of hers in their garage, either. After being targeted like that, I'm surprised he showed up to help us at all, but he's been faithful every day."

"Perhaps I should have been kinder," Donna sighed.

"What, Dear?"

"Oh, nothing. It's nothing." She looked again toward the houses along the quiet street, but Andy Davis was nowhere to be found.

*   *   *

Andy walked up to his brother who was standing in their back yard. "What you doing out here?"

Allen jumped at the sound of his brother's voice. "I . . . I was just looking for something."

"In the yard?"

"You been out here lately?"

"When I parked my car in the garage."

"You've got a car?"

Andy shook his head and smiled crookedly. "Yeah, it's right there in the garage."

"Yeah, I saw it. Didn't know where it came from." He paused for a long time. "That old garage needs to come down."

"I just fixed it up. You know, like I fixed the house you live in? That's what I do on my days off. What do you do?"

"Hmm," he answered noncommittally.

"Next week I got another load to haul down to California. I'll be gone a week or so."

"You know about that little girl?"

"Yeah, tough on the family."

Allen looked squarely at younger brother. It was the first time he seemed almost sober in nearly a year. "You know what happened?"

"What?" Andy shrugged.

"To the girl. Do you know what happened to her?"

"She's run away, maybe," Andy suppressed a smile, one eyebrow rising. "Do you know what happened?"

"You was gone almost all night the other night." He paused to wipe the sweat from his face. "Now you're out there helping them try to find her."

"I got a life, you know, I come and go as I please. And, as for helping neighbors, that's what sober neighbors do, Brother."

"Did you do something to that little girl?" Allen demanded, his voice rising and sweat pouring over his florid face. "I seen you talking to her before. It got me to thinking . . .

"What?" Andy laughed as he slowly walked toward the back door. "What you been thinking? Heck Man, you don't know half what goes on around here, and now, all of a sudden, you're thinking. You better crawl back into your bottle, Brother. It's safer for you there." He let the door slam behind him.

Allen stared at the back of the house for a few seconds, then turned and looked into the open garage. There wasn't much to see. Andy's car took up most of the space and there were a few tools hanging on one wall. Allen gazed up at the rafters and noted some old lumber and a piece of rope dangling along the far wall. He reached for the door handle and pulled, shutting off his vision of the inside of the old building. He rested his hands on the door, shaking his head lightly. "My mind's about gone, my brother's a lunatic," he turned and looked at the house. Tears coursed down his florid cheeks and he wiped at them with his soft, white hands. "It ain't worth it," he whispered. "It just ain't worth it."

Andy made himself scarce for the rest of the weekend, staying in a cheap motel on the outskirts of the city rather than going home to his drunk brother. He was done looking for lost girls and done trying to live with his brother. It was about time to go back to Missouri. His grandparents' old home was always a safe haven for him. Mother, who died in 1984, and her sister Sandy lived on the old place and his own sister Betty, lived not too far away. Aunt Sandy and Betty would be glad to see him, no matter what. He opened his journal and looked at the pages for the previous week. In the margin for the 29th of March he wrote, 'Wendy' in neat capital letters.

He drove back home on Monday, ready to say goodbye to Allen and his old neighborhood. After his run to California, he'd just keep driving back to Missouri. He pulled up in front of the old garage and got out to open the door so he could park his car. What he saw left him standing in silence, staring into the interior. Hanging there from one of the ceiling beams was Allen's lifeless body. It was April 4th, and Andy Davis was 24 years old, today.

Late Summer, 1988

Andy Davis sat on the porch of his little cottage in Missouri, and shot idly at a stray cat. His sister, Betty and her husband Ben, sat with him.

"Why do you kill those cats?" Ben asked.

"Cause they're helpless," Andy muttered as he took aim at another cat near the shed.

"Well, stop it, Anderson, really," put in his sister.

"They overrun the place just like a bunch of rats," he said, putting his .22 caliber handgun down on the swing.

Ben shifted his weight on the stoop. "You gonna go out on the road with that fancy rig?" He pointed at the new truck tractor Andy had just brought home. It gleamed bright red in the sunlight.

"Yep," he grinned, looking lovingly at the truck. "I've got a load to pick up out in Maine next week. If it works out, I'll run the east Appalachia's for a few months. Probably pay this place off before another year's out."

"You can make that kind of money?" Betty asked.

"Yeah, well I'll sleep in the truck and won't eat that much. I think I'll be able to swing it." He frowned at the small home behind him. "Paid too much as it is. Should've waited awhile and saved my money."

"You could've lived with Aunt Sandy," she commented.

"Nah. That would've been all right if Mama was still there, but not now."

"I'm sorry you had such a terrible time out in Seattle," Betty changed the subject. "Did you get a decent price for the old house? It wasn't in very good shape, I suppose."

"I fixed it up when I lived with Allen, you know. Gave me something to do on my days off. Allen was always too drunk to care."

"Did they ever find that O'Neal girl out there in Seattle?" Betty asked. "Do they know what happened to her?"

"Little pimple-face probably deserved what she got," he answered with a wicked laugh.

"Did you know her?" Betty frowned. "The girl would've been very young."

"No!" Andy got up and stretched before walking to the door. "Want something to drink, Ben?"

"No, we're gonna hit the road in a minute."

"I wish he wouldn't go out on the road in that truck. I wish he'd just find something around here, settle down and get married." Betty said in a near whisper to her husband.

"Let the man be," he said as he got up and dusted off the seat of his pants. "He'll work things out one of these days."

"But, a truck driver!" She continued. "He'll end up just like Allen." She dabbed at a tear in her eye.

"I ain't gonna be like Allen!" Andy boomed from behind her. "I'm already not like Allen. I don't drink for one thing. Allen was a lush who hid from life in a bottle. As for women," he got close to his sister and stared into her face. "Who needs 'em?"

"Anderson!" She complained. "I'm a woman."

"So you are," he commented, sitting on the stoop where Ben had been.

"Women always want men to be married," Ben explained with a half-grin. "She'll nag at you about it, but you go do what you need to do." He turned his attention to his wife, grabbing her hand. "We gotta be going. It's gonna be dark before we get home."

"Okay," Andy called after them as they walked hand-in-hand toward their car. "I'll send you a postcard from, um, Pennsylvania or Georgia, or someplace!"

He watched them drive away, then let his gaze sweep over the truck gleaming in the bright sunlight. He smiled and closed his eyes as a gentle breeze ruffled his unruly hair.

Anderson Davis spent the next four years driving in the eastern mountains and along the seaboard. His truck proudly sported the hand-made sign, 'A-D Trucking, Seattle, WA'. His new driver's license from West Virginia read, 'Cole Davis'.

Almost religiously, he sent a postcard to his sister on the 4th day of each month. He never said much, but he signed each one with a simple letter A, and they let Betty know where he was.

Tanya, 1990, Knoxville, TN

She was just a farm chick, hitchhiking along the highway. She was so small, only five-foot—two, and weighing in at less than 100 pounds, looking almost like a child. "How old are you, twelve?" He asked when she approached him at a rest area.

She smiled broadly, showing even white teeth. It caused her freckles, of which there was an abundance, to dance across her nose and cheeks. "Try nineteen," she laughed. "Everyone always thinks I'm a kid!"

He looked her over once again, noticing for the first time, the contour of her calves and her budding figure. "Okay, Miss Nineteen," he said. "I should have known by your body that you were older. Sorry about that." He appraised her with new interest.

She blushed just enough to again heighten the freckles. Her brown eyes gleamed with mischief. "So, where you headed?"

"Why, where you going?" He countered back.

"Up north, maybe," she answered thoughtfully. "I've got cousins in Pennsylvania. Sometimes I hitch a ride up there to see them."

He looked around the small park. No one seemed to notice him talking to the girl. "Where do you live, Girl?" He asked.

"Close. Why, you want to meet my folks or something?"

He backed up a step from the picnic table where he'd been lounging. "Uh, no. Not at all."

She laughed at his discomfiture. "I live around here, back in the hills a ways. You know, a couple of hollers over that way." She waved her hand toward the trees behind the rest park.

"And you just come over here and pick up men?"

She cocked her head prettily, looking at him thoughtfully. "Something like that, I guess. Truckers go places and see things. I like to travel around."

"Yeah, well I'm headed south right now. This here," he pointed to the road, "is the south-bound lane." He saw the disappointment in her face. "But I'll be back in a week or two. If you still want a ride, I guess I can take you up north with me."

"So, where you going down south?"

94

"This load goes to Georgia, but I'll pick up a couple of items down there and make some side runs into Florida and maybe Alabama."

"Wow, your company must do business everywhere," she commented.

"Well, I work for myself, you see. I arrange my own loads. That way, when I don't want to work for awhile, I can just go home, or whatever."

"Where's home?" She asked.

He frowned and looked at her again. "You're too nosey, Girl."

"The name's Tanya," she said. "Not Girl." A silence fell between them as he watched other truckers come and go. There were a few curious glances now. He'd spent too much time talking to this girl who looked like a child. He'd almost forgotten she was standing close by, so her next words startled him. "What's your name?"

"What?" He barked out at her. Her eyes hardened at the tone in his voice. "We aren't gonna become friends or anything, so what do you need to know my name for?"

Tanya's head came up, chin outthrust, her eyes darkening to obsidian. "I told you my name, now it's your turn. It's polite conversation." With that, she turned abruptly and walked to the women's restroom without a backwards glance. Her long, reddish-brown hair swung free behind her.

"Nasty little girl," he mumbled. He stretched his arms and bent over to touch his toes working his back muscles as he straightened up. The toothpick he'd been chewing on was in splinters. He spit, watching the pieces of wood hit the grass. Hiking up his pants, he lumbered over to his truck and did a walk around, checking the tires and wiping dust off the lights. He looked around the parking lot, noting that there were about fifteen trucks parked there. "Stupid, nasty girl!" He spat onto the pavement. "There's plenty of other men here, why's she talking to me?" He glared at the building housing the restrooms, opened the truck door, and swung up into the cab.

He turned up the radio, tapping on the steering wheel in time with the beat. But, flashes of faces seared through his brain. A thrill of excitement coursed through his body as he thought of his large hands against the smooth skin of a young throat. He turned the music up, trying to erase the images floating before him. Donna O'Neal singing her nasty little rhymes, his mother whining about bills, sweet tender little Wendy, so trusting and soft in his hands. Unconsciously, he began whistling the old tune he'd made up as a child. It was a long drive to Georgia and places beyond. He put the truck into gear and pulled slowly out onto the highway, leaving Tennessee behind.

Things didn't go as he planned, of course. After he delivered the load in Macon, Georgia, he traveled on to Albany where he was supposed to pick up a small load that was going to Jacksonville. The load was so small he almost left if on the dock. "I can't make a living like this," he complained to the foreman. "It was supposed to be at least twice this much."

"I dunno," the foreman shrugged. "This here's what they told me was being picked up today."

Andy slammed the heavy doors on the trailer, clicking the latches into place, and climbed back up into the truck. He pulled the rig up near the front of the building and climbed back down. He could see the secretary through the window. She was watching him, pretending to do some kind of paperwork on her desk. "She better have my check ready," he mumbled to himself as he brushed dust off his pants. He put on a smile before opening the door to the office.

"Just sign here," the woman said too brightly.

He looked down at the clipboard with the manifest on it. "Thought I was getting a bigger load," he said casually, not looking at her.

"Nope, this here's yore load, all right." She smiled like they were sharing a funny story.

Andy looked up and met her coal black eyes. She was forty or fifty years old with protruding teeth and a long nose. Her hair was a mousey brown, cut short and curled. *Maybe she really is just stupid,* he thought. He picked up the clipboard and signed the paper. "Just give me my check." He growled. "I won't be back."

"Oh, well, all right then," she said. She looked at the paper he'd signed, made a copy and handed him one with the check in an envelope. "The boss said to tell you the rest of that load is over there in Brunswick, if yore goin' that way."

"Say, what?" He scowled at her.

"I think there's a note in there about it, with yore check." She smiled at him like she'd just done him some kind of favor.

He stood for a moment rooted to the spot. He could feel the anger rising in him like a tidal wave. *Get out of here! Get out of here now!* Said the all too familiar voice in his head. "This is what happens when you let nice little kitties live," he choked out as he turned and blindly reached for the door handle. He jerked the door open and loped across the parking lot to his waiting truck. Once inside, he laid his head across his outstretched arms on the steering wheel. A picture floated into his mind of Wendy O'Neal. She was opening the box with the kitten in it. Now, a picture of the cute little gal up in Tennessee flitted across his tortured mind. "Nasty little girl," he whispered, glancing once more at the office window. "Some cats should've been shot before they got so old," he said aloud. His voice sounded dull in the cramped interior of his truck. The engine was already idling, so he put it into gear and pulled slowly out of the lot and onto the highway. "Man, it must be two hundred miles to Brunswick," he said. But, he knew he'd do it. He'd keep from going to Tennessee for as long as possible.

Andy spent a month going around the circle from Jacksonville to Tallahassee to Macon to Savannah. He found plenty of loads and more than made up for the loss that had been the beginning of this trip. It was finally time to start north once again. He couldn't forget the little gal in Tennessee, but he hoped that the encounter had been just a one time thing. But, if he really did see her again . . .

* * *

Tanya made many trips to the local rest stop. She talked to lots of strangers, even went for a couple of rides with a group of motorcyclists. But, she knew she was looking for *him*.

"Hey, Tanya!" Someone yelled from across the grassy area in front of the restroom building.

She looked up and waved at a semi-familiar face. But, she was still watching the trucks thundering down the interstate, going somewhere, doing something. *Not stuck here like me in this stupid corner of nowhere,* she thought for the hundredth time. She'd never gotten to go on a long ride with any of the truck drivers. It was a dream she talked up like it really happened, but no one was falling for it and no one was asking her to go anywhere. *If only HE would come back!* She thought of his blue eyes and handsome features.

"Tanya!" Barked a very familiar voice.

"Oh, Man," she breathed as she watched her brother striding toward her from his old Chevy pickup.

"What you doin' out here?"

"Nothin, just watching traffic go by."

"Yeah, well get your sorry butt into my truck so's I can take you home. Ma's been looking all over for you."

"How'd you find me, anyways?"

"After that little motorcycle stunt you pulled a couple of weeks ago? I knew you'd be here."

She walked silently to his old truck and slammed the door as she flounced onto the cracked leather seat.

"Why don't you find some nice local boy and settle down?" Her brother asked.

"Like Mama?" She frowned out the windshield.

"What's that mean?"

"You want me stuck here in these hills forever, like Mama?"

He shook his head in disgust. "That or get yourself kidnapped or something, you know? Mama worries. You're a worry to her and you're old enough to have been married and got a whole passle of kids."

"Ugh!"

"Man, if you was my kid I'd teach you a thing or two!"

"Oooh, I'm really scared." Tanya retorted. The minute the truck rolled to a stop, she jumped out and ran up the long, steep steps to their double-wide trailer set against the hills. Mama was sitting on the porch swing shelling peas.

"Where you bin, Tanya?" She asked in her soft voice.

Tanya settled next to her on the swing and grabbed a handful of peas. She knew better than to lie. "Out to the highway," she tried to sound like it didn't matter, like she'd been to the store or something.

Mama sighed, never stopping her work.

"I didn't do nothin' wrong, Mama."

"Ken Tucker stopped by. He wants you to come watch his young'uns whilst he goes to the horse auction."

"Ken Tucker wants a mama for them kids. And I ain't interested."

"He's a good man."

"When he ain't drunk, maybe."

"A growed woman out here don't have many good choices, Tanya."

"Well, that's for true. But, Mama, I want somethin' different, you know?"

Mama stared out over the hills and down the dirt road. "Yeah, I know," she said quietly.

"I been thinkin' I'd visit Aunt Carrie up there in Pennsylvania for awhile."

"Whatever for?" Mama frowned at the mention of her oldest sister.

"Just to see what it's like. I've never been anywhere, Mama."

"I don't have enough money for even a bus ticket . . ."

"That's okay. I'm sure I can get a ride."

"How?" Mama frowned mightily into the bowl of peas.

"Well, I met this really, really nice guy, uh, truck driver . . ."

"No!" Mama's peppered gray hair bounced with each shake of her head. "No, Tanya, I won't hear of it!"

"Some guy talking to you is gonna get a bustin' if I catch him," Tanya frowned at her brother who was leaning on the porch rail. "You can count on that, Little Sis." He nodded confidently before jumping up to sit on the railing.

"You never busted Ken Tucker," she pouted.

"Well, now that's different, ain't it?"

"I just don't want to be stuck here forever, Mama," Tanya whined. "And Aunt Carrie said I could come up there anytime, remember?"

Her brother laughed loud and long. "That was what, two or three years ago? She prob'ly don't even remember yore name, even."

"Charles, hush," said Mama. "Of course Carrie remembers Tanya. They were close when she lived down here. And, besides, she's family. You just don't up and forget you have family."

"Couldn't I go for just a little bit? I'd come home before winter, prob'ly."

"Tanya, I just don't have the money . . ."

"I CAN get the ride. This guy's really nice. He's clean and younger than most of the others . . ."

"Are you hard of hearing or just dumb?" Charles slapped his thigh. "Mama already said no to that."

"Charles," Mama said in a tired voice. Tanya stuck out her tongue and her brother threw a twig at her. It landed harmlessly on the porch only a few inches from the railing. "You stay home and be a good girl, you hear?" Mama patted her daughter's knee.

With a long sigh, Tanya answered. "Yes, Mama."

A horn honked over on the freeway a mile away, and Tanya shook her hair over her face while she concentrated on her lap full of peas. Charles slipped off the rail and headed for the barn. Mama hummed quietly as was her way when she made a decision and didn't want any more talk on the matter.

Tanya did stay home, being extra helpful for a whole week. She worked hard in the garden and helped with housework, too. She even helped Charles with the barn chores and to get in some hay, without complaint. It was easier to sleep and not hear the traffic noise at night when she tired herself out. She babysat for the Tucker children a couple of times, praying hard that their daddy wouldn't try to kiss her or something when he'd been drinking. But, the call of the traveling life was too strong. As she lay in her room one night, she could hear the cars and especially the trucks, only a mile away on the Interstate. She dreamed of going away. And in her dreams a blue-eyed stranger smiled making her heart flutter at the thought.

Early one morning Tanya scrawled a hasty note and walked away into the fog-shrouded forest. In less than an hour, she was sitting on a bench in the rest area park along the North bound lanes. Nobody else was there, not even one trucker. Well, there were a few cars, but not what she was looking for. She spent some time in the restroom, washing her face and hands and combing her hair. She sat at a picnic table and counted her money. She walked around the grassy area until her feet were sloppy with dew inside her shoes. At last, she put her backpack on one of the table benches near the back of the park and used it as a pillow.

*   *   *

Andy pulled into the small rest area and rolled to a stop. He wasn't really tired, but he figured if the girl was here, he'd take her along for fun. But on the other hand, he wasn't going to spend a lot of time just sitting around. After all, he had a load for New Jersey and a time line. He surveyed the park from behind the steering wheel. There wasn't much to see, a couple of cars parked near the building and two trucks that had followed him in. He sighed heavily, blowing air out in a long breath of relief and a little frustration. *Heck, it mighta been fun to take her along*, he thought, almost convincing himself that he could have a normal relationship with her. He climbed out of the truck and hitched his pants, swatting at the dust that always seemed to gather. "What was her name, anyway?" He mumbled at the small cloud of dust that was settling on his boots. He frowned, then opened the small side door of his truck cab and got out a soft rag. He put one foot on the step and started shining his western-style boots. He paused a moment and looked up at the sign on the door. "Tara or Toni, something like that." He contemplated.

"Hey, Red!" Some guy yelled. "You there, Cowboy!" Andy straightened and looked past his trailer to his right. *An overweight, sweaty excuse for a man,* he thought as he watched the other truck driver plod toward him.

"Yeah?"

"Hey, you gat a busted taillight on your trailer. Better check it out before some cop pulls you over." The grinning man puffed with the effort of talking and walking at the same time. Andy shook his head as he watched him go toward the restrooms.

"Thanks." He nodded as he changed feet on the running board and shined his second boot before stretching and rolling his shoulders and head. Driving was hard on a guy's back and neck. He put the cloth back in the 'boot' and slammed the door. Then he walked slowly back to the rear of the trailer. Sure enough, there was a broken taillight. What's more, there were pieces of the red lens lying on the pavement just below the truck. Andy knew a few drivers got some kind of perverse fun out of pulling pranks like this on other drivers. He shook his head and picked up the pieces. A familiar stirring of anger was welling up inside and he knew he better just get into his cab and go on down the road. "The heck with little girls!" He muttered.

"I knew you'd come back," a sweet voice said breathlessly from behind him.

He wheeled around and looked at the girl he'd been thinking about for over a month. "Get in if you're goin'", he motioned toward the front of the truck.

"Yes!" She whispered with her fists raised to the sky. She disappeared around the truck and was climbing into the cab before he could get his door opened. She put on her seatbelt and sat quietly, looking shyly at him from behind her long hair. A backpack sat awkwardly next to her feet.

"Throw that bag back on the bunk," he said as he prepared to leave. She heaved it over her shoulder and he heard the thunk as it hit the wall.

She glanced back briefly. "Sorry," she said.

They started rolling out onto the highway. He was acutely aware of her looking out the side window, then stealing a glance at him before she just stared forward at the road and traffic.

"Pennsylvania, huh?" He asked with a smile.

She grinned back. "If you don't mind, Sir." She quipped.

"Cole," Andy said, smiling broadly, absently patting his shirt pocket where his license rested.

She blushed and hid her face behind her hair. "Okay, Mister Cole. Thanks for taking me somewhere. Pennsylvania will do just fine."

"Well, I got a load for Jersey first, Honey. Then we'll see where the loads take us. I'll try to get one in P-A as soon as I can. But the one from N-J is gonna be in good ole Vermont."

"Really?" She was excited. "Wow, I didn't expect to get to do that. That's great!"

Andy, now calling himself Cole, nodded. "Okay, there's a bunk that pulls down over the bottom one, so on the next stop, we'll put your gear up there."

She looked around behind her at the single bunk and blushed again. She could see the handle for the pull-down bunk and nodded. "That'll work right good," she said.

Andy smiled and relaxed. *This might work out okay after all,* he thought. It did get lonely sometimes on the road and she was a nice kid. A picture of Wendy O'Neal's face flashed before him and he shook his head slightly to rid himself of the thought and the memories. *Naw, this is a nice girl. I think we'll have fun together. At least for a while.* "You like music?" He asked as he tuned to a country station on his radio.

Tanya nodded in time to the beat and smiled as she watched the world go by from the vantage of riding in a big rig. They settled into an easy conversation about trucks and driving. She asked good questions and Andy didn't mind answering. It was amusing and made the miles slide by faster. He didn't usually like to talk to people much, but she was smart and kind of fun to talk to. They stopped at a Truck Center and got a meal at the café. Andy liked to watch Tanya blush at the least little thing, like a wink from him or a compliment from another driver. *She's really a cute kid,* he thought more than once.

It was well past midnight when they pulled into the truck yard near Trenton, NJ. The guard at the gate let them in so Andy could unhitch the trailer and block it up. Tanya had been asleep in the bunk, but got out and helped him. She was a quick learner and really was a help. He nodded his approval and tousled her hair. She smiled shyly at him, but this time she didn't blush. She just looked straight at him and heck, he felt like HE might blush. "Get back in the truck!" He growled. She grinned innocently at him, but disappeared back into the bunk. Andy moved the truck to a WalMart parking lot and got some sleep himself. In the morning he would pick up another load and head for northern Vermont.

"Where's your family live in Pennsylvania?" He asked over a trucker's breakfast in the early morning.

Tanya swallowed before answering. "Outside Philly."

"Hmm," he nodded, taking a drink of the scalding hot coffee. He set the cup down carefully. "Well, you know, we're right there. Why don't you call them and get them to pick you up? I'll go on up north and around for a while, then take you home in a couple of weeks or maybe a month. Okay?"

Tanya frowned and swallowed hard to keep from tearing up. "Oh, sure, okay." She smiled up at him thinly. "Guess you're tired of me already, huh?"

"Look Kid, don't spoil it, okay? I'm used to being alone and I got things I gotta do." He paused, stirring the eggs around on his plate, frowning fiercely. "I'll be back for you in a while. I'll pick you up right here." He waved his fork around, indicating the restaurant. "If I keep you with me . . ." he shook his head. "Nope, I'll be back."

Tanya silently got up and went to a pay phone. She pulled a scrap of paper from her backpack and dialed the number. "Hello, Aunt Carrie? It's me, Tanya . . ."

Andy watched her make her phone call. He felt relief wash over him as he saw her talking to someone on the other end. He left money on the table and made a few calls of his own, arranging loads for the next two weeks.

Tanya walked out the door and stood awkwardly outside the truck stop. "I thought he was gonna take me with him," she mumbled, sniffling loudly and wiping away tears that were threatening. This wasn't exactly what she envisioned when she'd dreamed about him taking her away from home, but it would have to do for now. She was startled when he walked up beside her and put his arm around her shoulders.

"Got your ride?" He asked gently into her hair.

"Yeah, they only live a half hour or an hour away or something, so they'll be here soon." She looked up into those vibrant blue eyes and felt weakness overcome her. Their faces were only inches apart. She stood mute, staring into his handsome face, not daring to trust her voice.

"Good," he whispered. Then, before she could even blink, he kissed her. She'd never been kissed before this, she knew that now. This was a real kiss, a kiss of love, she was sure. She melted into him and felt his arms tighten around her. She hoped this moment would never end. But, of course it did, as abruptly as it began.

"Look for me in a couple of weeks, Miss Tanya." Andy let her loose, lightly running his hand over her hair and pulling it ever so gently as he strode to his truck, never looking back.

She shivered in the heat of the morning as she watched the red truck pull across the parking lot and out onto the highway. The fantasies began in earnest now. *He'll come back and we'll go on the road together. We'll get married and I'll stay home with the kids and he'll keep comin' home to me. It will be like a honeymoon all our lives.* She hugged herself to keep the vision real. But, all too soon she heard her aunt's voice calling her and in a trance got into their pickup truck, headed for the farm they owned on the outskirts of Philadelphia. "I thought you lived in the city," she commented with a slight frown.

"Well, we did for a lot of years, but you know what we found out? We're country folks. So, we bought the cutest little farm out here in the country. It'll remind you of home, Honey."

Tanya nodded and tried to smile. "Great," she muttered.

Aunt Carrie reached over and patted her knee. "We'll take you up to the city, don't you worry none," she laughed.

"*Mama was right. I'm gonna hate this,*" she thought. She looked out the window, wondering how far away Cole Davis was by now. She touched her lips as she remembered the kiss that seemed like so long ago already.

"Tanya! C'mon, Honey, get yourself up. You know what it's like on a farm, c'mon!" Tanya covered her head and wished her aunt would go away. But, now she could smell breakfast and she peeked out of the covers. It was barely daylight.

"Oh-h-h-h," she moaned as she swung her feet out onto the hardwood floor. "Why did I come here?" She shook her head and slumped along to the hallway where she could look toward the bathroom. No one was waiting, so she made her own trip to the toilet. She felt better after a quick shower and brushing her teeth. But, it was still a farm and still nowhere. Sure, they'd gone to the city a couple of times, but it wasn't like living there, she was sure of that. She still felt it must be exciting to live, work, and play in the bright lights, with so many stores and restaurants to go to whenever you wanted. She trudged back to her bedroom and looked at the calendar. "Hm-m-m, on Friday it'll be a month. Surely he'll be back by then," she mumbled. She'd been disappointed nearly two weeks ago when she'd had her aunt drop her off at the truck stop. She waited around for most of the day, but Cole never showed up.

"Who is this guy?" Aunt Carrie asked when she came back for her.

"Just a friend." Tanya said.

"Well, I gotta tell you, Tanya, that your mama's worried about you. I'm worried about you, too. She told me she doesn't even know who you're with. Is that true?"

Tanya nodded without looking up.

"Just talk to me, Honey." Her aunt coaxed. "I'll listen and try not to judge. I realize that you're over eighteen and can make your own decisions, but your family wants to help you make good ones. We all just want you to be safe and happy, you know?"

"Yeah, not happening," Tanya answered. There was a long silence before she opened up. "Okay, his name's Cole Davis and he's from West Virginia. He's a really nice guy who brought me all the way up here without asking me to pay or anything."

"Okay. How'd you meet him?"

Tanya sighed. "At a rest area near home. He promised to take me away somewhere, and he did." She paused again. "Right where I told him I wanted to go."

"How old is he?"

"I'm not too sure, but not so much older than me."

"What company does he drive for?"

"His own, I think."

"What kind of guy picks up young girls at a rest area, Tanya?"

"It's not like that. Cole is a gentleman. He's hardly even touched me at all, just a couple of pats on the head and one little kiss."

"He kissed you?"

Tanya nodded and sighed audibly. "Yeah, just before he said goodbye. It wasn't much to speak of, just kind of nice, you know?"

"And you really think he'll come back for you <u>and</u> take you home?"

"Yep!" Tanya nodded emphatically. "He said in two weeks or a month, so the next time we come, you can go on back home and I'll be fine."

"No, it doesn't work like that, Girl. I'll wait until I know you're on your way. Then, I'll go home and call your Mama to let her know you're in the truck. I'll let her know you're on your way back, and you'll call me when you get home. Okay?"

"Sure, whatever you want. That's okay."

"And now it's almost time," Tanya breathed into the early morning air, coming back out of her reminiscing.

"Tanya!" Her aunt called again.

"Coming!" She called back. Suddenly, the day didn't seem so dreary. She was looking forward to leaving and it wouldn't be long, just a couple of days. She hummed her way through the morning chores, not even minding so much the smell of the goats she was expected to milk. She peeked into the chicken house to see if the rooster was guarding the door, but he was evidently out with his harem of hens. She quickly got the eggs out of the nests, except for the one with the big red hen sitting on it. She knew her aunt used gloves to get the eggs just for this reason. The red hen stayed on the nest until you made her get off and she didn't go willingly. Tanya had scars on her hands from encounters with the hen's beak.

"Soon," she whispered. "Soon, no more chickens, no more goats, just the open road and a seat in a big red truck." She hummed a little bit as she made her way to the back porch where she would clean the eggs before putting them in the refrigerator. "Maybe he'll even consent to me going south with him, wouldn't that be something . . ."

*   *   *

Andy looked around the truck stop and heaved a sigh of relief. No girl and no worries. He needed to get his fuel and get back out on the road. He'd already stayed longer in the north than he should. A flash of memory ran across his line of vision. The big black bear had been aggressive and come for him instead of the prey that was offered. He touched his ribs gingerly, feeling the scabbed marks along his right side. It had been close, too close. "What was wrong with that old bear anyway?" He mumbled as he rubbed his hand lightly over his shirt. He'd made sure there was plenty of prey to choose from, but when the bear appeared in the valley Andy had carefully chosen, she was already agitated and came down the path in a hurry, running right for him. He'd backed away, but she grabbed him and raked his side with her powerful claws. He punched her in the face over and over until finally she'd backed off, towering above him as he lay prone on the bed of moss and leaves of the forest floor. She stood for a moment, sniffing the air, then lowered herself and walked slowly to his offering, growling once back in his direction. After a few moments he sat up, keeping a close eye on the bruin. But she was busy now, tearing into flesh and bone not fifty yards away. He came up against a tree behind him and stood, backed away slowly, inching his way in and around brush and trees down the trail to his rental car. He washed his side in a nearby creek, keeping a wary eye on the forest around him. When he was satisfied that the bleeding was slowing down, he dug an old towel out of his duffle bag in the trunk and wrapped it tightly around his ribs, grabbed a clean shirt to put on, and drove quickly to his destination. He spent a few minutes cleaning out the car, gassing it up and vacuuming the floor and seats. Then he drove to the drop off point for the rental car. He left it in the lot and put the keys in the drop box next to the door, then walked to the truck stop a couple of miles away and stowed his duffle back into his semi cab. He then put his bloody clothes in a plastic bag and stuffed it into the boot for disposal later. Now, here he was back in New Jersey, half looking for that girl, but glad that she wasn't there. He felt vulnerable and had to rethink things, so he took his journal out of its hiding place and leafed through the pages. He wrote two names in the margins of its pages and filled in some missing days.

"Hey, Cole," a sweet voice said from the ground.

He looked down at her upturned face and felt a familiar flutter in his stomach. *She's a cute thing,* he thought as he smiled *I forgot how cute she is*. "What'cha doin' Girl?" He asked.

"Just waiting for a ride home," she smiled up at him.

"I don't know, Tanya." He answered. "I'm not feeling too good about this."

"Oh," she looked down at her hands. "Well, I just need to get home. Maybe somebody else is going that way." She smiled weakly at him, then looked quickly at her hands, wringing them in front of her.

"Oh, c'mon," he growled. "Get in."

She was around the truck and climbing in before he could get out the words. She waved at someone in a pickup truck who waved back.

"Thanks, Cole," she breathed as she settled back into the seat. She'd already thrown her backpack into the upper bunk.

Andy moaned as he reached for the glove box and slipped his journal inside. He sat up and started the truck rolling out the driveway and onto the freeway.

"Are you okay?" She asked, a frown creasing her forehead.

"Yep, just had a bit of an accident the other day."

"You slip and fall or something?" She asked innocently, but with concern in her voice.

"Yeah, something," he mumbled. "It's really none of your business, Kid."

"Sorry," she said. "I know the rules."

They rode along quietly for miles and miles, not even music on the radio to invade their thoughts. He was involved with his driving and Tanya stared out the window at the passing scenery.

"You hungry?" He finally asked.

"Nope," she answered.

"This load's goin' to Knoxville, so that'll be close enough to home for you, huh?"

"Sure, that's my backyard."

"Yore mama expectin' you?"

"Sometime, I guess."

"I've got a partial to go on down to Georgia. Ever been there?"

Tanya controlled her voice. "Nope," she answered, hoping she sounded bored about the prospect.

"Well, we'll see," he said.

Again, they rode in silence. The miles rolled by and too soon they were in Tennessee. Tanya held herself still as they rolled into the state and then right by her favorite rest area. A smile stole its way across her face, but she looked out the side window and let her hair fall forward to cover the fleeting reaction to his driving on south with her.

When they stopped for the day, she was glad to climb up into the bunk and sleep. She was disturbed slightly when he got up and went to the restroom, then got back in and started down the road again, but the movement of the truck soon lulled her back to sleep. When she woke up, they were sitting alongside the freeway in a long line of trucks beside the off ramp, somewhere in Georgia. She could hear him in the bunk below her, softly snoring. She closed her eyes and dreamed of long roads and elusive kisses.

After Georgia, they went to Florida. Then he had a load in Alabama and they returned to Florida. They spent time looking at alligators and eating strange, spicy foods. She found that he had a great sense of humor, but that he hated cats and seemingly children. He treated her like a girlfriend and she thought of herself in that role. It was fun and all she dreamed it would be. She called her mother and told her how happy she was out on the road with her new friend. Even when he disappeared for four days, she wasn't worried. He'd put her up in a really nice hotel and left her with money for food and shopping. When he returned, he was moody and aloof, making it a difficult few days. Tanya was afraid he would leave her in Tennessee as they passed through, but he kept going.

Another month found them in Massachusetts, Vermont, and Pennsylvania. Suddenly, Cole couldn't seem to wait to get out of the northern states and back down to the south. Tanya didn't care. As long as she was with Cole, she was happy. They spent two days in North Carolina. That is, Tanya spent two days there in a condo on the beachfront. She wondered where he'd gone, but knew better than to question him. He was a very private person. So, she decided it was a good time to call her mother.

"Hi, Mama," she said.

"Tanya, where are you? Are you safe?"

"I'm flne, Mama . . ."

"When are you comin' home? I'm worried sick about you."

"We're on our way up north, Mama. It'll be awhile, I think."

"Tanya, I don't know anything about this man. Who is he? Who's his people? I don't even know where you are."

"I call you Mama."

"Who is he, Tanya?"

"Mama, I have to go. I told Aunt Carrie everything and she wasn't this paranoid about it. He's from West Virginia and his name is Cole. We're happy, Mama. We go to nice places, restaurants and such-like. He treats me real good."

"Tanya, I want you to come home."

"Mama, I'm twenty years old. I'm doing what I've dreamed of doing, traveling, seeing things. Cole is really good to me. Can you just be happy for me?" Quiet sobs on the other end of the phone made Tanya sigh. *Why do I call her?* She thought. "Mama . . ."

"No, Tanya, I just worry about you."

"I know. Well, I've gotta go. I'll call again one of these days." She didn't wait for an answer. She hung up quickly and went for a swim in the hotel pool.

The next two months were spent with a fast and furious schedule. There seemed to be plenty of work up in the northeast. Tanya and Cole went lobster fishing and to a real clam bake. She'd never been happier. These were things she would never get to do on a side-hill farm in the hills of Tennessee.

Finally, the day came to head south again. "How do you know when to get loads in the south or in the north?" She asked.

"Just do," he answered. He seemed sullen and withdrawn.

They traveled in virtual silence for most of the way to Florida. It was strange how his moods could change and she never knew how to expect him to be. In Florida, they went on a ride in an airboat. It was fast and skimmed along the waterways and through the tall savannah grasses with ease. Tanya laughed and laughed as they zoomed around in the swamps with their guide. They chased out Nutria and alligators and zipped around in circles until she was wet from splashing water and exhausted.

"Happy, Tanya?" Andy asked that night as they spent the night in a motel.

"Yes," she breathed. "It's like a fairytale, you know?"

She felt him stiffen next to her where they sat watching TV. "What?" He demanded.

"You know, it's like a story about Cinderella or something." She watched him as his frown deepened. "I've always wanted a life of travel and fun and you've brought that to me, so it's like a fairytale with a happy ending . . ." Her voice trailed off as she watched the emotions playing across his face. She wasn't sure if he was mad, or disappointed, or just what.

"Why is it girls have to spoil everything?" He asked, looking at the TV.

"I'm sorry, what did I do?"

He stood up and paced the length of the room between the bed and the sofa. "I thought you were different, Tanya. But, you're just like all the rhyme makers."

"The what?" She frowned as she tried to make sense of what he was saying. Andy ran his hands through his hair over and over again as he paced. His head shook. "Never mind. Never mind."

It was the first time in six months that she felt fear, fear of Cole. "I don't know what I've done, Cole. How can I make it okay? Please, just tell me the way."

Andy stopped in mid-stride. He stared at Tanya like he was seeing her for the very first time. "What did you say?" He asked, his voice hoarse and rasping.

"I, uh I, just want to make it up to you. Tell me what to do!" Her voice rose in desperation. She sat on the sofa with her knees drawn up to her chin and her arms hugging her legs close.

He stared at her. "You did it again, Tanya. Is this some kind of joke?"

"What did I do?" She asked barely above a whisper.

"Stop!" He ordered. "I'm going out and I may not be back tonight." He put up one hand to fend off her retort. "Don't! I've got to think and I can't do it here." With that, he walked out the door.

Tanya stared at the door for a long while. "What did I do?" She whimpered to herself. Absently she turned off the TV and sat on the bed. She thought about their conversation and couldn't come up with what had offended him. "I don't know what to do, Mama!" She whispered into her pillow. The tears came then, hot and bitter. She cried until she couldn't force another tear down her face, and finally fell into an exhausted, fitful sleep.

Cole woke her early in the morning. "If you're gonna get washed up or something, do it now. We're going to leave in about an hour. I'll be in the truck." His voice was a monotone she didn't recognize.

"At least he's not leaving me here," she mumbled as she dragged herself into the shower and got herself ready for the trip. She packed their things and carried both bags to the truck.

"Thanks," he said with no emotion and no smile.

"Where we going?" She asked, trying to keep her voice light.

Silence.

They didn't talk all the way to Tennessee. In the southern part of the state, he stopped the truck along the highway near a state park. "Let's walk," he said as he opened his door and climbed out. Tanya followed him. He slipped over the retaining wall along the edge of a hill. She clambered after him into the waiting forest below. He turned, offering his hand, a smile brightening his face for the first time in hours.

Tanya breathed a sigh of relief and put her hand in his. "You forgive me?" She asked timidly.

"I do."

They walked into the forest along dim animal trails for over an hour. Andy didn't talk and Tanya didn't either. She felt perfectly at ease, walking along with her hand firmly in his, feeling like he'd gotten over whatever had made him so angry. *I'll be more careful from now on,* she thought, even though she wasn't sure what it was that had set him off. They came to a spot where the edge of the trail broke off into a creek a few feet below. Andy stepped behind her and laid his hands gently on her shoulders. She crossed her arms in front of her chest and laid her head against his shoulder. They stood there, gently swaying for several minutes.

"It's the end of the road, Tanya," he whispered.

She cocked her head up at him, a smile lighting her face. "You mean the end of the trail?"

"No," he smiled down at her.

She was sure he was going to kiss her, so when the pressure came against her throat, it took her completely by surprise. She tried to remove his hands, but he was so strong. She saw red lights and white lights and . . . .

As Andy Davis (leaving his alias Cole Davis behind) pulled his red truck out onto the highway, he whistled a little tune he'd made up when he was a boy. "It's time for me to come home, Ma," he said to the windshield as he started out on a new route, one that would take him back to Missouri and his family home, a place of safety and refuge.

Ida and Yolanda
1990-1995, Spokane, WA

Ida Gonzales and Yolanda Herrera met in the sixth grade and became best friends forever. They wrote it everywhere, in their school lockers, on trees at the park, in their books and diaries. They both had rich, full, black hair and shining brown eyes, but Ida chose to have short hair. It always laid neatly around her ears and along the base of her neck. Yolanda's hair was long, almost to her waist. She brushed it twice a day for a hundred strokes on each side. It parted in the middle of her head, cascading across her shoulders like an ebony river.

The two girls smiled contagiously, befriended everyone, and made life fun for their families and school friends. Because of their attachment, their mothers became friends and their language changed. Now, the mothers ran their names together like one word, Idanlanda was what everyone began calling them because they were simply inseparable. They dressed alike, ate the same foods, tried the same fads and took the same classes in school.

When the girls became teenagers, they were still close, but their tastes were changing. Ida was interested in nursing and small children. Yolanda liked to style hair. She began spending time at the mall, eventually becoming a waitress at the food court so she could spend time near a hairdresser and learn some of the newest techniques. Ida got a job at a local hospital, first as a Candy Striper, then as a tech assistant for the lab. She basically ran errands, but it kept her in the hospital and on different floors so she could see what she liked best, while she finished high school and began college.

School and a few dances were the only places the girls had in common by the time they graduated, but the tie of love was still strong between them. Ida moved to Idaho where she attended college to become a nurse. Yolanda went to beauty school for a while, but finally dropped out to wait tables at a truck stop near her parent's home. Once in a while the girls would get together at a popular disco for dancing and a party. At those times, Ida wondered why their lives had to be so different. They were still like sisters, but they never got to see each other anymore.

"Why don't you move to Couer d'Alene?" She asked her friend.

"I'm not that far away," Yolanda would reply. "Why don't you come home?"

The answer was always the same. "Well, my mom's over here now . . ."

"I know. And my family's over there."

"At least we're not hundreds of miles apart," Ida would say.

"Yeah, and my job's pretty good." Yolanda said unconvincingly.

"Why don't you come over and go to college or something?"

Yolanda looked sadly at her friend. "I can't, Ida, you know I can't leave Mama with no income."

"But, there are programs . . ." Ida began, but stopped when Yolanda shook her head. It was a subject they never got to finish. Yolanda just wouldn't talk about it.

Both girls dated casually, but never found anyone they wanted to get serious about. "Someday, someone will come along and sweep us off our feet," Ida said one evening as they sat at the club.

"Gee, I hope there's more than one someone," Yolanda retorted with a sad kind of smile.

"You know what I mean!"

Yolanda laughed, her head back and long, black hair shining in the lights. "Some doctor in mind?" She asked.

Ida smiled shyly. "Well . . . not really, but I have gone out with a couple of interns. Have you been dating lately?"

"There's one truck driver who comes in sometimes. He's really handsome, but he's kind of old."

"You're not serious!" Ida protested.

"No," Yolanda shook her head lightly. "But, you know, talking to him is better than going out with Jerry all the time. Besides, Jerry's family doesn't like me."

"What's not to like?"

"I'm not like you, I'm just a waitress. They want something better for him, you know?"

"Yo, there's nobody better than you and me. Haven't we always said that?"

"Yeah, we've said that, but . . ."

"Hey! This is a party! Let's find a couple of guys and dance."

Yolanda smiled. It was like her friend to always want to dance and laugh. She suddenly realized that she didn't laugh as much as she used to. *Not even when I'm with Ida,* she thought.

A few days later, she went on her first date with Davis Baines. "I told my girlfriend about you," she said as they rode in his rented car.

He frowned slightly before answering. "Why?"

"Because Ida and I tell each other everything, and we've been best friends ever since the sixth grade."

"I never had a best friend." He said quietly.

She rubbed his arm lightly. "I'm sorry. Where're we going?"

"Just for a drive, I like the mountains." They drove along a country road for a few moments in silence.

"It beats going out to eat," she said. "I get tired of restaurant food."

"Me, too." He smiled disarmingly at her.

Yolanda felt a flutter in her chest. *He's so handsome and his smile makes me want to melt into the seat.* An alarm went off somewhere in the back of her mind, but she couldn't think straight when he smiled at her like that.

He parked the car near a copse of trees. "Let's walk for awhile, okay?"

They walked through the trees and talked about things she'd never even thought about. She'd never wondered about nature or the names of grasses and weeds. He knew the names of everything they saw. It opened up a whole new world to her view. She was pleased when he took her hand for the walk back to his car. He never kissed her or tried to touch her. He was a gentleman, and the first one she'd ever met. She couldn't wait to tell Ida.

It was a week later before she had the chance to see her friend. Ida took one look at her and said "You've found a guy," with a knowing look.

"Maybe," she said. They went into the club and found a table.

"Tell me about him," Ida encouraged. She had opened the flood gates.

"Oh, Ida," Yolanda breathed. "He's handsome, and smart, and he treats me like a lady. I think, well it's still too early to tell for sure, but I think I could really love this guy."

"How long have you been dating? I just saw you a couple or three weeks ago. What do you know about him? Do I know him?"

Yolanda smiled at all the questions. "Uh, one, we've only gone on one real date. Two, he's older and from California, I think, and he knows everything about trees and weeds and stuff. And three, no, you don't know him, not yet, anyway. I want you to meet him, but I never know when he'll come around."

"It isn't that truck driver, is it? Why can't you just go out with some of the old crowd, Yo?"

"Because the old crowd is all gone, married, or something, except Jerry and that's a dead subject, okay?"

"Okay, so when can I meet Mr. Right and Handsome?" Ida laughed at her friend.

"Make fun all you want, the next time he's in town I'll call you and we can all meet up."

"Okay, bring him here to dance."

Yolanda frowned. "No, he won't like that. Maybe we can go for a picnic somewhere. Your uncle might let us take his boat out on the lake, right?"

"Sure, that'd be fun. Just give me a call." They stayed at the club for an hour or so, but finally called it a night and parted.

It was several weeks before Davis showed up again at the restaurant. They didn't talk, just a simple hello as he came in and she showed him to a seat. When he left the restaurant she found a note written on the napkin. 'See you after work.' was all it said. She was anxious for her shift to end, but she was extra careful to do a good job and help clean up after the last patron left. Instinctively she knew that no one else would approve of her seeing this traveling man, so she didn't tell anyone about him. Maybe she would later if they really became a couple or something. But for now, she thought it was better that she just not say anything, not even much to her best friend, Ida.

"I thought you must've forgotten me," she said as they settled into his car when she finished work.

"You know I drive," he mumbled.

"Sorry," she murmured. *He must be having a bad day,* she thought to herself as she looked out the window. "It's faster if you just go up past the hospital to my apartment." She told him. "If you're taking me right home, that is."

"Hmmm," he answered.

"My friend and I would like to do something really special, you know, go out on a boat on the lake, or something. I thought you might like to go along . . ." She hesitated at the scowl on his face.

Yolanda turned her head to watch the city lights speed by as he drove along the streets to her apartment in complete silence. She loved the city, especially from the south hill where she could see it all spread out before her. She wondered why he'd bothered to pick her up if he was just going to be quiet and sullen. "Will I see you tomorrow?" She asked as they pulled up to the curb.

He turned off the engine and looked directly at her. "Yolanda with a Y, right?" He asked.

She frowned. "Yes . . ."

"And what's your friend's name?"

"What, you mean Ida?" This conversation was really confusing. What was he talking about? Why'd he want to know about Ida? Didn't he even remember her own name?

He laughed. "Ida from Idaho?"

She smiled and tried to relax. "Yeah, she laughs about that, too."

He nodded, looking past her into the night. "So, you've made plans, huh? You and your little friend?"

"I'm sorry, Davis. I just thought you might like to meet Ida because she's a very big part of my life. It's okay if you don't want to go."

"Oh, what the heck? I'm just being crazy." He said quietly. He looked at her and smiled sweetly. "Sure, we'll go. I'll meet your friend."

Yolanda relaxed and laid a hand on his cheek. "You're great, you know that?" With that, she opened the door and skipped up the steps to the apartment building. Before opening the door, she turned back and waved. *It's going to be good,* she thought. Humming, she ran up the steps instead of taking the elevator.

The following day was Saturday. Yolanda woke up early and helped her mother clean the apartment. "Who you say you're going with?" Mama asked.

"Ida, Mama," Yolanda answered. "We're taking a couple of friends out on the lake in her uncle's boat. It's fine. We'll have a good time and come back early. Okay?"

"What friends? You mean dates?"

"Mama, please! I'm not a child anymore. Yes, there will be guys." She looked pleadingly at her mother. "It's fine, people Ida and I know."

In the end, her mother quit fussing and gave her consent.

A week later, the day finally arrived. Ida brought a friend with her, too. They were waiting on the dock when Davis and Yolanda arrived at the lake home. "Hi!" Ida called and waved. "C'mon out here and meet James."

"Hello," Yolanda said, turning slightly to include her own date. "This is Davis." The man and boy shook hands awkwardly as the girls smiled and watched. "So, okay, are we ready to go?"

"Yep," Ida answered.

The men took over, untying the boat from the dock and shoving off. The four of them spent the rest of the day floating along on the lake, stopping from time to time to ski in the main channel or swim in a quiet bay. The men talked about fishing and the girls giggled about the men. Ida had prepared a picnic meal of chicken, potato salad, and some fresh vegetables, topped off with her almost-famous chocolate chip cookies. At last, the final dying rays of the sun touched them as they glided toward the dock and the end of an almost perfect date in the minds of the girls, at least.

Settled in the rental car, Yolanda talked and talked and talked. Davis drove in silence, staring straight ahead into the gathering night. The lights of the city loomed ahead and he sped up just a little. He turned off the engine when he'd parked in front of her mother's apartment building.

"Wanna get a coffee or something?" She asked brightly.

"No," he glowered at the steering wheel where his knuckles showed plainly that he was gripping the wheel. "Gotta go."

Yolanda watched him for a moment. "I'm sorry, Davis," she said sadly. "I've ruined it all by talking too much." She reached for the door handle and pulled it, letting in the warm night air. "I'll see ya around," she sighed as she stepped onto the pavement. She closed the door quietly, unbidden tears forming and running down her cheeks. *Like I'll ever see him again after today. He's older and this must have been awful for him, like a date with a teenager or something.*

His deep voice flowed over her like a spring shower. "Let's go for a hike in the mountains next time I come around, Yolanda with a Y," he said.

Yolanda turned and looked at him, sitting there in his rental car, looking like a movie star. "Okay," she said meekly, afraid to break the spell that she felt forming around her.

"Bring your friend," he smiled and drove away.

"Wait! Davis . . ." she called after the retreating car. "Where will we meet you?" She mumbled. She watched his car disappear then turned quickly and ran to the door. Letting herself in, she was greeted by a surprised mother.

"You're home much earlier than I thought," Mama smiled.

"Yes," she gave her a peck on the cheek and hurried to her room.

Mama followed. "Are you okay? Is something wrong?"

"No," Yolanda shook her head causing her hair to flow and shimmer in the light from her desk lamp. "Everything's fine, just fine." She plopped herself on her bed and looked up at her mother who had followed after her. "We're going hiking sometime soon," she said.

"Who?"

"What? Oh, well, um, Ida and me and these guys we met."

"Hiking where?"

"I'm not sure . . . someplace Davis, I mean one of the guys knows, I guess."

"On one of your days off, I hope?"

"No," she said too quickly. "I mean, it really doesn't matter. I can always trade with someone."

"Landa," her mother pleaded. "We need the money."

"I know, Mama. But just once can't I have some fun?" She paused. "I'll do a couple of double shifts to make up for it. They'll let me." Her dark eyes were pleading.

"What kind of man asks you to give up your livelihood for him, just to have fun?"

Now Yolanda's eyes flashed with fiery indignation. "Mama, I work all the time. I bring you home almost every dollar. I won't be spending any precious money and if I pull a couple of doubles the week after, I'll make more than just working one shift anyway!"

"Excuse me," her mother disappeared from the doorway.

Yolanda threw herself across the bed and wept bitter tears. *It isn't fair to yell at Mama. I'll make it all up to her, really I will.* She reached for her phone and called in to see how hard it would be to switch her schedule.

"When?" Hardy, the night manager asked.

"Well, sometime in the next couple of weeks, I think." She felt stupid by not even having a confirmed date. "It's okay, never mind. I'll call when I know more, but it may be at the last minute."

"Yeah, do that," Hardy snarled into the phone and hung up.

Yolanda sighed deeply and called Ida.

"Home already?" Came the rich, and familiar voice.

"Yeah, he's a real gentleman."

"He's a little old, you know."

"Old for what?"

Ida chuckled. "Okay, just a little older than I like them. Did you have a good time? James did and I think he really likes me."

"Oh, that's good. He seemed really nice." Yolanda was reluctant to discuss her own date. She was glad that Ida seemed anxious to talk about her own new boyfriend. It wasn't like she was ashamed of Davis or anything. There was just something that made her reluctant to share anything about him with anyone. Sometimes he acted so strange . . .

"Yeah, he's a student and we don't get to go out much with his hospital schedule. But, someday when he's a doctor, we'll be . . . well, that's a long ways off."

Since Ida was still talking, Yolanda let herself drift back to thoughts of Davis. She wondered if he was really her boyfriend or if he was just amusing himself while he was in the area. After all, he was a truck driver and would come and go as he pleased, he might have girlfriends all over the place, women who . . .

"Did you hear me?" Ida was asking.

"Sorry, I was day dreaming, I guess. So, you think you'll marry this guy some day, huh?"

"Could be, if his parents like me. Like I was saying, we're going to their place on James' next holiday."

"Ida, who wouldn't like you? You're so outgoing and lovable."

"Yeah, right. But, you know how it goes. You gotta pass the parent test sometime."

"Hey, do you want to go for a hike in the next few weeks? Davis asked me to see if you'd go with us."

"Can't. Gotta work and study. No time for the next couple of months. Where ya goin' hiking?"

"I'm not sure. Can't you switch schedules or something? That's what I'm doing."

"No, the hospital's not like that. If I'm scheduled and not dead, I'd better show up for my shift. Besides, I've got tests coming up at the college, too."

"Oh."

"Maybe after this term. It's not like we can't plan something else, right?"

"Yeah, sure. Well, gotta go and get some sleep. Talk to you later."

"Or sooner . . ." Ida signed off with the traditional words. They'd been doing that since they were in the seventh grade.

Yolanda smiled into the muted light of her room. She drifted into a sleep filled with dreams of hiking and boat rides and trucks and Davis. Most of all she dreamed of Davis.

Days rolled by and Yolanda worked and helped her mother with the laundry and housekeeping. She volunteered for double shifts as much as she could, in preparation for the day she'd take off. And waited, she waited for him to come back again. *I don't even know how to contact Davis,* she thought one day as she washed dishes. *This is crazy, pining after an older man and not even knowing anything about him. Maybe I should just call up Jerry and see what he's doing.* But visions of Davis and his sensual smile caused her to think again. "I'll wait. He'll be back, I know he will. It's only been three weeks, anyway."

On a hot and stuffy Friday, he waltzed into the restaurant as though he'd been coming in everyday. "How ya doin', Little Girl?" He asked with a loud laugh.

Yolanda shook her head and showed him to a table. "What can I get you tonight?" she asked.

"The special and a piece of that good pecan pie," he said, dismissing her by picking up the newspaper.

She felt confused and disappointed. He clearly didn't want to talk to her. *But that's usual, right? He never talks to me here. Relax, Yolanda, relax! You're expecting too much.*

She went about her work trying not to look at his booth every few seconds. She was only vaguely aware when he left, and was surprised at the relief she felt. She realized that she'd been nervous the whole time he sat there ignoring her. She finally got a few seconds to clear his table. And there it was, the note on the napkin. 'Hiking in the morning, right?'

The rest of the evening flew by in a haze. She barely remembered to talk to her supervisor and change shifts for tomorrow. She hated to work on Sundays, but it was the only switch that would work on such short notice. As she stepped out into the balmy night, she looked around the parking lot, but no rental car was waiting. Resolutely, she set out for the long walk home. "Someday I've got to get my car fixed," she mumbled to the street as she hurried along.

She awoke with a start as the first rays of morning sun peeked through her window. *What time did Davis want to go?* She thought frantically as she threw the covers aside and groped for her clothes. She looked out the window, moving to the left as far as she could, but still couldn't see the front street where he might be waiting even now. "Oh-h-h-h-h," she moaned. Her hand flew to her hair when she passed the brush lying on the dresser, but she hurried out the door and into the hallway to the upstairs bathroom. She listened but the apartment was quiet. *Good, I'm the only one awake.* She took a quick and almost silent shower, running the water at little more than a dribble. Wrapping herself in a towel, she tiptoed downstairs to the kitchen and rummaged through the basket of clean clothes for her favorite jeans and aqua t-shirt. Then, she sprinted for the stairs and closed herself into her room to dress and comb her hair. *A note, a note, I've got to leave Mama a note,* she reminded herself as she descended into the living area once again. She found a pen and used the note pad from the refrigerator.

"I'll be gone most of the day on this hike I told you about.
Ida couldn't go, but that's all right.
I love you. Landa"

Sure enough, Davis' white rental car was parked along the street across from the apartment building. She wondered idly if he always rented the same car since he was always in a white one. She decided to pay more attention to little details about him. Yolanda ran to the passenger door and climbed in. "I knew you'd be here early," she said breathlessly.

"Early?" He quipped. "Girl, the day's almost half gone!" He flashed her a disarming smile as he put the car into gear and rolled down the quiet street. "Hey, where's your friend? I thought we were gonna make this a three-some?"

"She couldn't get away. She works and has school . . ." Yolanda wondered if he didn't want to be alone with her, maybe.

"I see," he seemed to be thinking for a few seconds. "So, what's she know about me, anyway?"

"About you?" She shrugged as she thought that most guys were conceited, thinking all girls were interested in them. "Not much other than your name. She's pretty caught up in school, her job, and her own boyfriend." She hoped she'd made a point that Ida wasn't interested in him. *He's so handsome, I'll bet every girl in every restaurant all over the country is in love with him,* she thought, a frown monopolizing her pretty face.

Andy Davis looked at her, then back at the road. He shook his head slightly and smiled. "All right, Sweetheart, I'm gonna trust you on that.

Yolanda frowned even deeper, if that were possible. *What did that mean? Maybe he'll just turn around and take me home. I'm not sure I want to go anywhere today, anyways.*

But, he kept going, turning off the highway and following some county roads, and she kept quiet. She remembered how her chatter seemed to make him angry before. This time she wanted the date to be perfect. They drove for almost two hours before Davis seemed satisfied with the back roads he was taking. "Nothing like high mountain air early in the morning," he said as he pulled off onto an obscure track. "Are you scared, Little Girl?" His smile was almost vicious and his laugh was like something you'd hear in a horror movie.

Yolanda shuddered. *I shouldn't have come alone,* she thought. But, when Davis took her hand and kissed her fingers, she relaxed and smiled back. *He's just teasing me because I'm so much younger than he is.* "Are there trails up here?" She asked, nodding her head toward the deep forest before them. It was barely daylight and the trees were shrouded in shadow.

"Honey, there are always trails," he answered. He turned off the engine and kissed her hand once more. A frown crossed his flawless brow and he looked around the seat where Yolanda sat. "Where's your purse, your wallet?" He asked. His voice held an icy edge.

"I don't carry one," she shrugged, puzzled by the way his mood could change in only a couple of seconds.

"You don't have a driver's license or ID of some kind?" His voice rose and he looked almost angry.

Yolanda reached calmly into her back jeans pocket. "Sure, my license is right here," she held it up for him to see. "Why? Am I gonna be driving somewhere?"

A small sigh escaped him and he was once again wreathed in that beautiful smile that caught her first glance a few months ago when he'd come into the truck stop.

"No, Little Girl, you're not going to be driving. Let's see . . ." He got out a small red marker and circled her name on the license. "Now, let's walk." He blew on her license to dry the red ink and slipped it into her shirt pocket.

"Why'd you do that?" She indicated the front of her shirt. "I'll need it and now you've marked it up. Won't the police or someone be curious about that?"

He smiled and winked, but didn't say anything more about it, just tightened his grip on her hand and kissed it before releasing her to get out of the car. As he joined her beside her door, Davis grabbed for her hand once again. He didn't seem to be in any hurry and was happy just walking beside her, not saying a word. They walked along a very dim animal trail over windfalls and through dense brush. It wasn't like the last time when he told her the names of all the plants and trees they saw. This time he was strolling along steadily, seeming to have a goal in mind.

What am I doing out here with this man I don't really know? She asked herself as they climbed along a high ridge. *Mama doesn't even know where I am or who I'm with. I won't do this again. Mama deserves better behavior than this from me.*

"Jump, Yo," he said as he turned and held out his arms to her. She jumped down from a large boulder and came to a halt on the edge of a narrow cliff, twenty or more feet high. The forest opened before them, but what caught her attention was the meandering creek rushing along the forest floor, winding in and out of the trees, touching a misty meadow only a few hundred yards away. She felt his hands resting on her shoulders as they stood there gazing out at the wonderful sight below, and a sigh of contentment escaped her. "This is so beautiful," she whispered, craning her neck to look up into Davis' alluring blue eyes.

He leaned down and kissed her gently. "Trust me, Little Girl?" He whispered back.

Yolanda nodded. This man was as mesmerizing as he was unpredictable. She thought she must be falling in love.

Suddenly, he cupped his hands over her head and whistled two long high-pitched sounds. She looked up at him in askance, but he pointed to the creek and whispered into her hair. "Just watch. You'll see, just watch."

They stood quietly for several minutes. Yolanda was happily aware of him standing so close behind her, his breath fluttering through her hair. His hands were lying on her shoulders with his fingers almost touching together along the front of her throat. She looked more intently when she felt his body tighten behind her, his fingers digging in slightly just above her collarbone.

There, just lumbering out of the trees, only fifty feet away from them was the biggest bear she'd ever seen. *Stupid,* she thought. *Of course it's the biggest one you've ever seen, you've never seen a bear outside a zoo.* She drew a sharp breath and the animal seemed to pause in its measured steps. She pushed herself back against Davis glancing up at him as he stood immobile behind her. His face was unreadable, a picture of pleasure and pain, joy and what, hatred? She couldn't be sure. "Davis, I'm frightened. That bear could eat us right now and how would we ever stop him?" She whispered fiercely.

He held her closer and whispered. "Quiet now, she won't hurt you. She'll just walk along the creek and sit over there by that boulder. I've been here lots of times. She knows me and she won't eat you, not while I'm here and you're alive, she won't."

What does that mean? She thought while her face screwed up into a giant frown. She became aware of several things at once. Davis was laughing that maniacal sound that scared her in the car, the bear really did sit by the rock and was staring at them like she was waiting on something, and Davis' hands were now fully on her neck, his fingers laced against her throat and his thumbs pushing hard on her spine at the base of her skull.

Her breath came in small gasps as she realized the very real danger she was in. *Oh, please no,* she thought. She opened her mouth to scream, but no sound escaped her. She felt herself sliding down the hill into a black abyss.

*　　*　　*

Winter came and went, spring brought new flowers and warm days, but Yolanda never came home again. Her mother sat and rocked, looking out the window in the new apartment where she'd had to move after there was no more income from her daughter's work. She knew the police had given up, convinced that her sweet girl had run away. She wondered if it could be true, but an inner voice said no, Yolanda was a good girl. She left that note and she meant to come back. Both Ida and she had told the police about the truck driver friend Yolanda had made, but no one seemed to know where he was from or how to reach him.

"His name is Daniel or Dennis . . ." Ida told them. "No, wait! His name was David. He went with us on the boat once. I'm pretty sure his name was David and he's from the coast, maybe California or somewhere. I should have paid more attention, but I thought he was just a casual date. They didn't really seem like a couple, you know? He was so much older and never interacted with us very much the whole day."

Yolanda's co-workers didn't remember any guys she'd been interested in. "Sure, there's lots of flirty truck drivers," said another waitress. "It kind of goes with the territory, you know?" When questioned further, she remembered little more. "There was some white guy she used to date. Some guy from her high school, I think. But, he married and moved away or something a long time ago. His name was Jerry, I think."

Another waitress suddenly remembered something. "Hey, remember that dude from Oregon or California, I think it was? He and 'Landa talked about him a couple of times. I thought his accent was more from the deep south, though."

"'Landa wouldn't have gone out with him! He was old." The teenaged cook frowned at the girls.

"Yeah, you're just jealous cause she wouldn't look at you twice!" Everyone laughed at the embarrassment of the cook.

The investigation hit a brick wall. There just wasn't any convincing evidence that Yolanda didn't run away. Even her mother had to admit that she was restless and discontent, but she still didn't believe that her girl just ran away from home. After all, she'd left a note saying she would be back. Well, it didn't say exactly that she would be back, but it didn't say she meant to leave forever, either.

Nevertheless, the fact remained that Yolanda was gone. One set of clothes and her driver's license were all she took with her. The note she left didn't prove anything one way or another to the local police. Yolanda Herrera was never seen alive again.

It would be many years later that Mrs. Herrera would get a call from a Detective in Montana saying that Yolanda's bones and driver's license had been found on a mountain somewhere over there. Montana . . . it sounded so far away.

Harriet, Alberta, Canada
Summer, 1996

"Where's Harriet?" Her step-father asked on Saturday morning.

His wife shook her head. "Didn't come home last night." She said as she washed their five-year-old boy's face.

"Again?" He asked. "Left you with all the work to do, too, I see."

"No matter," she answered, thinking it was easier to do the work than to argue with her willful eighteen-year-old daughter.

"She out with that group from the lodge?"

"Maybe so."

"She comes in later you put her to work good and hard, you hear?" He grabbed his hat from the peg by the back door of their log cabin. "If you don't have enough to do, you send her out here to the barn. I'll find something to fill her time." He looked down at his son who stood staring up at him with his big brown eyes. "Come on, Josh, come help Papa."

They went out the door and down the path to the big log barn. She watched them through the window, then turned to the sink full of dirty dishes. "Yah, someday she won't be comin' home, I'm thinkin'," she said to the work before her.

As the days turned into weeks, those words became prophecy. Harriet didn't return. Her mother grieved in silence while her step-father raged about the embarrassment the girl was putting his family through, being a runaway.

Wasn't it hard enough, thought the woman, *just living day to day, scraping by a meager living off this scrub land? Did life have to be as barren as the rocky fields?* She sniffed as hot tears ran down her cheeks and dripped into the tepid dishwater. *Two living children out of seven and now one of them a runaway.* She thought sadly about the babies that were stillborn and the son who drowned at the age of ten along with his father, her first husband. *Well, mebbe we was just too hard on the girl,* she shook her head slowly as she finished the chore at the sink and moved on to mending. She looked out the window at her husband, older brother to the man who was Harriet's father, in his greasy overhauls, working on the tractor, again. "And maybe she'll come home someday with some kind of rich man and a passel of little ones. Maybe he'll treat her like a queen and she'll smile and say how grand life is . . ." She smiled slightly at the needlework in her hands until a great sigh slipped from her lips. "Prob'ly not, though." The silence of the house reminded her that her girl was gone, gone these many weeks . . .

Harriet had always been an adventurous sort of child, even more so than her boys. She climbed trees and haystacks, rocky crags in the mountains near their home and even to the top of the barn. She was the only survivor of the accident that took her father's life. She was smart, too. She'd finished her schooling at home when she was only sixteen and had been learning everything she could about housework and farm work, too. But, she was restless. She wanted to test the world. When they went to town, she was always the one running from store to store and the last one in the truck when it was time to go home.

Harriet had started sneaking out of the house to meet some of the tourists and town youth a couple of years before. It was easy for her to just wait until her folks were snoring up a storm, then walk out without even a backward glance. At first it was kind of exciting, going to impromptu parties and on forbidden dates. But, after a while, she was bored with the local farm boys and the little tourist village near their home. She wanted to go places and see things like the tourists at the local lodge were always talking about. She began babysitting for folks who were in town shopping, taking their children to the play equipment in the park while their folks bought their goods. It gave her a little spending money and didn't really require a lot of hard work like the farm at home.

Harriet's first venture to the ski lodge was to put in an application for work. Maybe she could earn some real money and go away to college, even. The only work available to a country girl was housekeeping or washing dishes in the restaurant. *I can do those things at home,* she thought. And they wanted to pay her so little! Working just didn't seem worth the effort while she could live at home for free. It wasn't like she had debts or anything to pay. She just wanted a little cash in her pocket to buy pretty things. So she continued babysitting for folks as the opportunities came up during the summer months. She dreaded the thoughts of winter and the months she'd spend practically chained to the farm while tons of snow closed off the roads and made going to town almost impossible.

She met a few interesting people at the lodge during the spring and summer of her eighteenth birthday. She went to some parties and got invited to spring ski and join youth groups for picnics. Once in a while, she got asked out on a real date by a stranger. That was the most exciting thing of all, riding around in fancy cars or hanging out at the pool near the lodge motel. But, getting home at a decent hour and being able to do her chores the next day was beginning to be a trial. Papa John was so demanding! "I don't know how Mama can stand that man!" She declared to the night as she trudged home after a date early one morning in the deep of summer. She crept to within a few feet of the log house set into the forested hill beyond. There was a light on in the kitchen already. With a sigh and a shrug she walked to the long, low log barn and prepared the stall for milking. She could hear Heidi, their brown swiss milk cow, just outside the wall walking in the muck of the barnyard. Harriet lit the kerosene lantern near the door and opened it to let the cow walk into her stall. She was a good cow, small and lean from foraging on hillside scrub. She walked methodically to the stall and stood patiently waiting, her tail flashing in the subdued light. Harriet smiled thinly as she shut the door. She walked to the small sink in the corner and wet a towel, which she stuck into her waistband, then she grabbed the one-legged stool and the bucket. She put her hand on the warm flank of the cow and bent over to wash the udders that were already dripping with the cream-thick milk. In only a few moments, the swish-swish sound of milk streaming into the metal bucket brought the barn cats out for their taste of the morning's treat. She heard her step-father come into the barn, felt him staring at her from across the straw littered floor.

"Gonna need another bucket?" His deep voice rumbled toward her.

"Yah, maybe," she nodded.

"Huh," he grunted before turning toward the storeroom for another metal pail.

I hope he's gonna be nice to me today, she thought as she waited for him to return. The bucket under the cow was filling fast. She aimed a teat at one of the cats and laughed as the feline caught the milk in midair and licked her face and paws.

"Here," Papa John thrust the new bucket at her from behind the cow. Harriet handed him the nearly full bucket and started on the new one. Swish, swish, swish the milk rang onto the metal. "You come out to the field when your chores are done," he said.

Harriet sighed. She hadn't gotten any sleep at all. "Papa John, I'm not feeling so awful good."

"Yah," his big head was nodding and he stared at her with a knowing look.

"I'll be along," she said quietly.

"Yah!" He said sharply as he turned around and headed for the door. "Don't you be too long, neither."

Harriet leaned her head against the cow's side as she finished the milking. The pungent aroma of fresh milk comforted her, but she knew she wouldn't get any rest this day. Papa John would work her until dark and she'd be glad to fall into her bed in the little loft room that was hers.

"Did you sleep?" Mama asked as she dished out some oatmeal for a hurried breakfast.

"No."

"Then eat up," she advised as she poured Harriet some orange juice. "You're going to need some energy today, I'm thinking."

"Yah," Harriet smiled gratefully.

A week later, Harriet met a truck driver along the highway and flagged him down. "Give a girl a ride to town?" She asked with her sweetest smile.

The face that looked down at her was lined with age and he had a full, almost-white beard. His hair was thinning on top, but he combed it forward to hide some of the balding. He frowned at her, then looked up and down the road. "Girl, does your family know where you are?"

Oh, great, he's gonna be just like Papa John, she thought. "I'll get another ride, Mister. It's fine." She started to walk away.

"What you going to do in town at this time of night, anyway?" He called after her.

"There's a party at the lodge!" She yelled back, half turning so her voice would carry back to him.

"Come on, then," he growled at her. "I don't want some cowboy getting ahold of you."

She grinned to herself, turned in one motion and fled back to the truck. As she settled in the passenger seat she sighed. "Thanks, Mister, it's kind of you."

"Do you have a ride home from this here party?" He asked, peering at her over his large nose.

"Oh, sure, I always get a ride home," she tossed her hair and rolled her eyes as she looked out the window toward the parking lot. There were a lot of trucks tonight and she had to pick one with an old man like her step-dad. She noticed one truck in particular, a red cab with a small white sign on the door. The driver was standing beside it and he seemed to be staring right at her. *Wow!* She almost breathed aloud. *Why couldn't I have picked that truck?* She stared back at the handsome man with his crooked smile.

"You stay away from that guy," said her driver. "There's something wrong with him."

"Like what?" She asked. She waved slowly in the side-view mirror and was pleased that the other man waved back.

"I mean it, Girl," the driver said sternly. "That guy has a few screws loose. He's like a snake or something and for you he's bad news. Remember that, okay?" He looked at Harriet, but she didn't look back at him. She looked at the road ahead.

"You can let me out about five miles down the road, there by the little soda shop," she said without taking her eyes from the road. "I appreciate the ride."

"The people at the soda shop know you?"

"Yeah, I grew up here."

"Hmmm."

They drove the rest of the way in silence. Harriet couldn't wait to jump out of the cab and run to the lodge a few blocks down the main street.

"How old are you, Girl?" He asked before she could get away.

"Eighteen," she answered, ready to flee.

"Well, then, you just watch yourself. Try not to get into trouble and don't worry your folks, you hear?"

"Yes, Sir. Thank you, Sir." She literally jumped from the seat and almost fell onto the pavement in her hurry to get away from the man who reminded her so much of her step-father. She didn't need that tonight! She'd had a week full of hard work and stern advise. Now, it was time to play!

Harriet walked into the soda shop and waited until the truck pulled away, headed back toward the highway. There were a few people she knew from school hanging out so she joined them for a while, but they were all going home early.

As soon as she could, she headed down the road toward the lodge. *Maybe there would be something fun going on with the tourists,* she thought. She heard a horn blare and turned to look back the way she'd come. There was the handsome man with the red truck! This might be her lucky night, after all. She walked backwards, sticking out her right thumb. He slowed the truck and motioned for her to get in. She was up the steps and onto the seat in a flash.

"My name's Harriet," she said right away.

He nodded. "Cole, Cole Anderson," he introduced himself.

"Nice to meet you, Mr. Cole Anderson," she smiled broadly at him.

"Where you going, Miss Harriet?"

"That all depends on where you're taking me, I guess."

He looked slowly over at her, a look of curiosity on his handsome face.

"Know any hiking trails around here?" He asked.

"Sure, there's lots of them," she answered, waving at the mountains surrounding them.

"Ever been up to Banff and Lake Louise?"

She clapped her hands in joy. "Wow! Um, yah when I was little and my Papa was alive. We used to go lots of places then."

He nodded. "Well, that's where I'm headed, so you're welcome to ride along."

She looked out the side window for a moment at the miles already rolling by. *I'm gonna miss chores for a few days,* she thought. She stole a quick glace at the truck driver. *Maybe I'll just keep going and never go back for a good, long time.* "Great!" She answered. "It's time for me to go somewhere besides this little valley." *I'm gonna be in so much trouble when I get back,* she thought. She looked at the driver again. *But maybe, just maybe Mr. Cole Anderson will be worth it and it doesn't matter any more.* She smiled into her hands lying in her lap.

Andy Davis, now assuming his role as Cole Anderson, nodded again and settled in for a long drive. At a roadside pullout, he showed her some rock formations and how the water of a roaring creek was creating new paths all the time. She was fascinated by his attention and his depth of knowledge about geological formations. If nothing else, this was going to be a trip of a lifetime. She was going to learn something, and that should please Papa John for once! She felt only a little guilt at the work she was leaving for her mother to do. *But, without me to eat and make a mess, Mama will actually have less to do,* she rationalized. As they continued their trip, she relaxed against the passenger seat of the truck and talked easily to the stranger beside her.

The tourist area around the popular area known as Banff, Alberta opened up before them on the following day. Cole had driven all night to get to there, like it was important to him. The place was busy, but not like in the winter when skiers came from all over the world to play in the snow.

Finally, Cole pulled into a truck parking area near some stores and local attractions and motioned her up into the top bunk. She was surprised, but secretly pleased that he was a gentleman. She remembered the words of the other truck driver . . . "There's something wrong with that guy," he'd said. Harriet decided the older man was jealous or something because Cole was real nice.

They slept away most of the morning. When Harriet emerged to find a restroom, she felt rested and happy. "I could get used to living like this," she whispered. "I hope he'll keep me with him for a long time."

Cole watched through nearly closed eyes as the girl climbed out of the truck and headed for the facilities. "Stupid little kitty," he mumbled. "They're always wanting to run away from home and picking up with the first tom cat that comes along." He reached under his bunk and rubbed his fingers along the barrel of his twenty-two rifle. It gave him comfort to know it was there, and it pleased him to know that he'd gotten it into Canada without anyone even checking. He absently rubbed his ribs until he felt where an old scar reminded him of a time when he could have used some protection like that gun. "But I won't need it for this puss," he smiled and stretched in the cramped quarters bringing his hands in front of his face and flexing his long fingers. "Nope, won't need any other tools for this job."

He stretched again before getting up, groping for his expensive, black western boots. He shoved his feet into them and climbed out across the driver's seat. As he slid out of the truck, he settled his feet firmly into his boots, stomping each one two or three times. He grabbed his hat and sunglasses from the side door and sauntered off toward a public restroom.

It was mid-afternoon when Cole finally came back to the truck. Harriet had amused herself by walking around the local shops and watching families hurrying from one store to the next. She felt relaxed and happy even though she didn't have any money, or even clean clothes. Her homespun dress was wrinkled and her shoes were scuffed, but somehow it just didn't matter today. She looked up occasionally to see if the truck was still there, and it always was. "I wonder where he went?" She asked a mannequin in a window. She looked at the truck again and started walking toward it. "It doesn't matter. He doesn't owe me any explanations." She smiled broadly when she saw him walking from the opposite direction and picked up her pace, half running to get to the truck at the same time as he did. "Hi," she said.

Cole stopped in mid stride. "Where you bin?"

"Just lookin' around."

"Who'd you talk to?"

Harriet frowned. "Nobody but an old mannequin in a window," she said.

"Well, get in the truck, we're going on down the road a piece." When they settled into the truck, he turned to face her. "You got some ID, Little Girl?"

"Yeah," she frowned at the question. "Right here in my pocket." She patted the small pocket on the side of her dress.

"Okay." He answered sharply, but softened it quickly with his crooked smile. "Good," he half mumbled. "That's good, then."

She wondered if she'd done something to displease him, but shrugged before settling into the seat, trying to get comfortable.

He turned back to the wheel without speaking, just started the truck and pulled out onto the highway. They drove only a few miles when he turned down a dirt side-road.

"Where's this go?" She asked with a frown. "Can you take big trucks down this way?"

"It's just a little side trip. I've been down this way before. It comes out on the highway twenty or so miles over that way." He pointed to the left and forward around a forested mountain. "There's hiking trails out there that I like."

"Cool," she responded, relaxing once again. *Everything's gonna be fine. I'm just a worrier like Ma.*

Cole drove several miles before he pulled the rig to a stop and backed into a dirt road. He didn't stop near the corner, but backed almost half a mile into the forest before shutting off the engine. "Get out," he said.

"What?" She asked, with a little fear.

He pointed to the trees beside her. "We're going for a little walk out there."

She smiled in relief. "Oh, okay," she said in a small voice. *Stupid!* She admonished herself. *Did you really think he was just going to dump you out here in the woods and drive away?* She giggled lightly to hide her embarrassment.

When Cole came around the truck, he grabbed her hand and pulled her along with him on a trail that was neatly hidden in the brush. She wanted to ask how he'd ever found it, but didn't want to break the mood of the moment. It was kind of a narrow track and she suspected it was more of an animal trail rather than one for hiking, but he seemed to know just where he was going and she was glad to be a part of his fun. They walked in silence for what seemed like a long time, but was really only fifteen minutes. It made her jump when he finally spoke. "See the waterfall?" He pointed to the rock cliff to her left.

She nodded. "It's beautiful. Can we go over there?"

"Nope," he said and pulled her along after him once again.

They finally came out into a long valley with a small, clear lake near the foot of a tall mountain. It was a beautiful sight. Harriet wondered if anyone had ever been here before. Except for Cole, that is. He'd obviously know about this special place.

"This is wonderful," she breathed. The pine scent in the air made her feel at home and if she listened closely she could hear the sound of falling water. They were too far from the waterfall they'd seen earlier, so she guessed there must be a creek that fed this little lake. A fish jumped making a splash and ripples fanned out in a wide circle. "If you count the ripples before they fade, you're wishes will come true." She said.

Cole snorted. "Where'd you ever hear a dumb thing like that? Is it some kind of little girl nursery story?"

"Well, that's mean of you," she said. "It's just something my Papa used to say when I was little."

"You live up in the mountains?" He asked.

"Yes, I do."

"You got bears and cougars at your place?"

"Of course."

"Yet, you still go out hitch hiking?"

"They don't bother me, not on the road, like they might if I was in the forest or something."

"Is that a fact?" He looked around at the towering mountains not far away.

"Where do you live?" She asked him.

"It's none of your business!" He snapped back, pulling the grass stem out of his mouth and throwing it on the ground. He bent down quickly and picked up a stone and flung it into the water. It made a splash and sunk to the rocky bottom.

"You gotta pick a flat stone to skip it," she explained, looking around for a specimen.

"I wasn't trying to skip it, only to drown it," he answered.

Harriet felt a chill at his words. She rubbed her arms to rid herself of the goose flesh that followed, but Cole didn't seem to notice.

A shift in the wind brought a strong odor to her nose. "Ewee!" She declared. "What's that awful smell?"

Cole put his head back and sniffed deeply. "Probably something a grizzly dug up," he said with a crooked smile.

"Doesn't it make you about half sick?" She asked. "Such a beautiful place ruined by a smell like that."

"The animals will take care of it, whatever it is," he said calmly. "Let's walk." He took her hand and pulled her along the shore to another trail. This one was steep and she had trouble keeping up.

"I don't have my hiking shoes," she explained, pointing down at her old, black flats.

"No matter," he said, helping her up the incline and onto a ledge high up into the trees. "We're not going far." True to his word, they stopped in only a few more feet where the way was blocked by a shoulder of the mountain.

She looked out over the treetops at the lake below them. "Wow, we came up quite a ways," she said in awe. The lake looked like a farm pond or an oversized puddle from here. She could see four or five buzzards flying nearby, swooping low into the trees between them and the lake, which was almost directly below their little ledge. She nodded sagely. "Yep, just like I figured, there's something dead down there." She pointed into the trees, moving around to see if she could see the ground.

Cole stepped up behind her and put his large hands around her slim waist. He could completely encircle her and it brought a smile to her face. She relaxed into his right arm and felt the flex of his biceps. A thrill coursed through her. *I'm glad he brought me here,* she mused. *This could be a new beginning for me, maybe for, well for us. Us, I like the sound of that.*

Cole pointed out a cave up high on one of the ridges across from them. "Bear den," he whispered.

"Have you been up there? Is it really bears, or cougars?"

"Bears," he said. "Didn't I just say so?" His grip tightened, but this time his hands were on her shoulders.

"Okay, okay, don't get mad," she said. "At home, we have cougars in caves and most of the bears hibernate in holes under windfalls and in the ground. I was just asking."

"Curious, huh?"

"Yeah, I guess so." She shrugged lightly, the mood gone now that he was being so testy. Suddenly she couldn't wait to go home. *He's too much like my step-dad,* she thought. *Thinks he knows everything about everything. Isn't there some man who would think that I know something, too?*

"Well," he said with a slow smile. "You know what they say about curiosity, right?"

"What?"

"That it killed the cat."

With that comment everything changed in Harriet's young life. When she looked up at Cole's face she saw a look of danger like she'd never seen before. It caused her to draw away from him and turn so that she was half facing him. "What?" She asked, alarm making her voice squeak.

Cole turned her back around so she faced the edge of the cliff where they stood. "Easy Little Kitty," he crooned as he rubbed her back. His hands rested lightly along her hips and she began to relax. Loons called in the distance.

Harriet looked out over the lake to see if a pair of the birds was floating on the water somewhere. "Ev . . . ever see loons?" She asked quietly.

He reached into her pocket for her ID card, slipping it into his own shirt pocket. She hadn't noticed before how close to the edge they were. Now it seemed like a sinister thing, the trees dark and menacing. She stood very still, trying to relax and recapture the joy she'd felt earlier or even the beginning calm of a few minutes ago. Cole's hands caressed her arms and he pulled her close to him. That helped her to feel safer in a way, yet there was something wrong and she couldn't quite grasp why she felt that way. *Why'd he take my ID?* She frowned with the effort to think, when she suddenly realized he was speaking.

"Relax little Kitten," he soothed. "Relax, now."

Harriet breathed deeply of the pine and rotting vegetation. She could still smell the acrid-sweetness of whatever was dead down in the trees, but the vagrant breeze had shifted again so it was faint. *I wonder what that is,* she thought as Cole's hands came to rest along the base of her throat. She relaxed into him, feeling the warmth of his body and his breath in her hair. There was no pain and only a little struggle as she succumbed to the quick pressure of those large, experienced hands. Her limp body slid gently off the ledge and down into the trees, coming to rest with the remains of others who'd been there before her. He drew out her license, marked her name with a red pen and flipped it into the trees below, with her.

Cole whistled his little tune as he hurried back to his truck. He climbed up quickly and sat with his hands gripping the wheel. After a moment he relaxed and started the engine. He pulled forward cautiously toward the country road. There was no traffic on the road, but still he drove slowly and carefully away from the parks and deep into Alberta, on his way east into Saskatchewan and on to Manitoba. It was time to head for home once again. He needed distance and time. Shaking off a feeling of melancholy, he whistled his song again for a little while. At his next fuel stop, he got out his journal and made a few entries, adding the name Harriet along the page margin. He idly flipped through the pages, looking for other names in the margins. With a sigh, he closed the book and tossed it onto his bunk. He gripped the wheel and rolled the truck slowly back out onto the highway as he smiled to himself. "Yep, it's high time to go home," he said softly.

Spring, 1997
The Four L's
Canada, nearing the Sault Ste. Marie Border Crossing

It had been a long month driving across Canada. Andy Davis only had a half load on the truck to deliver somewhere in Wisconsin. He hadn't been able to find another US cargo to pick up, not even an illegal one as he drove across Ontario. "Not like out west where loads are ready for the asking," he mumbled into his coffee. He sighed as he looked out the window at the countryside rolling by. "I've been gone more than long enough," he said. "It's time to go home for a bit." He smiled as he turned on the radio. He hadn't been back to Missouri for nearly five years.

At 7am, he rolled through the border crossing, talking easily with authorities, waiting patiently as they looked at his cargo, examined his manifest, and inspected his truck.

"You can go," said a Customs Inspector as he handed Andy his license and paperwork.

"Thanks," he smiled. "You guys have a great day." He whistled a little tune as he climbed into the cab and drove away. He knew better than to start that tune, a little ditty he'd begun as a child. "Let's see, when did I start that?" He mumbled as he drove along Highway 45. "Oh, yeah it was on my birthday, the one when the old man up and kicked the bucket." He shook his head as tears threatened. He whistled the tune again, louder this time. His mother's voice echoed somewhere in his tortured mind. 'Anderson always whistles when he's dealing with something. I know when he's okay. He starts up with his little song, and soon he'll be just fine.' Andy Davis laughed. "Yeah, I'm okay, Ma," he said aloud. "I'm A-okay." He whistled his way toward the state line and the wilderness area of Wisconsin.

He pulled in at a small restaurant around lunchtime. Looking around he smiled contentedly. There was a run down motel nearby where he could spend the rest of the day, maybe get to know some of the natives. He smiled again, spying the little village scattered among the scrub brush and trees.

Inside the restaurant, he was surprised at the volume of people for such a tiny place. "Must be good food here," he said to the pretty young waitress.

"We do our best. What can I get you?"

"Just some ham and eggs, Honey."

"Coffee?"

"Nope, I'll have some milk." He appraised her figure. "You look like a good farm girl. I'll bet you drink lots of milk." He smiled what he knew was a disarming smile.

She shook her head, her long silky hair waving along her back. "You truck drivers are all alike," she said.

"I'm hurt," he feigned a pout.

"Right," she laughed her way to the serving window behind the crowded bar.

Andy looked around the room and sized up the patrons who were busy doing the same about him. There were a bunch of farmers and ranch hands, a couple of drivers, maybe, and the local cop. No women, not one woman in the whole place, except for the waitress and the cook, who looked like she was no more than eighteen. Andy reached across to another table and grabbed the local paper. Not much to it, only ten or so pages. Well, it would serve as a shield if nothing else.

"Here's your lunch, Mister," his waitress said from the other side of the paper.

"That was fast," he nodded appreciatively at the mounded plate. "Looks good, too. Where'd the Little Girl learn to cook like this?"

"Linda?" She queried. "She's been cooking here for three years. You won't find better food than this even if you go clean to Milwaukee."

"Is that a fact?"

"Yes, it is," she nodded and smiled again.

He smiled back at her before asking "Say, who do I see about a room out there in the motel?"

The waitress turned. "Silas Edward Bean, you got a customer!" She hollered at the group of farmers.

A man about the age of a tree stood and ambled over to the table. "Want a room, ya say?" He asked in a spidery voice.

"Yep."

"Well, I got one left. Cost you twenty-five dollars a day, in advance."

Andy waited, but the old man just stood there staring at him as he wolfed down his food. He slowly laid down his fork and reached for his wallet, extracting a one hundred dollar bill. "I'll just pay for four nights, then."

The old man smiled revealing rotting and missing teeth. He snatched the money like it was the last of its kind. "That's mighty nice of you, Young Feller." The old man rushed out the door, letting it slam behind him.

"He'll be back with a key," the waitress said, looking fondly after the ancient.

"Good," Andy said around a mouthful of bread.

"My name's Lana. Who're you, with all the money to burn in a washed up old town?"

"Some call me Baines," he bantered, cocking his head to look up at her.

She sat at his table and looked searchingly at him. "What do others call you?"

He couldn't help but smile. She was sharp-witted, this farm girl. He put his hands behind his head and leaned his chair back. "Anderson. Some call me Anderson," he said.

"Hm-m-m. Well, Baines Anderson, or whatever your name is, welcome to our little corner of the world." She paused and looked around at the other customers. They all seemed mighty absorbed in a quiet conversation all their own. "Are you really staying four days or are you just jerking the old man's chain?"

"If there's stuff to do, I'll stay awhile," he answered as he drank the last of his milk.

She shook her head, her sharp features more prominent when she held her head high. "There's nothing to do around here, much. We don't even get good TV reception."

"What about camping, hiking, or fishing?"

She smiled at him. "Everybody in Wisconsin goes fishing."

"Know where I can rent a car?" He asked.

"Rent? Well, I guess I could rent you mine. My sister can drive me around for a couple of days."

"The cook your sister?" He nodded toward the kitchen.

"Linda?" Lana shook her head again. "No, she's not my sister. "We're neighbors, that's all."

As if on cue, the dark haired girl from the kitchen hollered out. "Gonna work or talk to the jerk?"

"I'll be along as sure as a song," Lana answered in a sing-song voice. When she turned back toward the stranger, she was shocked to see the look of meanness on the face of the man across the table from her. He was sitting upright now and looked like a thundercloud. "Sorry," she whispered. "We always tease each other like that. She," Lana pointed with her thumb at the kitchen. "She's always rhyming everything. You'll get used to it."

"I doubt it," he sputtered. Andy Davis, now Baines Anderson, swallowed hard, trying to keep the breakfast he'd just eaten from spewing across the table. *Evil little girls!* He thought as he watched Lana walk toward the bar and begin cleaning up some dishes. She glanced his way once, then busied herself with the dirty dishes and counter.

The old man startled Baines by showing up silently beside his elbow, shoving a dirty piece of paper in front of him that resembled a receipt, and a key with a large fob dangling from it, marked with the number four. Baines starred at the number for a long time before he grabbed it and left the restaurant. His head hurt. He needed to get some sleep.

The local cop was standing outside and followed him to the motel room. Andy never looked at him, just stuck the key into the ancient door lock and turned the rusty knob. Despite the age of the building, room number four was clean and sported a microwave and small fridge. Baines flipped through some snowy channels on the TV, but decided the girl Lana had been right. There wasn't anything worth watching anyway. He peered out the small window once, but the cop had gone on about his business and was nowhere to be seen. Andy closed the curtains and drew the shade down for privacy. "I'll not be staying around here," he mumbled.

At about nine o'clock there was a timid knock at the door. Baines drew aside the curtains and was surprised to see Lana and another girl standing outside his room. He slowly opened the door. He was even more surprised to see that the girls were very obviously twins, identical twins. "Hi," Lana said. At least he thought it was Lana.

"This is my sister Lynette," Lana pointed to her twin.

"Nice," he said, looking from one to the other.

"I brought you my car. You said you needed one for a few days. Is ten dollars a day too much?"

Baines reached for his wallet. "I only have a fifty," he said handing the bill to her.

"I don't have any change," she said with a slight frown.

"Nah, keep it," he said as he looked intently at the girls. At first glance they seemed lovely, but their features were sharp and that made them look hard and a little mean to his eyes. "I'd like to go camping for a few days, any suggestions?" His mouth felt dry and the words came out forced.

Lana and Lynette exchanged looks. "Well, there's a couple of lakes where camping is allowed, or up at the marsh," said Lynette. Her voice was softer than her sister's, but that seemed to be the only difference between them.

"Yeah, we're all going up to hike on the marsh trails this weekend, well we're actually headed up there tonight until Saturday or Sunday," Lana added. "I guess you're welcome to come up and hike, too."

"Aw, Man!" Muttered her sister, which earned her a glare from Lana.

"Who's we all?" He asked.

Lana pointed to her sister, then waved back at another car sitting alongside the road. "The two of us and the two of them."

Baines looked, expecting to see a couple of boys in the other car. To his further surprise he saw the cook, Linda and another girl. "Who's that?"

"It's Linda and her sister Laura. We're all twins. That is, two sets of twins. We do everything together."

Baines looked harder at the other car, then walked toward them, Lana and Lynette following. He was bare footed and the gravel hurt his tender feet. Sure enough, the girls in the car looked like another set of twins. "What is this, the Twin Twilight Zone?" He asked no one in particular. That set them all to laughing.

"We always surprise folks with our little jokes," spouted Linda. Her sister laughed even harder, a high-pitched, wheezing kind of laugh.

Baines closed his eyes and turned around to flee into his room. He was out of breath, a red haze blurred his vision.

"Sorry," said Lana when they got back to the door. "I know you don't really seem to like the rhyming thing, but she does it all the time, really." She paused, but he didn't turn around. "Well, you're welcome to join us. The trails are really great and we always have a lot of fun up there. I drew you a little map and left it on the front seat of the car just in case you'd be interested.

"Yeah, we don't get any strangers around here, so she latches onto everybody that stays long enough to say more than 'hi' to her," piped up Lynette.

Lana frowned as she handed him what was in her hand. "Um, here's the keys."

Baines turned around and snatched the keys from her slight hand. He looked at the car parked near his door. It was a 1965 Chevy Impala, old, but in good shape. "Yeah, I'll see about the hike," he said as he turned around and shut the door. He leaned heavily against the wooden door, before he shoved himself toward the bed where he collapsed in a heap of tears and anger. He pummeled the pillows until one burst into a cascade of feathers.

A couple of hours later, after a hot shower, Baines felt more relaxed and as he lay on the creaky old bed, he began to plan and scheme. *Two sets of little girl twins,* he thought. *Now there's a challenge for you. One's, even two's can be dealt with, but four?* He stared up at the ceiling. It needed new paint and some of the cracks fixed. He was distracted for a few moments thinking about the repairs this place could use. *Maybe I could come back up this way after I've had some time to get another few loads. I could just leave right now, tonight . . .* "Nah, who're you trying to kid?" He spat out into the darkened room. "You know you're gonna do it because of the L's and because of the challenge. Besides, they do everything together." That thought got him to laughing, long and loud into the night.

Later, in the wee hours of the morning while the little village lay sleeping, Baines donned a pair of tight-fitting gloves and drove Lana's car around the area, getting familiar with the county roads and the campground on the map she'd given him. He took her car to a deserted gravel road where he parked it, a road that was within walking distance of the marshland where the girls were going to be camped. As he hiked back to the motel, jogging and walking to pace himself, he breathed deeply of the fragrant night air. It was hardly any effort for the ten plus miles. Baines always kept himself in good physical shape.

Early on Friday morning, just before daylight, he pounded on the motel keeper's door. When the old man finally appeared, Baines gave his best smile. "Sorry I gotta leave your little joint. I got called on a run, so that's just the way it is. When there's a load, I hop to it."

"Too bad," the old man said, a worried look on his weathered brow.

"Just keep the money. Maybe I'll be back this way sometime." Baines smiled again and gave a little wave as he sprinted from the door to the truck on the other side of the restaurant where he'd left it. He smiled at the shiny red door, minus its sign. "You've been smarter than usual, Andy, old boy," he said to his reflection in the rearview mirror.

*   *   *

Lana was up early on Friday morning as well. She got a fire going in the ancient propane camp stove and began making pancakes for their breakfast.

"Lookee, lookee! Who's the morning cookie?" Linda piped from the tent door.

"Think the old man might want what's in the pan?"

"Linda, can you just stop with the rhymes for once in your life?" Lana spat back from the picnic table.

Linda stood for a moment with her head sticking out the tent door, cocked to one side. "You know me, it's how I'll always be," she said quietly.

"Yeah, and it's why you won't ever have any boyfriends, either!" Lana shot back.

Linda quickly disappeared inside the tent. Lana could hear her and the other girls talking animatedly, if softly. She felt guilty for having snapped at one of her dearest friends that way. "What's the matter with you?" She asked the pancake batter as she poured some of it onto the hot griddle.

"Do you really think he's gonna come out here?" Lynette said softly from behind her shoulder.

"Oh! You nearly scared me out of a year's growth!" Lana startled at the sight of her sister so close. "I didn't even hear you come out of the tent."

"He's old, Lana. Why must you flirt with every stranger who comes here?"

Lana looked squarely at her twin. "Someday, one of them is going to take me away from this place." She said in a near whisper. "All I want is to go away and never look back, don't you?"

"No, all I want is to have mama back so daddy will quit drinkin'."

"Yeah," Lana agreed. "Are those two ever gonna come out here for breakfast? The trails will be almost empty this early on a Friday, you know. We can have them all to ourselves for once."

Lynette and Lana both looked back toward the tent where they could hear subdued voices. The soft murmur was somehow comforting in the quiet morning air. Even the birds seemed to hush for awhile.

"Did you know she only makes rhymes when someone else is around?" Lynette suddenly asked. "She almost never rhymes when it's just her and Laura."

"Why is that, do you think?"

"I think she's nervous that she won't be liked and just makes a fool of herself so people will laugh and talk more to her. I don't know."

"Ever wish that their mama and our daddy would someday get married or something?"

"Are you kidding me? No, I've never even thought that!"

"We'd all be sisters, then." Lana sighed.

"It's better to be best friends. Sometimes I need a break from Linda's rhymes and Laura's asthma. Don't you?"

"Yeah, that's true. But if we were sisters, maybe Linda wouldn't rhyme with us all the time. And maybe daddy wouldn't drink so much if he had a woman in his life."

"You are such an airhead!" Lynette suppressed a chuckle. "Don't you know that daddy has plenty of women in his life?" She moved closer to her sister and dropped her voice to a whisper. "And that Mrs. Bailey's one of them?"

Lana turned to stare at her sister. "She is? Are you sure of that?"

"Uh, yeah."

"How have I missed that one?"

"Cause you're always dreaming about prince charming or someone, anyone for yourself. You have no idea the things our daddy does." Lynette retorted.

"And now we all know," came a deep voice from behind them.

The girls were both startled as they looked off to the left of the tent. There stood Baines, bigger than life. He was dressed in a pair of black jeans with a black western-style shirt, open at the neck. One foot was up on a stump and he was chewing on a toothpick.

"Aw, Man . . ." Lynette sighed. Lana smiled in true pleasure for the first time in two days. "I'll get the others," Lynette nearly dived into the tent.

"Good morning," Lana said heartily. "Want some pancakes?"

"Sure," he smiled back, showing even white teeth. "I'd like that." He moved his foot so he could sit on the stump watching Lana's every move.

"You can come to the table," Lana tilted her head toward the pair of tables they had set together for their camp.

"I'm fine right here," he answered, eyeing the soft dirt around the tables and camp area. "Got me a tent off in the woods, there a ways." He pointed over his shoulder with the toothpick, which he slipped into a shirt pocket.

"Butter and syrup?" Lana asked as she slid three pancakes onto a tin plate.

"Sure, but just use a paper plate for me, okay?" He asked.

Lana looked bewildered for a moment, but dug around in their camp basket for a paper or Styrofoam plate. She transferred the food onto the new plate and refilled the tin plate with one pancake for herself. Out of the corner of her eye she could see he had dragged a folding utensil from one of his pockets. It was a combination knife, fork, and spoon set.

"Wow, you come prepared," she said indicating his utensil and handing him his plate.

"I spend a lot of time camping and eating alone."

"Mind if I join you?" She nodded toward a log lying close by.

"Wouldn't have it any other way, Sweetie," He answered.

About that exact second, the other three girls came tumbling out of the tent, tripping over each other in their hurry. "Where'd they go, I'd like to know." Linda spouted. Lana watched as Baines' knuckles turned white, he was gripping the fork so hard, but he didn't look up or say a word.

"We're right here," she said loudly. "Get your breakfast and let's go hiking."

"Geez!" Laura jumped at the sound of Lana's voice. "You scared the bejeebies outta us!"

Everyone laughed as the girls dished up their food and sat at the table to eat, everyone, that is, except Baines and Lana. *He's a broody one,* Lana thought. *Maybe we can slip away from the rest of them while we're hiking.* She looked through her long lashes at the man near her. *Man, he's good looking, no matter how old he is!*

Soon, the camp was cleaned and all the food items were stowed in a metal cooler and locked in the trunk of Linda's car. The girls tidied up the tent, laughing and talking together as long-time friends do.

"I'll be back in a minute," Baines said before slipping away into the trees. *He's as silent as the deer of the forest,* Lana thought.

"That guy gives me the creeps," Laura was saying inside the tent.

"Yeah, well Lana likes him, so give it some time. Either he'll fade off into the sunset, or she'll make a go of it with him."

"Are you kidding? She'd do his bidding?" No question who that was talking.

"I'm just saying, back off and give them a chance to get to know one another. Maybe he's nice."

"What's an old man want with our Lan'?"

"That's enough, Linda," Laura chided softly. "Let's just have a good time this weekend."

With that, they spilled out of the tent one at a time like little children at a school picnic. Lana sat at one of the tables facing the door. Guilt was written over all three beautiful, young faces. Lana looked at each of them before she shook her head and looked away. "Family and friends; you gotta love them no matter what." She sighed.

"Let's go," the girls started down the trail.

"I'll be along in a minute," Lana called after the three. She looked nervously around the camp and peered into the trees where Baines Anderson had gone. She waited ten minutes, but there was no sign of him. "Another one bites the dust," she sighed as she heaved herself up from her seat and trudged toward the trails. "I wonder where he parked my car?" She thought idly. "I never even heard it pull into the parking lot." She kicked at a stone on the path. "Of course I wasn't listening for it, either." At the first fork in the trail, she looked at the tracks in the dirt, but couldn't decide which way her friends had gone. She looked up at the sign post to decide which way she wanted to go. All the trails intersected somewhere along the way, so she'd find them sooner or later. Besides, they were so loud she'd hear them before she ever saw them she guessed. *No wonder we never see any moose or bears,* she thought. *They make enough noise to wake the dead.* She was suddenly chilled and looked around to see if someone was watching her. *I'm not used to being alone, I guess.* She shrugged off the feeling, rubbed her arms and shook her hair away from her face. Turning to the right, she walked slowly down the grassy trail. "This one doesn't get used as much," she mumbled to herself.

"Then it's a good choice," Baines appeared before her from the surrounding bushes.

"You do like scaring people, don't you?" She blew out a breath to calm her racing heart.

He smiled and offered her a hand. Lana thought how small her hand was in his as they walked slowly down the path. "There's a little pond up here," he whispered into her hair. "If you're really quiet we might see some animals."

Lana felt a thrill course through her as Baines led her to the water's edge and hunkered down behind her. Her elbows came to rest on his knees as he placed his hands on her slight shoulders and quietly they waited. Sure enough, their wait was rewarded as a moose cow with twin calves splashed their way into the water for a morning graze of succulent water plants. Lana smiled, feeling the warmth of his hands as they moved to encircle her neck then back down to the tops of her shoulders. The spectacle of nature before her paled in comparison to the feelings rising within her heart and mind.

"Let's move on," he whispered against her right ear. "Show me the trails. This is as far as I've come."

She nodded and they rose as one. Baines' hands dropped to encircle her waist as they backed onto the trail a few feet behind them. They walked side-by-side down one trail after another, saying little, pointing out wildlife, peculiar tree formations, and twittering birds around them. *We are in perfect sync,* she thought. *We don't even need to talk, just be together. Oh, I really could fall for this man!* From around another bend in the trail, they could hear plainly the voices of the other girls. They were laughing and talking loudly, making Baines frown. He gripped Lana's hand and pulled her off into the bushes away from the trails where they waited until the girls had passed them by. He held her close to him, his right arm around her and his left parting bushes so they could see when the girls passed within a few feet of them.

"Let's go this way," Baines said as he pulled her around some boulders and away from the trail.

"There's no trails through here," she pulled back. "We could get really lost out in this swamp. Some people have, well they've gotten lost for a long time and had to be rescued."

Baines stepped up close to her and tilted her head so she looked right into his glacial blue eyes. "Trust me?"

She studied his face, so close to her own. "I, well I guess so, but . . ."

He stepped back and the moment was lost. In a voice chilly as winter's frost he spat out the words, pulling her back into the grassy hummocks. "Either you do or you don't, Lana."

She didn't have time to answer him. He rushed down the path the way they'd come, leaving her standing alone. "I'm sorry, Baines," she said, running to catch up with him. *He almost kissed you and you had to go and ruin it all!* She chided herself as she hurried around the twisting trail. But Baines was nowhere to be seen. At last, she came back to the camp. The other girls were there getting out some lunch.

"Where'd you go? We didn't see you anywhere." Lynette said around a bite of Twinkies.

"I had a wonderful, quiet walk," she smiled at her sister.

"Where's Mister Right? Did 'ja have a fight?" Spouted Linda.

Lana shook her head and busied herself with food of her own. Suddenly she felt hungry and realized that she'd missed the girls' company, even if they were loud. *What do you know about this guy, anyway?* She asked herself. *He's like a sneaky cat or bear or something.* A chill assailed her once again. She looked around, but couldn't see anyone. *He's so quiet, he could be lurking out there in the trees and bushes anywhere.*

"Hello-o-o, I'm talking to you," Laura was waving at Lana from across the table.

"Sorry. Hey, did you see the moose family in the pond?"

"There's a pond?" Lynette asked.

"Uh, yeah! Where do you think the mosquitoes come from?" Laura asked. Everyone else laughed.

"Well, we were quiet and got to see some moose, and a family of quails, and, well lots of stuff." Lana looked dreamily at the three facing her.

"Who's we? You and a tree?"

"No, Baines and I went walking down the trail you came back up."

"We didn't see you." Lynette was frowning. "Not until you stepped out of the trail head a minute ago."

"Yeah, and where's the guy?" Laura asked, looking around.

"Oh, never mind," Lana said, shaking her head at the bewildered look on all their faces. "What's the plan for after lunch?" She busied herself with the makings of a sandwich as the talk circled around all the things they could do with their time.

"Let's go up to the cliffs and climb around for awhile, then go for a swim in the lake," Lynette offered. It was agreed. The girls scrambled into the tent, two at a time to change into bathing suits under their jeans and shirts. "Lana gets to carry the backpack of towels cause she's the oldest," Lynette laughed, throwing the pack at her sister.

"By ten minutes," she quipped good naturedly.

"Do we need a rope?" Laura asked.

"No, let's just climb around at the base. There's plenty of arrowheads and bones and stuff to find down there. I don't want to go to the top, does anyone else?"

"No," agreed Linda. "Let's go!"

The trails to the cliffs and to the lake started from the main parking lot so the girls walked down the camp roadway to get there. Lana noticed her car wasn't parked anywhere in the small lot. There was only one pickup truck at the far end and an empty row of parking spaces. She sprinted ahead to see if her car was on the entrance road, but it wasn't there, and Baines wasn't anywhere around either. Lana's heart plummeted. *I really scared him off,* she thought. *He must've decided to go back to the motel. He'll probably just get into his truck and head on down the road, too.* She looked around once more, then walked back to the trail where the girls were waiting, talking about the heat of the day and how this was turning into a perfect weekend already. Lana forced herself to join in with the banter and giggling, but still a part of her wondered greatly at the man she'd spent the morning with. Already it was becoming like a dream. Had it really happened or was she just pretending and making it real in her mind? That was a scary thought. She shivered and shook off the feeling that she was being watched or that he was somewhere following them around on the trails. She felt she was being paranoid and would be ruining the weekend for the others if she didn't snap out of it. "I'll beat you all to the top of the hill!" She called and sprinted off ahead of the others. That caused a melee of sorts as the girls reacted to her play. They all ran and squealed in delight for the hundred yard dash up the incline in the trail. Lana won, of course. She had the advantage of surprise and a head start on all the others. Plus, they were laughing so hard running was almost impossible.

The rest of the afternoon was spent combing through the rocks at the base of a sixty-foot cliff that jutted out above the stunted trees and dense shrubs a hundred yards or so above a large, blue lake. Eventually they made their way to the sandy beach where they stripped down to their swimsuits and bathed in the cool water. They laughed and splashed one another, playing water tag, having swimming races to the buoy and simply paddling around in the beautiful lake.

At one point, Lana thought she saw Baines standing at the top of the cliffs, watching them. Self consciously, she buried her body in the water. She wasn't sure why, but he made her feel vulnerable. His behavior was beginning to worry her.

"Is that the creep, looking into the deep?" Linda quipped.

Lana looked at her and thought. *So, she feels it, too.* She looked back at the cliffs, but he wasn't there. "It might have been the game warden," she said lamely.

"Maybe," her sister agreed.

"Let's go back to camp," Laura whined. "I'm getting cold."

Lana felt a chill, too. *But, this isn't from being cold,* she thought. *This is from something else.* She looked up at the cliffs once again, but no one was there. At least no one was where you could see them.

"I win!" Lynette yelled as she stepped out onto the beach and grabbed her towel from the backpack.

"Who was racing?" Laura called back. She looked at Linda and Lana. "Were you racing her?"

Lana began laughing and shaking her head. "No," she said. "It's okay, Laura. You didn't miss anything." With that, Lana swam to shore, Linda and Laura close behind her. Lynette was still laughing at them all.

As Lana dried her hair, she stepped up close to her identical twin. "I love you," she said simply.

"I know!" Lynette said brightly. "That's why I also know we'll be together for always."

"Why? Was someone going somewhere?" Laura looked worriedly from one to the other of them.

"No," Lana said. She took her sister's hands in hers. "We're all going to be right here, together." The two sisters slowly twirled around, arms outstretched, hands clasped.

"Wait for us!" Laura laughed as she grabbed her sister and they did a similar dance on the wet sand.

Lana and Lynette moved over raising their clasped hands over Linda's head, so they were in a square. They twirled together that way until Laura bumped Lana and they all ended in a heap on the sand. "Together forever," Lynette said. They hugged all around before going back into the water to rinse off the sand.

It was a more subdued walk back to the camp, sisters holding hands, their clothes damp from the wet bathing suits underneath. They took turns dressing into their warm jogging clothes as an evening breeze wafted through the camp. A short rope strung between two trees near the tent served as a clothesline. Linda set about making supper of steaks and baked potatoes.

"A bonfire tonight?" Lana asked no one in particular.

"Yeah, let's sing some old songs and stuff like when we were kids," Laura offered.

Lana began building a fire in the provided pit between the ell formed by their tables. It was soon blazing brightly, crackling cheerily as they ate their supper.

"I'll help you with cleanup, Laura," Lynette offered.

Lana got out the ingredients for s'mores and Linda laid a blanket against the old log across from the fire. "This will be comfy," she commented.

"Hey, let's play hide and seek," Laura suggested after they'd had their fill of the gooey treats.

"There's only three of us to hide," Lana complained.

"I know, but it could still be fun," Laura pleaded. "C'mon, we used to play it all the time!"

"You're 'It'! Let's git!" Linda squealed as she fled into the dark.

"Stay in the campground!" Lana called. "No going off into the trees!"

"Well, duh!" Laura said. "We don't want to get lost, just hide from each other."

Lana smiled and ran off after the others while Laura laid her head on the table and counted to fifty. It didn't take long for her to find Lana hidden behind the car and for the others to get 'home free' while she wasn't looking. Lana took her turn as 'It' and found Lynette easily behind the nearby outhouse. The play went on for a long while until Linda couldn't be found.

"Linda, this isn't funny!" Lana called into the night.

"I . . . I can't feel her, you know?" Laura looked at the twins before her.

A frown of concern crossed Lana's face. "Should we get some help?"

"No, I just think she's too far away. Maybe she went down the trailhead . . ." They all looked toward the trail opening a few feet from their camp.

"Surely not," Lana said. "We said at the beginning not to go off into the trees."

"Well, maybe she didn't think the trails counted." Lynette said.

"We could walk a little ways and keep calling," Laura peered into the night.

"Well, okay, but we keep together, and if we don't find her in a little bit, I say we go for some help."

"I'll go down to the other end of the camp and ask those folks we saw earlier if they've seen her," Lynette said as she moved toward the roadway.

"No!" Lana panicked. "I mean, don't leave us. We've got to stay together."

"Lana, I'm just going to the other side of the parking lot. There're two campers up there near the end where the RV's and stuff go." She shoved a flashlight into her sister's hand. "Take this and look down the trail a bit, then we'll all meet back here."

"I don't want you to leave me," she looked quickly at Laura. "I mean us." Lana said.

"Stop it. Linda's gotten turned around somewhere and we just have to keep looking. We all know this place like the back of our hands. It's okay." Lynette soothed.

Lana took a deep breath. "Okay, I know you're right. There's just something that has me spooked. I can't describe it."

"If you don't stop, I'm gonna start crying," Laura said with a catch in her wheezy voice.

"Do you need your inhaler?" Lana asked.

Laura nodded. "I'd better get it. I think I left it in the glove box of the car."

"Hurry," Lana said as she stepped onto the familiar trail. She waited, tapping the flashlight on her left hand.

"Oh!" Laura exclaimed, somewhere out in the dark behind the tent.

Lana turned back peering past the dying fire toward the camp. She couldn't see the car because the tent was in her way. The camp seemed too quiet, the shadows too sinister. "Laura?" She called out weakly.

"I think I broke a fingernail," Laura came from behind the tent.

Lana breathed a sigh of relief. "Did you get your inhaler?"

"Yeah, it's right here," Laura waved it at her.

"I didn't even hear the car door.

"That's cause I remembered it was in my pants' pocket on the clothesline," she explained.

"Well, let's go down here as far as the 'Y', okay?" Lana shined the flashlight out in front of them.

They called and called for Linda, but there was only the sound of rustling leaves, their footfalls, and their own voices.

"Would she have gone clear around the loop?" Laura asked. "She knows the trail pretty well."

"Without a flashlight in this dark, though?"

"She might have our flashlight. I didn't look to see if it's still in the tent."

"Oh, Laura, you're such an airhead!" Said an exasperated Lana. "We'd better go back and see if it's there. I'm gonna kill her if she's gone off on the trails somewhere."

"Well, you only said not to go into the woods, not down the trails," Laura complained.

"I also said to stay in the campground, and the trails don't count as the campground," was Lana's terse reply. "Come on, let's get back to the tent."

Lynette wasn't back from her search at the other camps yet, so Laura and Lana sat at the picnic tables, poking sticks into the dying fire. Lana rose suddenly and put more wood on the embers, building the blaze higher.

"I really have to go to the bathroom," complained Laura.

"Go ahead, they're right there," Lana waved toward the outhouses a few yards away. "Lynette should be back any time with some help, I hope."

"It's so strange," Laura said as she rose and walked away from the firelight. "I feel like I'm all alone." A sudden chill caused her to rub her arms and hunch her shoulders as a shudder passed over her body.

Lana looked after her friend as she disappeared from the firelight. "I do too," she whispered aloud, rubbing the goose flesh on her own arms. She looked back at the flames and wondered at the feeling of loneliness that seemed to engulf her. A coughing sound somewhere in the trees caused her to look up. "Linda, is that you?" She asked into the dark. She shined the light toward the trees, but couldn't see anything but inky darkness away from the fire. "I suppose Lynette's talking to a bunch of people and I'll have to go looking for her, now." She mumbled toward the red glow from the pit. She added a few sticks of wood so the fire would light the area again. She looked toward the car, but couldn't see anything beyond the trunk. The fire was bright and everything else was like a black wall, closing in around her. "How long can you take in an outhouse?" She asked the fire. "We aren't even hunting for Linda. This is just bizarre." She raised her voice as she glanced toward the buildings. "Laura, are you done yet?"

"Hello, Lana," he said from just beyond the fire.

She looked up, a mask of panic showing plainly in her eyes. "Oh, Baines, thank God you've come." She jumped up and ran around the fire to him, but stopped short of falling into his arms.

"You and your little girl friends get tired of playing games?" He asked.

"What?" She shook her head and pushed her hair back from her face. "Linda's missing," she started. "That is, we were all hiding and we just can't find her." She looked back toward the car. "She might have wandered off down the trails, I guess, and her sister Laura just went to the bathroom. She'll be back in a moment, I think, but it's taking her forever. And Lynette's gone for some help from the folks over there," she waved out toward the campground. "If they're even still over there, that is." She gazed toward the parking lot. "I haven't heard a sound of anyone else for quite awhile." She turned back to face him. "I'm glad you're here. Please, can you help us?"

He looked slowly around the camp. "First of all, put out that fire." He nodded toward the blaze.

"Why?" She frowned, looking around at the fire pit.

"Because," he said patiently, as though she were a little child. "If we're going to be hunting for someone, we don't want the forest burning down around us."

"Oh," she said meekly. She kicked some dirt onto the fire as she walked by to get their bucket of water. "I guess that makes sense," she said. The fire hissed and a billow of smoke rose toward the heavens as she poured the water onto the burning wood. She set the bucket down on the ground and returned to Baines' side, stepping carefully over the log lying between them.

"Now, come with me, Little Girl," he said as he pulled her into the covering of the trees.

"Wait, the flashlight," she pulled back.

But, his grip on her hand was tight. "I've got all we need," he said.

"I can't leave Lynette and Laura. They won't know where I've gone," she stopped once again.

He reached out and placed his hand over her mouth. "I thought you were going to trust me, now," he whispered fiercely at her.

Lana could barely make out his form in the darkness that was closing in around them. She nodded mutely behind his hand. He turned into the trees, seemingly knowing just where he was going. She stumbled along behind him as he pulled her farther into the darkness. They fought their way through a bramble hedge, Andy holding one arm out to keep most of the branches from hitting her in the face.

"I don't think Linda would be out here, or are we going to your camp?" She asked.

"Sh-h-h!" He hissed at her.

As they came into a clearing in a deep thicket, Andy moved around behind her, his hands once again on her shoulders as they had been that morning. *Was that just this morning?* She thought.

"What is that?" She peered into the inky darkness before her. As she leaned forward, his hands slid up to the base of her throat, holding her back. It looked like people lying on the ground. *Why are they out here sleeping in the forest?* She thought. *What kind of people do that?* As he applied a little pressure, she straightened until she was almost leaning back against his chest.

"Silly, silly, evil little girl," Andy whispered against her right ear.

"What?" She started to turn toward him, but his grip tightened against her neck.

"Evil, evil little girls with your games and rhymes," he hissed as she crumpled before him. It was over in just seconds with little resistance. As she slumped under his hands, he slipped his arm down to support her weight and laid her out with her companions on the forest floor. He sprinted back to the camp, slipped on gloves, and hunted through their stuff until he found four ID's. In the glow of his pen flashlight he used a red marker on each card. He then went back to the bodies and slipped their driver's licenses under each of their folded and clasped hands on their stomachs. "Four wasn't so hard after all," he mumbled. He spread needles and leaves over the bodies, from a pile he'd made earlier, careful not to step in any dust. He whistled a little tune as he finally sauntered off into the trees, heading for his waiting truck and the open road. He smiled as the first few drops of rain splattered against his windshield. Feeling safe and comfortable in his beloved truck, he drove over a hundred miles before turning off at a truck stop for fuel and a shower. He ate a hearty meal and listened to the bantering play of truck drivers and waitresses before going back to his red truck. He pulled his magnetic sign out of the boot and lovingly brushed it off before he placed it on the door of the cab. Finally satisfied that it was straight, he climbed up into his comfortable and familiar seat. "It's time to go home," he said as he patted the steering wheel and drove off into the night leaving the little truck stop and rural Wisconsin behind. "Yep, it's time to go home for a good long spell."

D, C, B and A

Andy Davis looked once more at the entries in his current journal. He spent several minutes on the chart in the back of the book, marking and remarking, then smiled in satisfaction. It was almost over. *I'll be free soon,* he thought. "A-B-C-D", he murmured. "Now it's almost over for me." He smiled at his little rhyme. It didn't hurt anymore, the alphabet was almost done and he was at peace. He flipped through three of his journals, pausing at each name he found in the margins. "Just a bunch of little kitties," he whispered to the books. "And soon, very soon, it will all be done." He let his head loll backwards onto the headrest of his truck seat. With a huge sigh, he sat up and put his books away in the black metal box he carried with him on this particular trip. He placed it on the passenger seat with his other personal belongings, tightened his seatbelt, and pulled his big red semi-tractor out into traffic. He drove to a place called "Jim's Trucks" and pulled into the parking lot. A salesman came out of the little shed to meet him as he dropped himself onto the pavement from the top step of the truck.

"Howdy, Friend," said the balding, overweight man. "How can I help you?"

Andy looked lovingly at his truck, patting the spot where his magnetic sign usually rested, then looked back at the salesman. "Wanna buy her?" He pointed at his rig.

"Nice truck, but I couldn't give you much for her."

"Well, give me a figure and we'll see what happens," Andy countered.

The man grimaced. "Twenty-five grand," he said, shaking his head sadly. He was sure the fellow would just get back into his truck and drive away, maybe even call him a few names in the process.

Andy had been standing with his foot up on the step. He slammed it down hard and looked more directly at the man before a smile spread across his face. "A hundred," he said.

"Huh! It's kinda old. Nobody's gonna give you a hundred for it."

"She's in real good shape, though."

"Mebbe," the salesman began walking around the truck, noting the almost new tires and shining chrome. It was a good rig, he could tell. He approached Andy again. "How many miles?"

"Only a hundred thousand. I traded for this one about a year or so ago, I guess."

"Forty, then."

"Nope. Gotta be at least eighty."

"What 'cha owe on it?"

"Nothing. I've got the title right here in my pocket."

"Hm-m-m, well I might could do fifty-five, you know."

Andy grinned. He didn't really care about the price of the truck. He needed to sell it and get done with his plans. "I'll tell you what, you make it sixty and we've got a deal."

The salesman almost fainted, he was so excited. This was a good rig and he would double his money, maybe even triple it. "I'll get the paperwork made up. It'll be a couple of days, but I'll get a bank draft for you, all right."

Andy arranged for the payment to go to his sister. "Send it in about a month," he instructed. "It'll be a surprise for Betty and Ben." He winked. "I'm gonna trust you, now. You've got my truck and my money. All's I've got here is this flimsy piece of paper."

"Oh, yes Sir, yes Sir!" Spluttered the older man. "You can count on it. I'll get this bank draft made out to your sister and put it right into the mail. Like you said, in about a month from today. I surely will." He circled a date on his calendar in red.

Andy looked at the circled date for a few seconds, seeming unable to pull his eyes from the page. He finally realized the man was talking to him and drew out a paper of his own with Betty's address on it.

At last the deal was made and the salesman had Betty's address to send the money to. He figured it was the best deal of his entire career. The more he thought about it, he knew lots of ways to get double or triple the money out of such a babied piece of machinery.

Andy was happy, too. He called a cab to take him and his belongings to the apartment, after a couple of stops for some supplies he needed.

"Anderson, what on earth?" Denise questioned as he arrived home. "She looked past him at the retreating taxicab.

"Is everybody ready for a hike?" He looked past Denise at his girls. They nodded in response.

"Where's the truck?" She asked.

He frowned. "Never mind," he said. "Let's get into the car and get going." He paused before going out the door. "Don't forget your driver's license."

"O-okay . . ." she stumbled over the word. Anderson never let her drive anywhere. She was surprised he even remembered that she owned a license. She dug in her purse and put her license into her jeans pocket. *What on earth can this be about?* She thought before putting on a smile and joining the girls in the car.

They drove for a couple of hours before Anderson turned off the main road and onto a track into the swamp near Henderson, LA. He seemed to know just where he was going, winding around through the sand and grasses. He finally parked in a small graveled area surrounded by trees and swamp.

"Are we going for a hike now, Daddy?" Carrie asked as she unbuckled both her and her sister from their car seats.

He turned and winked at her. "Yep, that we are. A walk and a little picnic near the river."

"What about alligators?" Denise looked around them at the grass and tall trees beyond. "And snakes?"

Anderson cupped her chin and kissed her soundly. "You don't worry your pretty head about anything any more, okay?" He smiled and looked deeply into her eyes.

She melted against him like she always did. They stood close like that for a few moments before he pushed away from her and opened the trunk of the car. He fished out a basket and blanket. "What's that?" She asked, a smile on her face.

"A picnic, what else?" He answered.

"A pic . . . Anderson, you're crazy!" She and the girls laughed and chattered as they followed him on winding paths to the river's edge. They spent the rest of the afternoon eating the snack food he'd bought and walking around the trails. He pointed out plants and explained their uses and names to the girls. He even built a small reed boat and helped them float it on the rushing river.

After their activities and another snack, Anderson insisted that they all take a nap on the blanket. "It's late, Anderson," Denise said looking around at the river. "I don't want to be out here so far from the car when the animals do start moving around."

"Didn't I say not to worry?" He asked, laying a gentle finger across her lips. "Come on, it'll be fine. "Trust me like you used to, okay?" He gave her a boyish smile and cocked his head to one side.

Denise sank down with the girls on the blanket. It was warm from the sun and she had to admit to herself that it felt good.

Anderson lay down next to her and took her hand in his own. He kissed her knuckles lightly. "It's been a good enough life, hasn't it?" He asked softly.

"I love you, Anderson," she responded. "Whatever is bothering you, I love you and it will all be okay. I think you're right. We should go home now."

Anderson smiled, then he laughed out loud. It took her by surprise. "Do you know, I love you too, Denise? I really do."

She squeezed his hand. They lay in silence for several minutes before she finally dozed off just like the girls.

Anderson waited until nearly dark before he sat up and walked to a nearby thicket. He looked down at the still form there on the ground then closed his eyes and began humming softly. He walked back to his family and swiftly choked the life out of his wife's body. It was easier than he expected. She never struggled, just opened her eyes in surprise for a fleet moment before she became limp. "D," he whispered. Next he moved to his youngest daughter. This was harder as she gagged and choked, thrashing about in his hands. But soon, she too stopped moving. "C," he said on the quiet evening air. He looked at Brianne, her obsidian eyes looking solemnly back at him. She only whimpered a little as he placed his hands around her wee throat. In only a moment that task was done, too. "And B," he said to her quiet body. He took a moment to slip Denise's ID out of her pants pocket and into his own, as he laid them out lovingly together, picked up their belongings, and walked calmly to the car. He sat quietly for a moment with his hands on the wheel. "It's done," he said as a long sigh escaped his mouth. He groped in the glove box for his latest journal, took a pen out of his pocket and wrote a few notes.

Back at the apartment, Anderson wrote a note to his sister before he packed up the few things he intended to take with him. He left a note for their landlord that they'd moved away and wouldn't be returning, along with money for another month's rent, double checked that he'd paid all the current bills, and grabbed some bottled water for his trip.

He could hardly wait to get on the Interstate Highway to take him home to Missouri. He hummed his little tune as he drove off into the night, stopping only once to throw Denise's purse and some personal toiletries in a dumpster. He took his time, arriving home late the following evening. He parked the car in the barn and got his black box out of the trunk. Lovingly, he spread his journals in the trunk before going up to the house. He grabbed a hammer from next to the barn door as he passed it, so he could open up a window or two and get in the front door. As dawn was breaking on a new day, he turned to look at the rising sun. "Good-bye world," he breathed as he shut the door and turned the lock.

Part Three

CLOSURES

Pennsylvania, 1996 (from 1992)

Early in the spring, a black bear stuck her nose out of her den in a side hill along a rushing river. There was still some snow in the shadows of the trees and a chill in the spring air. She shook her big head and grunted, snuffled at the roots of the big overturned tree that protected the opening to her den, then rubbed her side along a scraggly tendril of root as she brushed by it heading for the river and a much needed drink. She was barely aware of the two sleepy little bear faces watching her from the den mouth. They blinked their big eyes but didn't venture out into the world. She growled a low coaxing sound as she walked away, pretending not to notice them. First one, then the other of the little bodies ventured out of the hole under the log before they both raced away down the hill toward the river, tumbling over one another in their rush to be with the mother bear.

After a long draught of the murky spring water, the bear started out through the forest with her two offspring. Now would begin the long time of teaching them to become self-sufficient. It would take about two years before she would chase them high up into a tree somewhere and leave them for the last time. Meanwhile, she had much to show them. She headed for a secluded depression deep in the forest, barked sharply at her cubs, sending them scurrying up a nearby tree, then she lay quietly on the top of a hill for several minutes, watching the bottom of the long ravine with its little wagon trail. There was no sight or sound of men. She sniffed the wind for the telltale smells of human flesh, but there was nothing. The cubs slid down the tree and were playing nosily at the bottom of the hill behind her. Irritated suddenly, she went charging down the hill to give them a swat for their noise and generally because she was hungry and irritable herself. Once the cubs were subdued, she laid back and allowed them to nurse. It didn't do much to make her feel better, but they would be quiet. And she needed them to be quiet. She didn't wait long after they were sleeping before she moseyed down the hill into the dense thicket. She rummaged around through the bones and torn bits of cloth, but found nothing left after the melting of winter snow. She sniffed the air once again, but still caught no odor of man. Irritably, she swatted a skull against a tree, then turned back up the hillside to her sleepy cubs. She swatted them too, as she lumbered past, going to a small meadow where she could find voles and other mice to help assuage her hunger. There was a rocky hillside housing marmots that eventually became their meal. Over the course of the next few weeks, the bear kept a close watch on her little valley, but there was nothing new, no fresh bodies as there had been in the past, no rotting remains tucked inside bones or half buried in the moldering ground.

She took her cubs in a wide arc around the forest to campground after campground, but didn't see a familiar face or hear the whistled tune that let her know an easy meal was to be had. It had been a very long time and her memory was fading. What she did hear in the forest was a cacophony of voices and sounds from groups of men and children enjoying the wilderness areas. She growled a low, menacing rumble, a sound which sent her cubs up a tree immediately. They watched as their mother stood on her hind legs and sniffed the air, pawing lightly at a few pesky bees and flies. "Harumph," she moaned as she let herself back down on all fours. The cubs slid easily from the tree and went about the business of bear cubs, chasing one another around the forest. As the summer rolled on, the bear ranged farther and farther from her usual habitat. But this was risky business because it put her in territory prowled by other bears and they meant to keep their own areas to themselves. She half-heartedly fought a couple of sows and even had a run-in with an old boar. But, she didn't want to fight, so she backed off and finally headed back to her own territory. This was her hunting ground, had been her mother's hunting ground before she was shot by humans and dragged away. She brought her growing cubs to the valley, but still there wasn't anything new for them to find. After a few days of foraging, the bruin started watching groups of small people as they hiked and swam and played. She paid particular attention to the ones who strayed alone into the forests, carefully sizing them up and tracking them. Fortunately for the children she watched, none of them wandered very far and soon turned back to be with the group. Or, an adult would call them back before they were out of sight.

The old bear's mouth watered and saliva dripped from her chin as she thought of the other bodies she'd already had. She checked her valley once more to be sure there was nothing there, then she turned her full attention to the camps of men. Although she'd never killed a person before, she had a taste for human flesh and nothing filled her desires like the thought of that taste. Her opportunity finally came when two boys wandered off on their own hike, away from the camp. She followed them to the creek where they were frolicking in the cold water. It was a simple task to kill one of them. The other ran into the forest, screaming and crying. She let the cubs chase him while she dragged her kill to the valley where she felt comfortable with her human prey. She knew the cubs would follow after her and this was an important lesson for them. They could fill their bellies before the new winter snows drove them into the cave once again. After some time, she heard human shouts in the forest, but they were still far away. When the cubs didn't follow after her, she pushed her prey under a dense thicket and went in search of them. After finding them she at first encouraged her cubs to chase after the running prey, but it became a tiresome game when the small person climbed a large tree and batted at the cubs with a stick when they followed him up the narrow branches. That and the lure of the fresh kill pulled her carnivorous mind away to her favorite spot. Frustrated with the game and eager to begin her feed, she demanded the cubs to follow and leave their quarry for the one already waiting. The cubs were wary at first, the overpowering smell of man didn't appeal, but their mother was insistent and they followed her lead. Introducing them to the new flavors, she growled as she tore into the warm flesh.

*　　*　　*

"Kevin! Benjamin!" The shouts rang out over the hills and through the trees of the forest.

"Where have those two scamps gone now?" One of the scout leaders said in exasperation.

One of the boys answered timidly. "Right after supper they said they wanted to go hand fishin . . .'"

One of the leaders smiled weakly. "Guess I shouldn't have told so many Indian stories around the campfire."

It's not your fault," another man spoke up quickly. "They're the adventurous ones, always getting into some kind of mischief, anyway."

Some of the men hunted into the night for the wayward boys while others stayed with the rest of the scouts. But they found nothing to help them as darkness quickly overtook the area. Exhausted at last, they made their way back into camp to await help and daylight. One man sat away from the group, listening into the darkness for any sounds or calls for help that might lead him to the boys. There was only the eerie silence of the forest.

*　　*　　*

Benjamin sat huddled against a tree trunk, about twenty feet off the forest floor. He whimpered slightly, fear keeping him awake even though his body slumped with weariness. He could hear the bears below him, still waiting for him to climb down.

Once in a while, one of the cubs would climb up and snuffle at his dangling foot. Ben had a stick that he slapped the bears with when they touched him. So far, that had kept them away. They would yelp like hurt puppies and scurry down the tree trunk to the safety below. Time seemed to go faster after the last light of the day faded into pitch dark. After what seemed like a very long time in the dark, Ben heard the mother bear approaching, her large paws making soft thudding sounds on the pine needles and leaves on the ground. He could actually feel the pounding of her feet through the tree trunk and it made him shake with greater fear as well as the cold of the night.

The older bear growled and swatted the cubs, sending them rushing up the tree. They passed Ben in their hurry to calm their parent. It happened so fast that Ben hardly had time to react. Instinctively, he knew not to hurt the cubs or surely the older bear would come up and eat him. He wondered briefly if she'd already eaten his friend Kevin, and he shuddered at the thought.

The bear cubs whined above him and were answered with a growl from their mother. One of the babies yelped back and the mother bear slapped the tree, growling fiercely. The tree, big as it was, shuddered at the impact. Ben held on, but one of the cubs slipped down almost into his lap, its claws scraping the bark and snapping a small twig growing out of the trunk just above his shoulder. Ben shrieked, sending the cub scampering back up to be with its sibling, trembling in surprise and anxiety. The mother bear huffed below as she stretched up the trunk of the tree, reaching with her massive front paws. She was only inches away from Ben's dangling right foot, but she didn't touch it, and possibly didn't know in the dark, how close she really was to reaching him. She slid her body down onto all fours and walked around the tree. Once again her cubs whined plaintively. She huffed, bounced her front paws on the ground a couple of times, and walked away, a low pleading kind of growl flowing back to the tree.

The cubs hesitated, knowing the danger that lurked between them and the ground, but finally followed their mother, sliding down the tree on the opposite side from Ben. Ben felt their paws slide past his own fingers and had a curious desire to reach out and pet them. *They're just babies,* he thought. *They don't know I'm not food. The old, mean bear made them chase me and scratch me.* He reached down and felt his leg where the scratches were still raw. The foot in his right shoe was sticky with blood, but the scratches seemed to be scabbing over already. He didn't know just how lucky he had been this night. He was too tired to think of anything deep, and too afraid to let his mind wander. Finally, exhaustion overtook him and his head lolled onto his shoulder in fitful sleep.

In the early gray of morning, eleven-year-old Ben climbed down from his perch and sat for a moment among the leaves and needles on the soft, mossy ground. He looked up the trunk of the old fir tree and shuddered at the claw marks in the bark, going high, high into the branches. She had come even closer than he'd realized in the dark of night. Ben felt his injured leg and winced at the pain. It was bad, a flap of skin lying loose against his ankle. He took out his neckerchief and wrapped it around the wound standing slowly and gingerly. It hurt to walk on it, but he felt an urgency to get away. He peered around the trunk of the tree, the way he thought the bears had gone. Then he walked into the woods as far as he could in the opposite direction. He feared he was walking away from the Boy Scout camp, but the bears had gone that way and he knew that someone would eventually find him. He finally had to remove his make-shift bandage because it was loose and kept rubbing on the wound. He carefully folded the cloth and put it into his back pants pocket. "I wish I'd brought my knife," he mumbled. "A scout should always be prepared." He hung his head and stood for a little while, looking out into the trees and unfamiliar area. He was standing on the crest of a hill and could see a pond below him, choked all around with brambles. He suddenly realized that he was really thirsty, but instinctively he knew he couldn't drink this black, still-looking water. He wrinkled his nose and licked his lips. They felt dry. "What did Mr. Jim say?" He said aloud. "Find a small pebble and suck on that until you find water, and you won't be so thirsty." He began a quest to survive.

*   *   *

In the light of a new day, it wasn't hard for the search party to find the bears and the remains of the boy named Kevin. Fish and Wildlife personnel had to euthanize the bears, for the deed they'd so obviously done. But, look as they might, the search party could only find the remains of one boy. That meant, of course, that Ben was still out there somewhere, or at least his body was still out there. The weary search party looked for signs of Benjamin, but couldn't determine any clear evidence or a real trail that wasn't covered with bear tracks. What they did find made their blood boil and their minds whirl. This wasn't the first time this bear or some other one had had human flesh here in this place. A forensics team was called in to investigate the area after the men found over half a dozen old human skulls and bones scattered around the little bowl of a valley. Among the debris of torn cloth they found identity cards and driver's licenses. Each of them had a red circle drawn around the name.

Meanwhile, the search for Benjamin went on. Mr. Jim, the best known tracker in the area was brought along to find the trail the bears used. He had little trouble tracing them back to the large conifer where Ben had spent his first night alone. "He's hurt," Mr. Jim pointed to dried blood on the tree trunk, and he smiled slightly. "But he ain't dead."

"Well, at least he wasn't when he was here," said another of the searchers in a quiet voice. The men looked knowingly at one another, fear etched onto each of their faces. The situation just didn't look good. Only two men still put their hearts into trying to find Benjamin, Mr. Jim and Ben's father. The rest were looking for remains.

Two days and very little sleep later, Mr. Jim stumbled across the boy huddled into a ball inside the burned out trunk of an old pine tree. He whimpered slightly when the man picked him up to carry him out. He was emaciated, dirty, and shivering with hypothermia, but, he was alive! After handing Ben over to his father and others, Mr. Jim stood silently for a moment and looked at the crude nest the boy had made in the tree trunk. A short distance away was a stream with cattails growing along it.

The stalks and tops of many cattails were found inside the tree trunk, making it a snug nest. The boy had also used plantain leaves inside a crude bandage on his leg, to help the healing of his injured ankle. Mr. Jim nodded in grim pleasure at the survival techniques the boy had used during his four-day ordeal.

At the hospital, Ben told his tale of hiding by night and hunting for food during the day. He made traps for rabbits and a spear to catch fish, but he'd only gotten one real meal for all of his efforts. He hadn't had fire, so the fish he had was raw and not to his liking, other than the cattail tubers he'd dug out of the mud, but it kept him from being too hungry.

Officials pored over the evidence they'd uncovered, tracking down missing persons and old, open cases. Other than their young scout, the remains were of women, eight women from twenty to forty years old. They had all probably been strangled, autopsy told them. That fact and the ID's marked in red were the only common denominators among them.

"This is about murder," one man said. "Eight broken necks is no coincidence."

"Supposed broken necks, but years of murder is right," agreed the County Sheriff.

"How old was the newest one do you think?"

"Two to three years, I'm told."

"So," added the Fish and Wildlife Agent, "our bear was used to human food and when it wasn't supplied, she finally hunted down one of her own."

"Yeah, something like that," said the Sheriff. "Whoever did this here, is responsible for that boy too. At least in my mind he is."

They all nodded in agreement.

"While detectives try to figure out who's responsible, we'll set up a watch on that part of the park, close it down to the general public, but not cordon it off or anything. Just like the bear, we'll wait for the killer to return."

"He might be dead himself," someone offered. "If it's been a couple of years already, things might have changed. I don't think we'll get much out of such a stake out."

"You could be right," the Sheriff nodded. "But, we'll try for a while anyway, just to cover our bases."

With that agreement being made, the meeting broke up. A watch was kept up for a year, then half-heartedly for part of another. Finally, it became too expensive to do and the assignment was cut. There were no results anyway, so they couldn't justify the cost any longer. The case went cold and the files were placed in storage.

Finally, nine long years later, the County Sheriff opened the file one more time. He called a new meeting and presented the evidence he'd received from an investigation in Texas. The new evidence fit their own profile so absolutely that they formally closed the cold cases, contacting families one more time to let them know the killer had been caught and was dead himself.

As the sheriff put the information back into the file, he looked over each page one last time. *How could a man do this over and over without being caught?* He thought as he looked at each of the packaged licenses. He shook his head slowly, put the last of the evidence in the file and laid it on top of a cabinet with other cases that were going to be filed away. "Closed," he mumbled. "After all this time, the only thing I have to say about these lives is that their cases are closed."

"Excuse me, Sheriff," his secretary interrupted his thoughts. "There's an accident out in the county that needs your attention."

He wiped his hand over his face and went to work.

Tennessee, 1999 (from 1990)

The Gimball family was enjoying their week long vacation at a mountain park. Sonja hadn't wanted to come, but now she was glad they had. She looked at the other families from their little church group. Everyone was playing in the small waterfall on the creek near their campsite. Her six-year-old son was wandering down the creek bed, chasing a frog or something. "Not too far, Jeremy!" She called.

"Okay, Mama!" He yelled back, splashing in the shallow water.

She sat back on the bank and let the sun fall onto her upturned face. She turned her head slightly and looked down at her two-year-old daughter snuggled next to her on the beach towel. Finding her youngest sleeping, she looked once again up stream for her son who was nearly out of sight.

"Jeremy! Not so far!" She called, but he didn't answer. "Jeremy!" She stood up and looked around the bushes that choked the bank. Turning back to the towel, she picked up the baby and ran down the bank and into the water toward where she'd last seen her boy. As she rounded a bend in the creek, she saw him splashing in the water near a steep slope of the bank.

Jeremy looked up as he heard his mother call. "I'm right here, Mama," he answered plaintively. "Come see the big fish," he beckoned to her to join him.

The baby was heavy, so Sonja sat her next to a big log on the bank and waded the few feet to her son. "Where?" She asked, peering into the sun sparkling water.

"There!" He squealed as he splashed and jumped backwards, slipping on the rocks and falling into the water with a big splash.

"Are you hurt?" Sonja laughed. An eerie feeling crept up her back and caused her to shudder involuntarily. She turned to look at the baby, but she wasn't where she thought she'd left her. Frantic with fear, Sonja turned and ran to the bank, looking in the water for her daughter. A scream and cry made her look up into the trees and she froze to the spot, the world suddenly slowing to a crawl. In the haze and slow-motion of fear, she saw her 2-year-old in the jaws of a big old black bear.

Instinctively, Sonja picked up a rock and threw it at the bear. He paused, momentarily losing his grip on the child as he growled at the attacking adult. Sonja ran toward the bruin, flinging rocks and sticks, anything she could get her hands on. She heard someone screaming hysterically before realizing it was herself. The bear looked at her coming at him from the creek, shook his big head, huffed at her, and loped off into the trees. Sonja was to her baby in three long strides. "No, no, no," she cried as she picked up the limp, bloody form. The baby whimpered softly, causing Sonja to fall to her knees, cradling the girl to her bosom.

Others adults had reached them, drawn by the screams of fear. One of the group was a nurse who gently took the baby into her own arms. She looked her over, giving orders for someone to get her a wet cloth. After cleaning the blood off, she was able to find only a few scratches and two actual puncture wounds on her body. "I think she's going to be fine," she said softly, reaching out for Sonja's arm.

Sonja nodded numbly, opening her mouth, but unable to utter another sound.

The nurse looked around. "Where's Jeremy?" She asked.

"Jeremy?" Sonja mumbled. Suddenly her eyes flew open as she remembered she'd left her son in the creek. "He's, he's looking at fish in the creek," she said in a squeaky voice.

"I'll get him," someone said.

The hunt went on for several hours, but Jeremy couldn't be found. Some blood on the bank indicated that the bear might have circled around and taken the older child while so much fuss was being made over the baby.

One of the men in the group went for help and the rest of them talked quietly as they waited. Several broke away from the main group to pray or look with terror and sadness at the darkening forest. Sonja sat numbly, not able to move or to communicate with anyone, just staring straight ahead, her eyes dull and listless. She had to be taken to a hospital for shock as she tried to absorb the day's events. Her daughter was recovering from puncture wounds, abrasions and bruises, but would be okay. As time passed, Sonja was moved to a sanitarium as she lost control, suffering from a mental break down at the loss of her son and the trauma of the bear encounter with her daughter.

"What caused the attack?" A reporter asked of witnesses.

"We don't know." A spokesperson volunteered. "We'd been out here all week and hadn't even seen a bear. It was sudden and, and well, you can see the results."

"It's not natural for a bear to just up and attack humans," someone offered. "This is crazy, like out of a movie or something."

"What do you think caused it?" the reporter persisted.

"I don't know," said the man. "Maybe the bear was old and just thought the kids looked like easy food."

"But, we were all close by and making all kinds of noise. It's not normal for a bear to do this, is it?" A worried mother asked.

"No, no it's not," a park ranger stepped up and answered. "This is completely out of character for one of our bears to do." He looked pointedly at the reporter. "I'm not sure how you got here so fast, but these folks need to pack up the rest of their stuff and leave the camp. We're isolating this area and everyone needs to go." He walked the group to their belongings and helped them get their vehicles packed.

*   *   *

Bob Nevins was a park ranger who normally investigated bear encounters with campers and hikers in the wilderness reserve. He hated it when people encroached on bear territory then blamed the bear for acting like a bear. On this occasion he talked to the father of the missing boy and dispatched a team to track the bear down. It wasn't hard to find him. The old bruin left a bloody trail to a secluded old dugout in a hillside where he denned up for winter. The remains of the boy's body were there and the old bear was feisty, giving the men no choice but to shoot him. It always made Ben sad when a bear had to be put down, but you couldn't have a bear attacking families. It wasn't like a black bear to attack people, especially with others in close proximity to the victim. He scratched his head in wonder.

"Hey, Bob," Hugh Bender approached his colleague.

"What is it?"

"Would you come and look at something?"

"Sure," he rubbed his hand over his stubbly chin. "Don't tell me there's another bear or something up there."

"No, Sir," Hugh answered. "No more bears, but there is something."

They walked the few feet to the den area. Scattered among the moldering leaves and pine needles were some rags and bones. Hugh moved the leaves around with the toe of his boot.

"What is that? It isn't a human skull, is it? Surely this must be some kind of bear graveyard, or something . . ." His voice trailed off as his friend confirmed the worst news.

"Yes, Sir." Hugh sighed. "And there's more of them."

"Human skulls? Is that really what we're lookin' at? Couldn't it be some kind of bear graveyard? Are you sure, Hugh?"

"Yep," his friend hung his head and almost whispered the answer.

Bob started looking around at the scattered debris; what he was looking at weren't just animal bones, they were human ones. "How many are there, do you know?"

"I think there's five of these older kills besides the body of the boy, but I'm not sure. We've found two driver's licenses so far, too." He handed over the licenses.

"Did you mark on these?" Bob asked, indicating the red circle on each one.

"No, Sir. They were both like that."

"Keep me posted when you know more," he handed the licenses back to Hugh and walked to his pickup truck to call in the local PD's. They, in turn, investigated the crimes and found the families of the missing women, some of who's bones showed the tell-tale signs of strangulation. Of the eight women who'd been killed and dumped in Tennessee, only two were from the state. There seemed to be no connection between any of the women, no common thread to help solve their murders. After a few months, the case went cold and the paperwork sat on a basement shelf in a box, gathering dust.

Five years later, in the spring of 2004, Bob sat in his office chair and shook off the memories. He looked again at the letter in his hands from an investigative team in Texas. He scanned the contents of the letter making mental notes. Then he called his friend Hugh. "Come on in here," he said. "I've got a story you aren't never gonna believe!"

After Hugh looked over the information about a killer named Anderson Davis, he looked up at his friend. "Is this for real? I mean I know it is, but are we really to believe it? Some truck driver was dumping bodies in the forest for that old bear and when there weren't any more, the bear went hunting?"

Bob nodded wearily. "It seems so."

"Why?"

"I guess to cover his crimes. I talked to one of the investigators from Texas. They've found spots all over the states with the same kinds of remains, driver's licenses, and they had similar problems with bears, cougars, and what-not-all that got the taste for human flesh and wanted more when this here driver moved on."

"These kills are old."

"I know. He'd evidently been about this business for quite a spell." Bob looked down at the scribbled notes he'd made. "Some seventeen or eighteen years, I guess."

"So, he killed these here eight women, outright killed them," Hugh said quietly. "But you know he's just as guilty of the death of this here boy, too." He looked up with a great sadness etched into his eyes.

"Yeah," answered Bob with a long sigh. "And he won't even pay for that crime at all."

"They got him in jail down there in Texas?"

"No," Bob sighed. "No, they say he up and did himself in, too. Hung himself after killing his own family. If you want to read the report, it's right there in the folder," he tapped the paperwork on his desk.

"You gonna call Mr. Gimball, or you want me to do that?"

"If you don't mind, Hugh, could you do that? I'm not sure knowing all this will help their family, but maybe having a reason for the bear's attack will ease the load for them."

Hugh nodded as he picked up the file and looked through it. The two men sat in silence, each caught up in their own thoughts, each trying to make sense of the crimes that had fallen in their paths, each man thinking of their own families and how uncertain life can be . . . .

Wisconsin, 2002(from 1998)

"The four L's, we called them, you know." Inspector Michaels told the group around the table. "In the summer of 1996, these girls went missing. There were four of them, two sets of twins, and all their names began with the letter L." He wiped at his chin and stared above the heads of those seated before him. "When we found them, let's see, that was three years ago, back in 2002, there wasn't a whole lot left to make a good ID. Mostly there was bones and teeth and a few fragments of cloth. We did find their driver's licenses though." He passed around a sealed bag with the licenses in it. Each one had a red circle on the name. "Never knew what to make of any of it until now."

Officer Katie Thompson passed around copies of a report out of Texas. "Please read this report and note the items we've highlighted. We believe this man was responsible for the deaths of our girls almost ten years ago. What we found seems to fit his MO and from our own investigation, we discovered that there had been a truck driver that showed up back then for a few days. The only one who'd even remembered him from back then was Silas, and his memory was too shaky to rely on. He thought the guy's name might have been Barney, or maybe Benny. You all know how Silas did business, there wasn't anything signed or anything like that, or if there was, he never kept anything like records, he always trusted everybody. Anyway, we didn't have any solid information to go on and the case went cold. Some said the girls had run away, others thought we didn't try hard enough. Some people said they'd seen the girls at the park, but one of the girl's cars was found miles away and the other one was out in the old gravel pit. No one had ever seen a semi truck or a truck driver around the camping area. We do have trucks going down the highway, so it could have been any one of those." She paused to wipe her nose with a Kleenex. "Of course, we did finally find the remains of their bodies in the park over six years later. A hiker found some bare bones and that led to a new search. It was them, all right." Katie sat back in her chair and drew a deep breath.

"Why didn't we ever search the park in the first place?" One of the men around the table asked.

Inspector Michaels answered the question. "We thought the girls had gone up to the quarry to camp. They often camped in various spots and we went out there where we found the car and camping gear. Nobody we talked to for a long time said they were in the park."

"So, this guy moved their stuff, or did he move them?"

"It would seem so, wouldn't it? Something was surely moved. It wasn't the bodies, though. He killed them right there in the park and covered them up with dirt and leaves. It looked just like it always did, the leaves and twigs on the ground and boulders all around, some of them sticking up a little . . ." He nodded at each of them, his eyes sad and faraway looking. He cleared his throat and went on. "Someone did move the girl's stuff and there were prints everywhere, but at this time I'm betting on this truck driver for killing them." Inspector Michaels pointed to the report before him. "This guy here, this Anderson Davis."

"Didn't we arrest some guy for this?"

"Yeah, what about those two punk kids who were questioned?"

"If you'll take the time to read the report that Katie put before you, you'll see that the boys confessed to moving the car and camping stuff. They thought it was a great joke at the time. Thought the girls were off hiking or swimming and they moved their stuff, even spent the night in the girl's tent, I guess. Then they got scared when we couldn't find the girls and they hid the car and tried to act like they didn't know anything about the whole affair. We had their prints, though, all over everything. When they did say they'd moved the car from the park, there was snow five feet deep." He cleared his throat and got out a handkerchief to blow his nose loudly. Everyone squirmed in their seats.

"Well, who got arrested? What happened to that guy?"

"He was just some drifter who came through at the time. He didn't know anything about anything, didn't know the girls, nothing. His prints weren't on anything, he had no known connections here. Silas said he never saw the guy before, for what that was worth, so we had to let him go finally. He was never formally arrested, just held for a little while."

"So, now after all this time, you think this guy did it?" The questioner tapped on the report in front of him.

"I believe he did. Old Silas isn't around anymore, so we can't verify if it's this guy pictured here, if Silas could even help with that, but the MO fits."

"Were his prints at the scene?"

"No, we identified all the prints as either the girls or the teenagers." He cleared his throat once again. "From the report here, he doesn't leave much in the way of evidence, except the driver's licenses marked in red. Those we have. He also kills by strangulation, and the coroner verified that that's what happened to our girls."

A silence filled the room for a few moments while everyone went over the reports before them on the long, mahogany table.

"So, we can lay this to rest and the families can have some kind of peace over the matter, I guess," Katie put in. "At least, no one here did it. It was a stranger. People can quit looking at their neighbors and wondering. And maybe those boys can get on with life, too."

"Yeah, but why? That's what I want to know," said the Mayor. "Why'd this guy come here and kill these four innocent girls?"

"If you read this report, it tells you why, at least in a way it does. We all know how those girls loved their rhymes and silliness. Well, as it turns out, this guy had some mental issue with the alphabet and rhyming, or something like that. I know it isn't perfect, but it seems to be the only half-way plausible answer to this age-old mystery. I'm ready to say the case is no longer a cold case, but a closed one." Katie looked up at Inspector Michaels, who was nodding in thought.

"I believe that's true," he added.

The meeting broke up shortly afterward and everyone left the police office except one man. He sat silently, reading the report and lightly tapping the table with his fingers. He finally looked up at Katie and Inspector Michaels. "Two of them were my cousins, you know."

"Yes," Katie said softly.

"I'll talk to the parents and maybe we'll have a little wake or something." He shook his head slightly. "After all this time, it was a stranger after all."

"The folks here can quit looking at each other and asking silent questions of their neighbors, like Katie said," Inspector Michaels put in.

The man laughed without humor. "That's true," he agreed. "Some guy just came wandering in off the highway, a guy who had a phobia against the alphabet and rhyming. Like we said earlier, we all know how much those girls liked to joke and rhyme and stuff like that, especially Linda. She made a rhyme out of almost every sentence she said. Innocent, beautiful girl-children and somehow, he up and kills them all." He paused, then snapped his fingers. The crack of his hand seemed like a rifle shot in the still room. "Just like that," he said. "Like they were nothing to him or anyone else in the world."

"Yeah . . ."

"It didn't say anything about him being a molester or anything. Do we know . . . ?" He left the question unfinished.

"I did call and talk to the investigative team in Texas and asked that very question. Our boy wasn't anything like that, his agenda was to kill the alphabet. Our girls just represented the letter L to him, that's all. And I guess the rhyming didn't help. He was one crazy fellow."

"At least there's that," he commented as he stood to leave.

"Yes," Katie said. "At least they died innocent as babes."

"How'd he manage to kill all of them? Why didn't one of them run away and get help?"

Inspector Michaels shook his head. "There are some things we'll never know in this life, I guess. I don't know how he did it. Maybe he got them one at a time when they went to the outhouse in the night or maybe he nabbed them off one of the trails one at a time. I can't figure it out, that's for sure. I don't know how this guy's mind worked."

"Yeah, well I guess that's that, then." He rose to leave. "I want to thank both of you. I think you did all you could and now we know . . ." He walked away as they watched him go out the door and down the hallway.

Calgary, Alberta, Canada, 2002 (from 1996-1997)

Constable Jerry Jones sat back in his chair and looked out the window at the traffic along the busy street. "Barbara, would you get me that red file off the shelf, please?" He called out the open office door to his secretary.

She brought it in promptly. "Some news?" She inquired.

"It just might be, after all this time." He tapped the letter he'd opened moments earlier. "This just came from Texas down in the States," he said.

"Texas, you say?" She shook her head in wonder. "And it has something to do with these poor, dead girls? Is it from those folks who were here a few weeks ago?"

"Yes, the very same ones. Makes me want to close the borders and never let another truck driver into our fine country," he said.

"Some American came up here and killed them, then?" She sat in the chair near the front of his desk.

"It seems like it," he answered.

"And he came from all the way down there in Texas? What in the world for, don't we have enough of our own truck drivers and criminals?" She shook her head again.

Jerry thought back to the day they were called by an RCMP unit up near Lake Louise in BC. Some hikers had found the remains of a body, it seemed. When they went out to the scene, it was worse than they thought at first. There wasn't just one body out there along the shore of a small mountain lake, but the remains of six young girls. There wasn't much left of them, animals having done their damage, and the elements, too. About the only thing left were some faded driver's licenses and old bones and teeth. It was a macabre sight scattered out across the forest floor, some of the bones half buried in the moss.

They investigated and found out who the girls had been, but no one had any clues as to what happened to cause them all to end up dead in a remote part of Canada's forested mountains, and the families could offer no real help. The girls had all been from farms or small towns, headstrong and wanting to break free from the wilderness life of their families. All but one, she was a true farm girl who just disappeared from a vegetable stand along one of the busy roads in the tourist-laden parks region. They'd all died the same summer, but none of the families knew one another. As far as it was known, none of the girls had ever met, either. Yet, their bones were dumped together like so much rubbish.

Constable Jones read the letter from Texas once again, looking at the accompanying charts and excerpts from the diaries of a madman. He looked up at his secretary and long-time friend. "When I'm done with this, I'll let you read through it. It's unbelievable. I guess we'd better call the families and let them all know that we've gotten information about the killer."

"Is he in jail down there in Texas?" She asked.

"No," he wiped his hand over his face. "No, he went and hung himself, I guess. It's a crazy tale and I'd best let you read it for yourself. I couldn't begin to tell it, it's that crazy."

"Do you want me to make those calls?" She asked gently.

He looked at her for a moment before answering. A small smile played across his lips. "No, thanks, I'll do it. It's best if I do it."

She nodded, rising from her seat and walking out. "Let me know if you need anything else."

He was already reaching for the phone.

"John?" He said into the black receiver. "This is Constable Jones in Calgary. How are you, Sir?"

"What do you want now?" Growled the older man.

"Well, Sir, we've found the man who killed your daughter, Harriet. I just thought you and your wife would want to know that."

"What?" The older man yelled into the phone. "Harriet's been gone for years. We told you that and you ain't ever done anything to find her! What's that you're trying to say now?"

"John," the Constable raised his own voice. "Is your wife there? Could I speak with her?"

"Sure, she's here, but she don't know any more than me!" John yelled. "That girl kept running off and then she up and got herself disappeared and killed. I told her she'd better do right or no good would come to her."

"Who is that?" His wife asked in the background.

"Why it's that Constable fella down there in Calgary. He's asking about Harriet after all these years."

"What?" She said. "Give me that phone. Hello. Hello, who is this?"

"Ah, Grace how are you?" Constable Jones lowered his voice a notch. "This is Jerry Jones."

"Oh, Jerry, how's your mother? She was feeling poorly the last time I saw her."

"Yes, well she's doing just fine now, thanks for asking." He coughed before going on. "Say, Grace, we've received some news about Harriet's killer."

"After all this time," she murmured into the phone as she sat down quickly. He could hear the squeak of a chair through the receiver.

"What's he saying?" John demanded from across the room.

"Yes, well it's taken a long time to find him, that's true. But, I wanted to tell you and John, and some others that he's dead. He died down in Missouri, in the States, you know."

"Why, what was he doing away down there?"

"He was an American, Grace. He was an American truck driver who came through this area all those long years ago."

"And he killed our Harriet, you say?"

"It sure looks like it, yes."

"I wonder why," she mused. "How would she have even met up with such a man, eh?"

"We may never know all the answers, Grace," he mopped at his face again.

"But it does seem like he's the one and that he's not going to hurt anyone else, ever." He paused for a moment, but when she didn't answer he went on. "I have the information here in the office. If you want to know anything about him, I could send a copy of this to you . . ."

"No!" She broke in. "No, we don't need to know anything more. It's finally over and we can leave it at that. She shouldn't have kept running off to town, but she just didn't take to farming after her Papa died. Well, thank you for your call. Be sure to take good care of your Mama, Jerry." She hung up.

Constable Jones sat and stared at the receiver in his hand. Grace and John were long time friends of his parents. He'd known John's younger brother Harry, Grace's first husband and Harriet's father, too. They were the ones he had to tell first, the hardest ones because he knew them so well. He was only ten years older than Harriet and had grown up in the same community. It was the one story in this whole mess that touched his heart. He was sure the others were just as tragic for their families, but this one was personal for him. He made the rest of the calls, then laid the files on Barbara's desk for her to read. "I'm going to take the rest of the day off," he said. "I need to go out to see my mother."

"Is she ill?" Barbara looked up at him with concern.

"No, no, I just want to spend some time with her. Call my wife and let her know I'm on the way and I'll pick her and the children up and we'll go for a little visit."

Montana, 2005 (from 2001)

"Lieutenant Barnes, this is Agent Mack Johnson. I'm a Special Crime Investigator from Texas. My team works almost exclusively on serial murders."

"Yes, I've already talked to one of your Agents. What can I do for you, Sir?"

"Well, it's more like something I can do for you. I'll be sending you some paperwork so you can close your multiple homicide case from 2003 out there."

Lt. Barnes sat upright in his chair and took a drink from a cup on his desk. His palms suddenly felt sweaty and his mouth dry. He coughed slightly. "You've caught him, then?" It wasn't really a question, but a statement of fact, spouted out after years of holding onto that hope. "Tell me, was it Baines Anderson, after all?"

"That's the name you knew him by, yes, Sir. His full name was Anderson Baines Cole Davis."

"Was? You mean he's dead?" He sighed in resignation and slumped back in his chair.

"He is."

"Did he confess before he died?"

"In a manner of speaking, yes, he's confessed."

"What's that mean? Did he confess to killing my d . . . my victims or not?"

"I'm getting to that, Sir." Mack mopped at his perspiring face. *I hate this part of the job,* he thought. *Should've had Jared or Meg do this.* "I'm sending you a copy of one of his diaries. I believe it'll lay your case to rest."

"He kept diaries?"

"Yes."

"We never found one when we searched his truck. Are you sure about this? We searched his truck on two different occasions, you know."

"I know your did, Sir, and yes, yes, we're sure it's him and he did keep diaries."

"I see." A short silence ensued while each was caught up in their own thoughts. "Did he say why? One, uh, one of them was my daughter, you know. Did he . . . did he say why?"

"No, not specifically. It's my belief he was trying to kill the alphabet, Sir. To him, your daughter was only an H. It wasn't personal, just an insane idea that got a hold on a boy and never let him go."

"Hmmm, so it wasn't about lust or anger, just about pure murder?"

"More or less, that's about right."

Lieutenant Ken Barnes opened his desk drawer and pulled out the old file. Inside, on top, were copies of the ID's he'd found so long ago. He began to read through them. "Hannah, Katie, Laurie, Norma, Opal, Roberta, no, wait! There's two R's, Agent Johnson. Are you sure about this? Or should I be looking at last names?"

"We're sure he went by first names. He kept killing others as he looked for the letters X and Z. I guess killing was a habit by then, I don't know. He'd gotten away with it for so long. He found a Z in 1997, but only found the X this past year. I guess maybe if he dated them, he killed them, but that's just a guess, you see. We don't know what his motivation was besides the alphabet angle and something about rhymes."

"So, you're saying, that somewhere in time he just started with someone randomly whose name began with an A and worked his way through the alphabet? That sounds pretty far fetched."

"I know it does, you're right about that." Mack started looking through the windows of his office into the main office area. "You know what? Let me have you talk to one of my agents who has more details. Hang on a minute." He covered the phone and yelled. "Jared!"

Jared looked up from his computer at his frantically waving boss. "Why doesn't he ever use the intercom?" He said aside to Meg Riley.

Meg smiled. "Because he doesn't have to." She replied sweetly.

He stood and ambled to Mack's office door, opening it slightly. "Yeah, Mack?"

"Talk to this guy. He wants more details than I've got here."

"Who is it?"

"Lieutenant Barnes from Montana."

"Okay, sure. I'll get it from my desk where I've got all the notes and stuff. Put him on hold." Mack scrutinized the phone, his large hand hovering over the many buttons. Jared smiled as he reached across the desk and pushed the hold button. "Okay, now hang it up, I'll get it in there," he said before he hurried back to his desk and picked up the phone. He looked up through the glass at his boss who was still holding the receiver and nodded at him to hang it up as he spoke. He heard the click when he started his conversation. "Lieutenant Barnes, is that you? This is Jared Sanders. We spoke a few weeks ago. How are you, Sir?"

"Ah, Mr. Sanders. Say, tell me about these murders. This alphabet thing sounds like a pretty good stretch to me."

"I'm sure it does. It's been a bizarre case."

"Can you give me details? How'd he pick his victims? How does the alphabet come into play?"

"Sure. Well, he kept notes in journals and put names along the margins of pages after he killed them, so we've built a kind of chart of the spree he was on."

"So he just started with A and kept going, or what?"

"No, he saved A for last. That was himself. He hung himself after he'd found all the others." Jared paused. "He seemed to hate a couple of things here, the alphabet and rhymes, and cats and girls. All with about the same intensity, it seems."

"So he used his last name, but everyone else's first names? What kind of logic does that make?"

"What? No, you see his first name was Anderson, not his last one. Andy Davis, that was his name."

"Yes, yes, your boss did say that. I can't help but think of him as Baines Anderson, you know." There was a significant pause as he obviously tried to get control of his emotions. "So, his body's there in Texas?"

"No, Sir, he lived in Missouri."

"Not in Seattle or in Texas, but in Missouri?"

"Yes, well it's complicated. We're in Texas and we were called in on the case as the closest US Marshall's Office that handles serial killers. Andy Davis, he grew up in Seattle, but his family moved to Missouri when he was still a teenager. I believe he may have had a brother who died out there in Seattle; hung himself too, I think his sister said. He kind of drifted back and forth it seems until his brother died."

"His sister, his brother, a family; yes, I suppose people loved him." His voice sounded tired and sad. "When we looked at him, his truck said Seattle, Washington. He had ID from there, too."

"Yeah, he never changed his sign. It was one of those stick-on ones he'd made himself. But, Missouri was his home, where he had family and the place he went back to every so often. That's where he went to finish the job he'd started, where he hung himself. He had multiple licenses, too. Used his own name, but scrambled it up so in one state he was Cole Anderson and in another Davis Baines, stuff like that."

Kenny Barnes sighed. "I knew it was him. All that time, I knew it was him. But, I could never prove it. I looked into those blue eyes of his and I could see it there. I wish we'd found that diary last year when we questioned him. Where'd he keep it?"

"We can't be sure about that, Sir. He'd laid them all out in the trunk of his car before he did himself in, sort of a ceremony or a confession even, you know?"

"And you say my Hannah's name is written in one of those journals? He did keep a record of his murders?"

"Yes, he did. He didn't take trophies like some murderers, but he did make notes about his victims. We'll overnight this stuff to you."

"Tell me, Jared, how many were there?"

Jared paused. "Sixty . . ."

"Sixty? My God, he killed sixty people?"

"Yes, over about 16 years, and from coast to coast. Yours weren't the first, or the last."

Another pause, this time from Lt. Barnes. "How many after Hannah, or I mean, after 2001?"

"Uh, let's see," Jared shuffled through his papers until he found the chart he wanted. "There were your twelve between 2001 and 2003. Then he took a break for most of 2004. That's when he found Xenia Davis in Louisiana. It was the end for him. He'd found the letter X."

"I see. So, Zinnia began with an X. Was she a relative he'd overlooked? You said her name was Davis, and his was too."

"No, the last name Davis was a coincidence, I guess because they were definitely not related. But, from his journal entries, it certainly influenced him to finish the alphabet once and for all. He felt it was a sign that his 'job' was done."

"But, why?" Lt. Barnes voice took on an edge of whining.

"Well, because of his own name, Sir, Anderson Baines Cole Davis, A-B-C-D."

"And for that he killed my Hannah?"

"I'm afraid so," Jared said softly. He could hear the grief in the older man's voice and knew he was probably crying. "It looks like he didn't really concentrate on the alphabet until oh, around 1996 or 1997, I guess, at least not consciously. It was then we think he made his little chart and realized he'd covered most of the alphabet. He left A, B, C, and D until last. His wife's name was Denise and his two daughters were named Carrie and Brianne."

"So, he killed his own wife and daughters, too?" The grief and pain were very evident in the older man's voice.

"Yes, Sir, he did that, and sent a note off to his sister about it. I've included a copy of the note in this file. I'll send it out today and maybe it will help. I'm very sorry for your loss, Sir."

"Thanks, Young Man. I really do appreciate all you've done. I wish we could've held him on something, anything. But, he didn't break any laws . . . . I mean, well you know what I mean."

"Yes, Sir, I do. Thank you and well, good-bye."

There was a muffled reply then the phone line went silent. Jared looked at the phone in his hand. *How can one man cause so much pain? But, then he was suffering as much as the families he hurt.* He threw the package to Montana into the parcel bin and started gathering all the notes and evidence to put back into the box for storage. He wrote the word 'closed' on the end of the box and dated it. He placed it on a cart with other boxes and turned away. It was all now a statistic, closed and done, sixteen years of silent terror; alligators, bears, and bones, it all boiled down to that, and a few scraps of cloth, plastic, and teeth. All those lives and this one box was all that was left. Jared sat at his desk and looked thoughtfully at the box across the room. "How does his own sister live with all this?" He mumbled softly. "She's such a nice lady."

*   *   *

Betty Myers sat swinging on her patio. She sighed again as she stared out over her lovely flower garden. A slight breeze ruffled her hair, but she didn't notice. She just pushed gently on the flagstone flooring with her feet, causing the swing to move back and forth slowly, ever so slowly.

She thought of her father and how much he aged after the twins died. He'd never allowed himself to get close to Anderson and she wondered if he'd secretly hated the boy, maybe blamed him for the girls' deaths, him being born that day and all. "Oh, that's just silly!" She spat out, pushing the swing harder for a moment.

"Of course, Mother always babied him," she murmured, her thoughts pulled back to the past. "Always made excuses for him, too, even when he was clearly in the wrong." She frowned mightily for a few moments, lost in memories of Anderson as a little boy, whining to mother and nearly always getting his way. The swing moved her slowly back and forth, back and forth, but she barely seemed to notice.

Her husband, Ben, came out of the house and sat next to her. He sat quietly for several moments, his bulk and feet planted firmly on the ground holding the swing still. He looked at Betty from the corner of his eyes. "Did you read that stuff from Texas?"

Betty nodded, tears threatening to spill over her cheeks once again. "I did," she whispered.

"I see," he answered. "And?"

"Oh, Ben!" She reached out to touch his arm. "Could that monster in those papers have been <u>my</u> Anderson? Could it really?"

Ben wiped a hand over his perspiring face. "I truly don't know, Dear. I saw that boy's body hanging there in the pantry and it looked like someone else. I still can't believe it was him, but I know that it is. Does that make sense?" He hung his head, silent tears of his own running down his florid face. He wiped at it with the back of one of his large hands, ineffectively.

"I know," she said. "I know you saw that awful sight." A shudder passed over her slight frame. "I'm so glad I didn't see him like that. And I'm glad the casket was closed for the funeral, too."

A bird twittered in a nearby tree causing them to both look. "Carrie used to love birds, so," Betty said after a moment.

"And Brianne would pick your flowers every chance she got," he added with a humorless smile.

"Yes, Denise scolded her, but what did it matter?" They held each other and cried softly. "When did he go insane?" Betty asked, looking deep into her husband's eyes. "How could he have hidden it for all those years?"

"I think, you know, it's always been there. No one ever knew it, that's all, because he was always so withdrawn, even when he seemed to relax around family, well us, of course."

"Perhaps," she replied. "Perhaps when he saw Daddy dead there in the living room, it did something to him, too. Then there was Allen hanging in the garage, oh, my!"

"It might have," he agreed. "We'll never know for sure which thing or if all of it caused him to do what he did; not in this world, we won't."

"No, no we won't," she said firmly, taking a deep breath. She kissed him on the cheek. "I love you, Ben. I guess I always have."

He smiled warmly. "I know that, Dear. I love you, too. I guess I loved you even back when you had pigtails," he rubbed his hand over her short curls.

She nodded, a smile playing at the corner of her mouth as she looked adoringly at him.

Suddenly, Ben got up and walked to the flower bed where he proceeded to pick a handful of blooms from the large variety available. He brought the bouquet to Betty and handed them to her. "Dees for you," he said, imitating their niece Brianne to perfection.

Betty couldn't contain the laughter as she accepted the flowers. "Thank you," she said finally, taking Ben's large hand in her free one. "Oh, thank you, Ben."

He pulled her close. "May we never forget," he whispered into her hair.

They walked arm in arm into the house, allowing the door to slam shut after them.

*   *   *

Back in Texas:

"Jared!" Mack yelled from inside his office. "There's a killer in Arizona we need to find!"

Jared Sanders smiled grimly as he rose from his chair and sauntered to the office door. "Yes, Sir," he said. "What's up?"

The End

Chronology of Anderson Baines
Cole Davis

Anderson:

April 4, 1964—birth
April 4, 1974—death of father
1980—moved to Missouri
1981—visited Allen for 6 months, began working as deliveryman
1982-1984—Served in the Army
1984—visited Allen for a year, worked at handy man jobs, then as a truck driver
1985—worked in Missouri for a trucking firm, driving local deliveries
1986—moved to Seattle to live with Allen, drove long haul trucks
April 4, 1988—Allen hung himself in the garage
1988—16 yr old, Wendy O'Neal found buried in leaves in the Snoqualamie Forest. She'd been strangled. Lived in Allen's neighborhood and showed an interest in Andy.
1989—Andy sold the house and moved back to Missouri where he became a long haul truck driver. On the road, he used the name <u>Cole Davis</u> for 5 years.
Trip #1—He drove the I-95 Corridor from Maine to Georgia. Made weekend side trips with rental vehicles.
14 unsolved murders of females, all manual strangulation whose bodies were left in the forest. ID was found in their clothing with the names circled in red.
April, 1994—went home to Missouri in time for the death of his mother. He and his sister reestablished a relationship. He complained to her that there was some kind of curse on his life having to do with the number 4 and the alphabet. He would send her postcards and short notes for the rest of his life.

1995—Went back out on the road, this time from Wisconsin to Washington. On the road, he used the name <u>Davis Baines</u> for 5 years.

Trip #2—He drove I-90 and I-94 across the north and northwest Corridors, and Canada 1 for a single trip back to the mid-west. He made weekend side trips with rental vehicles.

24 unsolved murders of females in the US and Canada and 4 in Wisconsin, all manual strangulation, bodies left in the forest. ID was found in their clothing with the names circled in red.

April, 1999—went home to Missouri where he married a local farm girl, Denise. She delivered their first child, a girl she named Brianna.

2000—Andy and Denise took a road trip from Nauvoo, IL to Salt Lake City, UT along the old Mormon Trail.

He went back to long haul driving in December, from Montana to Northern California. On the road, he used the name <u>Baines Anderson</u> for three years. Denise visited him in both Montana and California.

Trip #3—He drove the I-5 Corridor along the west coast. He made side trips with rental vehicles.

12 unsolved murders of females, all manual strangulations, bodies left in the forest, ID left in their clothing. Their names were circled on the ID's in red.

April, 2001—birth of second child, a girl Denise named Carrie.

2003—Andy went home to Missouri.

April, 2004—the family moved to New Orleans

April, 2005—Andy moved back to Missouri.

April 4, 2005—Andy committed suicide. He left a note for his sister.

April 6, 2005—bodies discovered near Henderson, LA. One body, a young black woman named Xenia, was strangled. The other three, a woman and two female children had been strangled and laid neatly on a blanket near the river. ID for the black woman was in her clothing. Xenia's name was circled in red on her ID.

Notations and Rhymes

Andy kept detailed journals from the time he was 12 years old, and his truck logs were meticulous, often with details added in the margins about dispatcher or vendor attitudes. In the margins of his journals were names written in red ink. They were all females.

The journal entries gave Special Agent Johnson, a detective from Houston, TX, goose flesh as he read through them. But the detailed notes and names gave his team the information to match the notations with unsolved murders all over the country.

On the back flyleaf of the last journal was written the alphabet from E to Z, squared off in blocks. There were two or more check marks on each letter except Z and X. The letter Z was circled in green ink. The letter X was circled in red and marked with a red star. The check mark in this box was also in red ink, made fat and dark. A reference note at the bottom of the page, also marked with a red star and green box, contained numbers listed in a row; years that were important to Davis' scheme.

E√√√	F√√	G√√√	H√√√	I√√√	J√√√√
K√√	L√√√√	M√√√√√	N√√√	O√√	P√√
Q√√	R√√√	S√√	T√√	U√√	V√√
W√√√	Ⓧ✔ ☆ Y√√	Ⓩ√			

1997■, 1998, 1999, 2000, 2001, 2002, 2003, 2004. ☆

Note left to his sister before he hung himself:

2004
And now I've made my A-B-C's
Aren't you very proud of me?
Only 20 years to find them all.
Now it's over. I'm the last to fall.
A.

Rhymes found throughout his journals:

1997
A, B, C, D.
They don't exist for me.
E all the way to Z;
One by one, that's the key.
A

1999
Q and X are hard to see,
Always hiding away from me.
Wait and watch as years go by,
Oh look! I've found another 'eye'!
A.

2000
Where is that little letter X?
Not here nor there or by or next.
I've almost doubled all the rest,
Save the first for last, and the best.
A.

2001
A, B, C, D.
Will this ALWAYS haunt me?
First my mother, now my wife;
Rhymes to taunt my tortured life.
A.

2004
It's done, complete,
From A to Z.
The alphabet's finally dead.
And I will soon be free!
A.